2 50

TWICE THE LEAD, TWICE THE LOVIN' IN ONE GIANT SPECIAL EDITION!

RUSTLER'S BLOOD

"Forget it, Josh," Morgan said. "You're the cattle buyer who has been buying rustled cattle with three or four brands and rushing them right through into cattle cars before anyone can find them."

Josh put his fork down. He adjusted his black tie and straighened his dark jacket. "I don't know what you're talking about."

"Five thousand head of prime beef. That's over two hundred thousand dollars worth. That jog your memory?"

"Last year I bought ten times that number of cattle. The cattle shipping season hasn't started yet."

"No, but the rustling season is in full swing. That's the part you know about. You're the only cattle buyer in town, so you have to be buying the rustled stock and putting them on the train to the St. Paul stockyards."

"Speculation. Scurrilous unfounded charges that could get you in real trouble if you repeat them in the presence of more than three other persons."

Morgan stood and loomed over the shorter man. "I won't deal in the law, little man. First time I catch you with rustled cattle on your sales receipt or your bill of lading, I'll start shooting as I would with any other rustler. Do we understand each other?"

BUCKSKIN
SHOTGUN!
Kit Dalton

LEISURE BOOKS **NEW YORK CITY**

A LEISURE BOOK®

January 1995

Published by

Dorchester Publishing Co., Inc.
276 Fifth Avenue
New York, NY 10001

Printed in the United States of America.

BUCKSKIN
SHOTGUN!

Chapter One

"Hey, cowboy, you been wading in stinkweed or sleeping with a skunk? You smell like shit warmed over." The speaker stood at the bar of the Boots & Saddles Saloon, his right hand dangling beside worn iron showing from a weathered holster. His face was grim and clean shaven; he had no hat. He wore the trademark clothes of the gambler—shiny boots, creased black pants, white shirt and a fancy red checkered vest with gold watch chain and fob.

"You deaf, cowboy? I'm talking to you." The gambler spoke again with a bite to the words.

The cowboy target of the gambler's words looked over at the man, shrugged and turned back to his half-filled mug of beer. He had on patched and bedraggled range pants, scruffy boots, a blue shirt with one sleeve cut off and a neckerchief that had seen too much dust and rain. He had a week's growth of black stubble that only partly hid the sunburn below his eyes, where his wide-brimmed Stetson couldn't protect the rest of his face.

His black low-crowned hat had been badly used, showing one bullet hole, a crushed crown and a brim that had fallen on the left side, drooping two inches below its rightful position. Bloodshot eyes turned once more toward the gambler.

"You talkin' at me, little man?" the cowboy asked, a serious Southern drawl flavoring the words.

"Hell, yes. Who said you could come into my saloon?"

The cowboy turned back to his beer, took a big swallow, then banged the mug down on the bar so hard the glass cracked.

"Nobody said I couldn't come in," the cowboy drawled. He stared at the gambler with listless eyes, his hands resting at ease on the bar.

"I'm saying I don't want you in my saloon, cowboy. You're a mess, you stink and I don't want you smelling up my place."

The cowboy snorted and shook his head sadly. "Supposin' y'all want to try to throw me out?"

"Might come to that. Be reasonable. You need a bath, a shave, some clothes—"

The cowboy turned this time with anger painted on his face. "Go hump your sister, you bastard, and leave me alone."

The blond saloon owner frowned; then his right hand came up slowly from his side. He hesitated, then reached for his vest pocket.

The cowboy saw the move. His right hand snaked off the bar, drew his six-gun and blasted a round through the chimney of the lit coal-oil lamp hanging over the saloon proprietor's head. Shattered glass showered down on the owner and the next two men along the bar. The saloon echoed with the heavy report of the .45 exploding. Men held their ears and shook their heads. Nobody could hear anything for half a minute.

The gambler's hand had only half pulled the derringer from the pocket inside his vest. The cowboy's face cracked into a sardonic smile. When the sound faded he grinned.

"Now, little man with a little gun, you were telling me that you wanted me to do something. What in hell did you say again?"

The gambler took a long breath, eased the hideout back into the inside pocket and withdrew his right hand slowly, turning it palm out to show the cowboy that it was empty.

"No reason for gunfire, cowboy. I asked you kindly and with no rancor to leave my saloon. I still think it's a good idea, and it'll cost you sixty cents for a new chimney for that lamp."

The cowboy nodded, eased the Colt back into well-used leather on his right hip and tossed a silver dollar on the counter. "Should cover it. If you ever want to use that little lady gun in your vest pocket there, tenderfoot, learn how to draw it fast. Either that or, next time you try that slow draw of yours, you'll probably end up with at least one deadly bullet hole in your worthless hide. Almost anything beats being dead."

The cowboy stepped back from the bar, looked at the dozen or so cowboys and townsmen in the place and shrugged. "Hell, if'n you don't want me here, I can spend my hard-earned money any damn place in town." He turned from the bar, putting his back to the unhappy saloon owner and walked unsteadily out through the door. A moment later, a man wearing a derby finished his beer and hurried outside, following the cowboy who smelled like a skunk had sprayed him.

A few feet past the saloon's door, the cowboy slowed his pace and stopped, then leaned against the wall. He took a long, deep breath and scowled. It wasn't any fun being thrown out of one saloon after another.

The man in the derby who had left just after the cowboy came up to him, passed him, then turned and came back. He stopped six feet away and watched the cowboy.

"You're pretty good with that iron," the man said. He had a mustache and chin whiskers.

The cowboy stared at him, squinted and stared again. It was four in the afternoon, but he squinted as if darkness had fallen.

The derby man had a white shirt with four-in-hand tie, a pin in his lapel and a white handkerchief showing in his jacket top pocket. He smelled of bay rum. His dark eyes stared at the cowboy.

Shotgun!

"I know you?" the cowboy asked.

"No. You're new in town, I'd bet. I noticed you in the last saloon, then saw your little handiwork with the Colt in there. I'd venture that you're out of work."

"Might be." The cowboy's eyes squinted more and he scowled. "I don't take no damned charity."

"None offered." The derby man grinned. "Might have a job for you. You any good with a rope? You a real cowboy or just pretending?"

"Not a horse I can't ride, not a steer I can't corral. I been a cowboy in six states and part of Mexico if'n it's any of your damned business."

"You have any better clothes?"

"Not so you could notice. Sold my good shirt for a quarter. That was just after I sold my horse a week ago."

"Long walk between stops out here."

"Yeah, I found that out." The cowboy still squinted at the smaller man. "You say something about a job?"

"Cowboy work. Only three or four days but the pay is good."

"Three or four days? Ain't roundup time yet."

"Want a job or not?"

"Yeah, sure. Straight riding work. No fences, no barn mending, none of that sodbuster work."

The derby man grinned. "You sound about right. Only thing is, if I hire you, after the job, you have to ride on down the line somewhere."

The cowboy moved away from the wall. He swayed a moment, then held himself straight and tall. "Hell, what's one more town. I been in a hundred of 'em lately. Yeah, I'd like the job."

"You have a name?"

"Call me Lee. What's your moniker?"

"You don't need to know." He held out a five dollar bill. "Here's an advance on your wages. We ride tomorrow about noon. Get yourself cleaned up, take a bath, buy yourself a good pair of pants and a shirt. I'll see you at the livery at noon to rent you a horse. Any questions?"

"Straight riding work. No gunhand stuff. I don't do no gun work for no stinking thirty dollars a month."

"Right, no gunhand work. Just some cattle to move. Get cleaned up and have a good night's sleep. You'll need it before you get back. Noon tomorrow at the livery." The neatly dressed man pointed across the street. "You can stay at the Delmonico Hotel tonight. I'll pay. First thing you do is get yourself a bath. You have a fight with a skunk?"

The cowboy had leaned back against the wall. He shook his head. "No fight. He saw me first is all. Yeah, I'll wash it off."

They walked across the street to the hotel and the derby man paid for one night and had the cowboy print his first name in the register. Then the well-dressed man left.

The cowboy did as he was told. He took a bath,

ordered more water and took another bath. Then he relaxed in his room. An hour later he checked the hallway to make sure no one was there. Then he hurried down the hall, unlocked another door and went inside. There he took new pants and a shirt from a leather traveling case and put them on. He kept the hat, but brushed it off and straightened the crushed crown. Finally, he took out polish and spiffed up his brown cowboy boots so they were halfway presentable. After a big supper at a nearby cafe, the cowboy returned to the hotel and went up to the room the derby man had paid for.

In the lobby the man with the derby nodded, folded the paper he had been reading and walked quickly out of the hotel.

The next morning just before noon, the cowboy showed up at the Lamar Livery and looked around. The derby man sat on a chair just inside the big wagon doors. When he saw the cowboy, he stood and walked forward.

"Bad news for you, Lee. The job's been canceled. Might not be any work for another two weeks. Sorry to lose you. Figure you'd be a good steady hand."

"They can't just cancel cow work. Cow work's got to be done."

"Like I say, I'm sorry. You know how it is on these big ranches. Nobody knows what the other hands are doing."

Lee reached in his new jeans pocket and took

out a dollar bill and seventy cents in change. He handed it to the derby man.

"Here's what's left of the fiver. I don't take no charity. I'll pay you for these duds if you tell me where you stay. Get a job here swamping out a saloon and pay you off. I never take charity. Not a damned dime!"

The man in the derby grinned and shook his head. "No, just keep the clothes as your pay for getting canceled on the job. We're six-twelve and even. Might see you around town here in Big Bend in a week or two for another job." The derby man tried to push away the change, but Lee insisted. At last the fancy dresser took the money and the cowboy wandered off mumbling to himself. Morgan looked back at the man in the derby once and then nodded. He had the man's face and body style imprinted on his memory.

Back in the hotel, the cowboy moved out of the second room and into the first one he had rented the day before. He shaved, used some scissors and clipped his hair into a shorter style, raised his sideburns and soon was smooth shaven.

He opened the clothing case and took out his usual working clothes—black pants, blue shirt with a black leather vest and a low-crowned brown Stetson with a checkered headband. He changed into cowboy boots and put on his belt and a gunbelt, then tied the bottom of the holster low on his right leg.

The transition from a down-and-out cowboy

looking for some quick money to Buckskin Lee Morgan took only a few minutes. The new clothes and shave had changed his appearance enough so there wasn't a chance that the derby man would recognize him.

Morgan turned to the pad of paper in his traveling bag and looked through the pages. He'd been in town for two days, wandering in his down-and-out-cowboy disguise from one saloon to another, asking about work, waiting for someone to contact him.

The derby man sounded like the one he wanted, but now the work was canceled. That was the worst news for Morgan. He had hoped to get on the crew of one of the rustler gangs and stop the thieving bastards. If he could only find the right contact and get on one of the rustling crews the rest of his job would be easy. At lest he had learned something. It looked like the top brain behind this massive rustling operation hired a new crew of five or six wandering cowboys for each job, paid them off and made sure they rode on down the trail. That way there were no witnesses who could testify against the rustling plotters.

Morgan settled down at the table with his notes and went back over how this job started. He'd been in Denver taking a few days off after a tough case in Arizona. A wire came for him from Miles City, Montana Territory, from the Miles City District of the Montana Stockgrowers Association. They had a problem. Was he available for a job?

They offered him 5,000 dollars if he could solve their problem within a month. Morgan had wired back that he was on his way and took the next train to the cow capital of Montana, Miles City.

In the Cattleman's Hotel, he met the five members of the executive committee of the district. The leader of the five seemed to be Isaiah Roundtree, the man with the second largest outfit in Montana. He was about 50, tanned and rugged. He looked as if he spent every day in the saddle. He had one tooth missing in the front and often talked with one hand partly over his mouth to hide the fact.

"Morgan, we got big problems here and they needed to be stopped last Friday. Rustling, young feller. Must a been what you figured when you cut and run out here so damned fast. We figure that, among the twenty-three ranches in our district, we're losing something like a thousand head a week."

Roundtree scowled and slapped his hand on the polished oak table. "That translates into forty thousand dollars a week! The big ranchers don't like it, and some of the little outfits are going to go flat broke if we don't get this stopped damned quick."

Morgan stood and walked around the big table. It was filled with food and several bottles of whiskey. "A thousand head a week? How do you know this, Mr. Roundtree? Your district is thirty miles wide and one hundred thirty miles long. You have twenty-three ranchers. You haven't had a roundup since last fall. How do you know you're losing that many cattle?"

"Easy. Mostly we make spot checks in areas where we know how many head we have. Last week one of my pastures lost over two hundred head. It don't take no genius to figure out I've been rustled."

"Estimations, I can understand," Morgan said.

Another man waved him silent. "No, boy, we got more than that." The speaker had introduced himself as Lorne Dempsy, he had the largest ranch in the district. Dempsy was shorter than Isaiah and fat. He probably never rode a horse anymore. He was at least 280 pounds, most of which was below his chest. He had a pale complexion and soft blue eyes. Morgan figured the man could smile at a man and cut his heart out at the same time.

Morgan had wired a friend in Billings, who had provided him short descriptions and resumes on the four largest cattlemen in the Miles City district. He had characterized Dempsy as a scoundrel and a vicious man who had to have his own way or else.

"Boy, we know how many cattle they steal because the railroad tells us. I've got a contact in St. Paul at the stockyards where most of our critters go. It's over there in Minnesota. He gets figures on how many cattle come in every day and where they come from. He can tell us down to a dozen how many we've lost.

"The railroad doesn't know how the setup works, but somehow the shipments get mixed in with legitimate ones. We don't know where the rustlers load the cattle, who buys them or who in the train crews is taking bribes. It has to be that way or we could pin it down without your expensive help."

Dempsy glared at Morgan. "I didn't want to hire you. I got voted down four to one. Damn democracy. The biggest ranchers should call the play."

"We did, Lorne," Isaiah said with a touch of impatience. "We've been over this again and again. I sided with the other three and together we have more damn cattle than you do. We're going by your own rules, so calm down."

Daggers of fury sped between the two men as they stared at each other. Isaiah looked away first.

"So that's about it, Morgan," Isaiah said. "You have an expense account of twenty dollars a day, more if you need it. We've got a thousand in cash for you now. We want this all settled and sorted out before our roundup in just a month and a half. That date is a guess, hoping that the rains will start and bring some grass to get the critters out in the open, where we can find them easier."

Morgan went back to his chair and sat. "Nothing on paper. No numbers of lost cattle. No suspects. I need something to start working with. Where do you guess that the cattle were loaded? To the east or west of Miles City? I know you must have followed tracks of rustled stock. Which way were they driven? How many shod horses trailed each bunch?"

Harry Nelson waved and Morgan stopped.

"We've got some of that." He tossed an envelope to Morgan. "Not a lot there, but I did two weeks of work trying to find out what happened to the steers. Didn't get far. Oh, we hired one detective out of Billings."

"Shut up, Nelson," Dempsy roared.

"Yes, I know about him," Morgan said. "The man who was found murdered two days after he started asking questions about the rustlers. I wondered if you would tell me. Since you did tell me, Mr. Nelson, you just saved your association another five thousand dollar fee. I don't like being tricked, and a murdered detective is the worst kind of secret you can keep from me."

Morgan looked around the table. "You have any more little bits of information like that which I should know?" No one spoke. The last two men, who had said little, shook their heads.

"Anything else I should know before I get started?"

"From what I found out, most of the steers from this area are moved to the west and loaded somewhere at one of the various sidings between here and Billings," Nelson said. "That's near a hundred thirty or forty miles. Probably the loading is done closer to us than the other end, we think."

Morgan looked at the men again, each in turn. When none of them spoke he nodded.

"I guess that's it. As I told you in my wire, I want my hiring to be kept a closely guarded secret. Tell no one. I'd rather not be the second detective killed on this job."

"Agreed," Isaiah said. He handed Morgan a fat envelope. "No bill larger than a ten. That way you won't have trouble spending it and you won't appear to be throwing lots of money around."

Buckskin pushed the envelope in his inside jacket pocket and stood up. The rest of them rose. "I'll be in touch with you with a sealed envelope at the hotel here addressed to the Montana Stockgrowers Association. To get messages to me, send them to me here at the hotel to room 212 under the name Buck Leslie." He looked around and saw the men nod.

He went out a side door and down the hotel's back stairway to the ground floor, then around to the front door.

Morgan went up to his second-floor room and checked the hall, then pushed the door open. No guns went off. He looked inside, then stepped through the door, closed and locked it. The cattlemen would drift down from the fourth floor one at a time and go out different doors. He'd made the contact with the men as safe as he could.

That meeting had been three days ago. Now he was back at the small desk in his hotel room in Big Bend. He went over the material from the committee again. He had a report from the dead detective who worked the case. It showed little Morgan didn't already know.

The stolen cattle had been driven to the west of Miles City to a point where they were loaded on the rail cars dropped off by a cooperating train crew. Somebody had gone to a lot of trouble to earn a few hundred thousand dollars. Who?

Morgan didn't have much to work with, but he figured he'd try to take it from the railroad siding and go backward to the rustlers. The rail men were a clannish lot and it would take some cultivation to get to know even one of them who would tell Morgan what was going on. He'd tried for six hours one day and come up empty-handed even after spending three dollars on beer for a train crew. They either knew nothing or would say nothing.

Right now, the derby man was Morgan's best contact. He didn't know the man's name and it would be dangerous in this little town to ask any questions. He would watch and listen.

Big Bend had a rail siding that wasn't used much. A quick look at it two days ago showed some of the rails had turned from rusty tops to bright silver where they had been spun against by the drive wheels of a big coal-fired locomotive.

This could be one of the shipping points.

Buckskin eased his way down to the lobby, then checked the dining room. He saw a familiar black derby resting on the side of a table for one. Yes, it was the man who had hired him and fired him in 24 hours. As Morgan watched, the man stood, carried his hat and paid his tab at the counter. Then he went and talked with the room clerk. He picked up one traveling bag from the clerk and hurried out the door. Morgan walked to the front desk and held a folded dollar bill in his hand. He let the clerk see it.

"The gentleman in the derby who just left. Where was he heading?"

"We can't give out that information," the clerk said. He wrote something on a piece of paper and pushed it where Morgan could see it. Morgan read the name and destination: "Selby Holt to Miles City train."

"Oh, by the way, when does the next eastbound come through town?"

"In just a little over an hour. You'll have plenty of time to catch it."

Buckskin dropped the folded bill on the desk, checked out of the hotel and caught the train with ten minutes to spare. There were only two passenger coaches and the rest of the long train were filled cattle cars. He looked over the first coach, then found Selby Holt halfway along in the second one. He was leaning back and snoring softly as the train thundered along toward Miles City at 35 miles an hour.

Why was Holt heading for Miles City? And what was his connection to the rustling ring? Morgan had all sorts of questions but no answers yet.

Chapter Two

There seemed little chance to lose a man in Miles City, a nice little town, but certainly no metropolis. However, one moment the derby man strolled along the boardwalk ahead of Morgan. But after Morgan took a quick look at an attractive woman walking by, the derby man had vanished. Morgan stopped and stared in a store window. Where could he have gone?

The street had a dozen buildings in that area, including a hardware, a general store, a seamstress, the newspaper and a land and real-estate office. The derby man could have turned into any one of them. Buckskin decided not to push it. If the man thought he was being followed, Buckskin didn't want to be pegged as the man doing the tailing.

He'd find the derby man again. It was still early, not yet three o'clock. He took his one traveling bag and dropped it in his room at the

Cattleman's Hotel. Then he walked the street, hoping for an idea.

Just beyond the hardware he saw a saloon and pushed through the doors. It was early afternoon but the place looked busy. A long bar extended down one side of the narrow room, and a lunch counter down the other side. Between sat two dozen tables and chairs for poker and other games of chance.

The place seemed strange. Morgan couldn't figure out why. Little smoke, no wild raucous laughter or yelling. Some men stood at the bar. A stairway at the end of the long room led upstairs but he saw no fancy women.

He stepped up to the lunch counter and asked for a cup of coffee. It came at once, hot and strong. He paid a nickel and the waitress grinned.

"Figured you for a big tipper," she said and hurried away.

He sipped the brew and got a feel for the place. Then he saw a sign over the bar.

Hannah's Place.
No swearing. No fighting. No whores. No arguments. Gambling and drinking permitted. It's my place. You don't like the rules, get out. I won't serve anyone I don't want to.

The waitress came back and put both hands on the counter and stared at him. That was when he saw her eyes, sharp and green with an intensity

25

that sent shivers down his backside. Her hair glistened carrot red, tumbling all around her face and shoulders and down her back. She had high cheekbones, a strong chin and full red lips. Her waist looked small enough to circle with his hands and the white blouse stood out, fully filled. She grinned.

"Yep, like I figured, you're new in town. Ain't never seen you before."

Morgan chuckled. "You know everyone in town?"

"Damn near."

He pointed to the sign. "No swearing, miss. The owner will kick you out of here."

"Ain't likely. Nobody pays much mind to that sign no more."

"Why not?"

"Hannah is getting soft. She don't grab miscreants by the ear and run them out the door like she used to."

"She sounds like an interesting lady."

The redhead snorted. "She's no lady, for damn sure. She started out dirt poor, struggled to get a few dollars, then had them ripped out of her hands and had to start over. She ain't about to be poor again."

"Sounds like you know her."

"Better than anyone. You want a doughnut to go with that black coffee?"

"Another nickel?"

"No, a dime. Made these myself." She reached

under the counter and brought up a fat doughnut glazed with sugar icing and put it on a small plate. Morgan dropped a dime on the counter and she pushed it back at him.

"On the house. A little welcome to town party. We don't get a lot of visitors, excepting cowboys who still stink of steer hide and manure."

"Hannah won't like you giving food away."

"This time she won't mind. You take care of yourself. I got me some other work to do."

She turned and left and evidently didn't hear Morgan's last question. "You have a name?" he asked. She was down the counter, filling a coffee cup. Then she vanished into the back.

Maybe she'd be back. Morgan surveyed the saloon. Twenty men there now; business was picking up. Some drinking, some eating, one card game going near the back. It was softly muted—that was the difference. No loud talk or screeching. No piano pounding. No squealing by the upstairs girls. It must be Hannah's delicate touch on the place.

Buckskin finished his coffee and doughnut and headed outside. He didn't see the redheaded waitress anywhere.

Back to work. He missed what could have been getting hired on what sounded like a rustling crew. The railroad men were closemouthed and the derby man had vanished. What did he try next?

How had the detective been killed? That might

offer some gauge of what Morgan was up against.

The county courthouse crouched half a block west of Hannah's on the same side of the street. The sheriff's name was Chris Attucks. Buckskin knew nothing about the sheriff but there should be a report of some kind on the murder. He crossed the dirt-packed Fourth Street, barely missing a plodding wagon team.

The sheriff's office held down a ground-floor space in back. It had a desk, two chairs, a small heating stove and a deputy who looked as if he wished he had stayed home in bed.

The inquiry about the detective's death brought a scowl, then a reluctant answer with a bit of information.

"We don't know much about it. Happened two weeks ago. Found him in his hotel room, naked on his bed. He'd been robbed and killed with a knife through his side. Doc said it probably went all the way into his heart. Thin little blade, not more than half an inch wide. So it must have been ten, twelve inches long."

"A Chicago ice pick," Morgan said.

"Huh? what's that?"

Morgan ignored the question. "Any signs that there had been a woman in the room?"

"A woman? What the hell for—oh. Yeah, I see. Don't know. I wasn't on the scene. Nothing in the report said anything about a woman being there."

"Who found him?"

Shotgun!

"The hotel maid who went in to make up the bed. Gave her quite a turn. She's my cousin."

"I'm a friend of the dead man. Just wondered how it happened. You find out who did it?"

"Not a chance. Nothing left in the room. Nobody saw anyone come in or go out of his room. We'll never catch the killer."

Buckskin shook his head in wonder as he left the office. How a detective could let himself be suckered in that way was a surprise. Seduction and maybe some knockout drops he'd heard about would have done it.

So this could be a more sophisticated group of rustlers than he had figured. It wasn't a quick hit-and-run operation. Someone did a lot of planning and groundwork. That would take a lot of money and many people, and that meant there could be weak links somewhere. That was what he needed to find.

Miles City had a big cattle-loading area out of town along the tracks. Morgan went out there looking for the brand inspector. In most areas a brand inspector was hired by the cattleman's association to inspect brands and accept for sale only those cattle from a given brand. Any other branded critters were cut out and usually taken back to a central point or to the other ranch where they belonged.

The brand inspector on a big operation like this was an important man. Here in Miles City he would be hired by the Montana Stockgrowers

Association. Had he been bought or turned his head the other way?

Buckskin slowed his pace. There would be no use talking to a brand inspector. He functioned in a legitimate operation where some brands might get mixed up on a cattle drive or on the range.

On this kind of an outlaw operation there would be no brand inspector. All they needed was a cattle buyer with contacts with the railroad. Buckskin stopped in midstride, turned around and headed back to the center of town.

It wasn't cattle-shipping time yet in Montana. A few herds on south might be sending some early roundup cattle to market, but not here. That meant there wouldn't be any need for a cattle buyer in Miles City. No herds for sale, no cattle buyer.

The problem was, the rustler operation needed a cattle buyer in order to make a profit. They certainly didn't give the rustled cattle to the railroad.

Most of the cattle buyers Buckskin had known or heard about spent little time at the loading chutes. Most set up shop in a local saloon, held court for trail-drive bosses and now and then went out to look over a herd just arrived. They were company men, working for the big meat-packing plants and stockyards in the east.

Morgan made another turn and headed for the train depot. There he wrote out a message and handed it to the telegraph operator.

Shotgun!

*To: St. Paul Stockyards Manager. How do
I go about talking to a cattle buyer in Miles
City? Will have herd here within a week
ready for shipment. Please advise soonest.
Buck Leslie, Cattleman's Hotel, Miles City,
Montana Territory.*

The operator looked at it and raised his brows.
"Little early for shipping, ain't it?"

"Early or not, I'm ready. Send the wire. You
know of any other way to get a cattle buyer out
here?"

The operator lifted his brows. "Might," he said.
Then he sent the wire. When the clicks stopped,
the telegrapher turned back to Morgan. "Say
you've got a herd? Where's it from?"

"None of your business. Got me some beef to
sell and I need a buyer from St. Paul or Chicago.
I don't care."

"Don't get huffy. No fault of mine. If you really
need a buyer, St. Paul ain't gonna send you one.
Chicago might on the outside chance you had a
big herd." He stared at Morgan and squinted,
then shrugged. "Reckon I could talk to a gent
who does business now and again with St. Paul
stockyards."

Morgan's interest picked up markedly. "Yeah.
Sounds good. I ain't particular about who I do
business with, just so it can be done quiet and
fast."

31

"This gent goes by the name of Josh Eagleston. He's also a part-time bartender over at Lord Willy's Saloon and Entertainment Center."

"He might have the contacts. Does he have the money to buy cattle? I ain't no charity outfit."

"How in hell should I know? Go ask him. You didn't hear nothing from me. Understand?"

"Yeah, if I heard anything at all."

The clicker on the key began tapping out a message. The operator took his pencil and wrote down letters on a piece of paper as fast as they came in. When he finished he handed the message to Morgan.

To: Buck Leslie, Cattleman's Hotel, Miles City. We have no on-site buyer there until later. Maybe within a month. Josh Eagleston sometimes makes contacts and arrangements for us. Former employee. Talk to him.

It was over the name of J. B. Carter, director, St. Paul Stockyards.

Morgan bobbed his head at the operator. "I didn't hear a thing from you."

He left the depot and looked up and down the street hunting the Lord Willy Saloon. It wasn't hard to find. The first two cowboys he asked told him the direction. It stood half a block north of Hannah's Place and on the other side of the street. Morgan had a beer at the bar and asked if Josh was in. The man stared at him hard.

Shotgun!

"I'm Josh, but I don't know who the hell you are."

Josh looked to be about 30. He had blond hair and a reddish mustache, pale skin and a sunken chest. Brown eyes stared at Morgan.

Morgan laughed. "Get down off your nervous-Nellie horse, Josh. Nothing serious. Friend of mine said Josh knew where the best whores in town were. Friend likes them young. Know what I mean? He goes for first timers, or at least one who pretends it's her first time. You help me out?"

Josh let out a long breath, polished a beer mug, then filled it and set it in front of Morgan.

"That's a dime." He took the coin and put it in the cash drawer and came back polishing the bartop.

"Yeah, there's one or two around town. None here. Our whores are so old they got daughters who are whores. One night I got a mother and daughter inside of a half hour, same damn bed. Now that was a night."

"I'm a one-shot man myself. Where are they?"

"Yeah, well, they got a young one over at Matilda Jane's place. It's a real cathouse, out back of the Cattleman's Hotel. On the street behind the hotel. A Street, I think they call it. Change the damn street names fast as they switch whores. Give it a try."

"Do that, soon as it gets dark. I'm funny that way." he sipped his beer and when Josh came back the next time he lifted his mug. "Josh, you know of any good cowhands looking for work? I got me a week-long job moving a small herd. Could use two good men."

Josh twisted his mouth to one side and squinted as he thought about it. He rubbed his large nose and then scratched his ear. "Not offhand. I'll watch for some riders. With spring coming they'll soon all be working the roundups."

"I figured. Want to get my job done before the big outfits. I'm new to this range. How in hell do I get hold of a cattle buyer when I need one? Anybody out here from Chicago? Or is it the St. Paul stockyards that get the play?"

Josh's interest picked up. He polished another glass. "Most of the stock around here goes to St. Paul. Good market there. Folks say it's a penny or two more than Chicago, but the packers save on the freight charges." He put the glass down and found a mug that needed attention. "How many critters you talking about?"

"Near as I can tell about three hundred head, all prime steers."

Josh shook his head. "St. Paul won't send a man way out here for a small bunch like that. Now if the DD outfit wanted to ship some off season, they'd send out a buyer for like five or six thousand."

"I heard there might be another way to get the steers sold, something about a part-time buyer."

Josh looked at him squarely and lied through

34

his thin mustache. "Ain't heard of any arrangements like that." He put the mug down and reached for another one. A cowboy down the bar banged his empty beer mug on the bar and Josh refilled it for him.

When Josh came back to Morgan, he leaned closer across the bar. "These steers of yours would all have the same brand, I'd guess."

Morgan cleared his throat and looked around. No one stood near them. He moved the mug on the bar twice then looked up. "Guy I bought the ranch from said there might be a problem that way. He put a vent mark on his brand on most of them, but I have some other brands, about three all together I'd say."

"Bill of sale?"

"Had one, but the damn thing got lost somewhere. I ain't too good at that sort of paperwork."

Josh grinned. "Might be I could contact St. Paul about buying your herd without too much trouble for shipment on the rails. Course it has to be done quick and dirty. Not here in town, about twenty miles east. Since you don't look like no rancher I ever seen I'm gonna level with you. I can offer you twenty dollars an animal instead of going by weight. Not a lot of weight stations along this line."

Morgan sucked in a long breath. He looked around again, then leaned in closer. "Twenty? They're worth forty, maybe forty-five. Twenty?"

"Usual price for stock, like these. I'm taking

a risk. I don't know where these critters come from. Could get my neck in a noose. Twenty is the best I can do. Taking a damn lot of risks. You should know about risks, trying to move a three-brand herd."

Morgan stood back and finished his beer. He put the mug down easily and nodded. "Might work. I got a partner I'll have to talk to. He does the fieldwork. I'm more of a negotiator."

Josh chuckled. "Know what you mean. A man can get filthy out there driving a herd of cattle." He nodded. "You let me hear. You have a name?"

"Name isn't important. Beef is what pays the old muskrat. Need to do this sudden. Like two, three days the most. I'll be talking to you tomorrow."

Morgan left the partly finished beer and walked outside. He might have hit another good contact. Nobody said the cattle in his herd of 300 were stolen, but that was the general impression. Josh didn't mind, and he had set the price at half the normal one. He must be a general free-lancer in selling stolen cattle. Maybe he worked for anyone and not for the rustler organization riddling the other ranchers.

Morgan would find out for sure tomorrow. Make all the arrangements. Be sure the train was set to stop at a certain place at a certain time. Then he could nail the crew and the buyer. Without an outlet for the stolen cattle the rustling

Shotgun!

plot would be chopped off at the gonads.

Buckskin had an early dinner about five o'clock and went back to his hotel room. He'd put away his notes and papers, hiding them in the fake bottom of his carpetbag. But he'd learned early in this game he couldn't be too careful.

He had just closed the door to room 212, lit the lamp and checked to be sure everything was the way he had left it. Then a knock sounded on his door. He drew the Colt .45 from leather and stepped silently to the wall near the doorknob.

"Yes?" he asked.

The knock came again, more insistent this time.

He touched the knob and turned it, letting the door open an inch. He saw a woman and frowned. She pushed the door open and smiled. The waitress from Hannah's Place. She walked into his room, closed the door and leaned against it.

"Well, is this any way to welcome a lady. I had to wait an hour in the lobby for you to come. If you were any kind of a gentleman you'd give me a better welcome than this."

37

Chapter Three

Buckskin Lee Morgan looked at the pretty red-head who had just barged into his room. He kept his face in neutral. "You don't mind if the door is closed?"

"I prefer it that way. Closed and locked. Do you have the key?"

Morgan handed her the key. She locked the door and left the key turned halfway in the key-hole; a key from the other side couldn't push it out and open the door.

Morgan watched her as she moved like some sensuous wild tiger. Her glorious mane of red hair flowed around her shoulders and back like a spring freshet. Her waist looked even smaller than before, accenting the size of her full breasts. She smiled and her intense green eyes stared hard at him. Her full reddened lips moved.

"I hope you don't mind my invading your room this way. I haven't seen anyone like you for a year or more. When I see a man I want, I go after him. Any objections?"

She walked up to him so close that her breasts brushed his chest. She reached up and kissed him hard on the mouth. Then her mouth opened and she met his open lips and gave a soft moan as she pressed pointed breasts hard into his chest. Her arms went around him and held him as her mouth chewed and sucked on his. Then her tongue stabbed deeply inside of him and she walked him slowly back toward the bed.

When Morgan's legs touched the bed, he turned her around and let her down gently, then lay beside her.

"Surprised?" she asked.

"Pleased," he said.

She rolled over on top of him and kissed him again, long and hard, her slender body writhing on top of him, causing a sudden swelling at his crotch.

"Oh, yes," she said as she let his mouth come free. "Oh, yes, now that's what I like."

She sat up, straddling him, letting her long skirt billow up around her waist exposing part of her silk bloomers. She watched him spread out below her.

Her eyes glinted and she opened the top button of the dress. She kept opening them until she came to the last one at her waist. Then she caught his hands, pulled them up and put them on her breasts.

"Oh, yes," Buckskin said.

Her breasts came out of the fabric as she slipped the dress off her shoulders. The twin peaks hovered over him, full, heavily nippled and with three-inch areolas of palest pink.

She leaned forward, letting the orbs swing down until one came to his face. He opened his mouth and she moaned as he took half of her inside.

"Yes, chew on me. Suck on me. It feels wonderful. I like it that way, love it, love it. I talk sometimes when I get feeling real sexy. I guess I'm talking again 'cause I sure as hell feel sexy. Oh, yes, switch to my other baby. Don't be partial. They both love you. Yes, yes, yes."

She swept one leg over him and came away from his mouth and sat up beside him. Her hands worked at the buttons on his vest, then his shirt.

"I want to see you bare assed and beautiful," she whispered and nodded. "Oh, damn, yes, fucking bare assed and beautiful. That will be before. I hope you can wait. Hope you have some staying power. I've got all night. We can make love and explore and get to know each other all night long."

She tugged the shirt and vest off him and threw them on the floor. Then she pulled at his belt until he opened it for her. She worked at his fly buttons and growled deep in her throat.

"I'm so hot right now I could fry in heaven and St. Peter would never know it. Damn, but I love this!"

Shotgun!

She finished the buttons and pushed back both sides of his pants. He wore briefs made of soft cotton under the pants. She giggled. "I ain't never seen anything like these. They new?"

"We call them briefs in Denver. Underpants."

"Yeah, I guess. Help me get them down."

Together they tugged and pulled. Soon his boots and pants and underpants lay on the floor. He wore only a pair of brown socks.

"Them, too," she said. I want you buck naked." She bent and took the socks off. Then she stood and pulled the dress off over her head, making her bountiful red hair do strange little dances as it came streaming back down around her shoulders after the dress had pulled it upward.

"Glorious," he said, catching her falling hair.

"Anything that helps," she said.

He wanted to ask about her name, but she pushed him gently to the bed and lowered herself on top of him. His erection had come full now. She grinned, caught it with both hands and played with it.

She looked up at him, her green eyes flashing, teeth gleaming white. "He's so huge. Not a chance he'll fit inside my little hole. Not a chance. I'll have to give him lots of slippery juices."

She grinned and went down on Morgan, taking him halfway in her mouth until she nearly gagged. She came away and licked him, then took small bites at his purple head and caught his heavy balls.

"These balls are good for five times tonight," she said.

"Been known to happen. Depends on how sexy you can get."

She dropped on him hard where he lay on his back, ground her hips against his erection, kissed him and held it a long time.

"I'll try hard to keep you hard." She laughed softly and rose to her hands and knees, backing up toward him, showing her soft round bottom.

"Let's do the doggie," she said, looking at him over her shoulder. "You know, you're a big stud dog on the prowl and I'm a poor little bitch in heat, panting for it." She laughed. "I can tell you that I'm damn close to panting just waiting to get your big cock inside me."

Buckskin came off his back to his knees behind her. He spread her knees a little more, then rubbed her heartland and waited for her reaction. She humped backward at him. He found her juicy slot and the small node over it. Twice he twanged it and she looked back and shook her head.

"Later. Right now I want you buried up to your hilt right dead center in my little cunnie. Right goddamn now."

He worked closer, bent a little more forward and found the right hole. In one sudden stroke he had lanced deeply inside her. She moaned and looked back at him and nodded.

"More," she said. "Deeper, more, all you've got."

Shotgun!

Two strokes after he entered her she wailed and screeched and then collapsed forward on her stomach as her body tore into a series of rattles and shakes. She vibrated and then spasmed as she wailed each time the tremors darted through her.

Once she quieted down and he thought she was through. Then it began all over again from the first soft cries to the panting and the shattering series of hip-pounding climaxes that tore through her slender, pumping, humping body.

When the last spasms subsided, she dropped her head on the bed and let out a long breath. Then she closed her eyes and Morgan wasn't sure if she slept or not. He watched her. He stroked her gently, and her eyes popped open.

"Do that again, cowboy. That's glorious."

He did. Then he set up a serious program of humping her, pulling the tip of his weapon all the way out and then pushing back in until he was buried all the way down to his own roots. She responded by grinding backward against him.

"Now that's some kind of wild fuck," she whispered, watching him over her shoulder. "I collapsed again, huh?"

"Yeah, early on."

"Damn, it's sometimes better to stay up on the old hands and knees and let you get in farther."

Then there was no time to talk. She was panting again and he felt her moving toward another climax. He pounded hard now, thinking only about the urge to get the job done, to plant the seed, to stroke and pound and hump her until that final moment.

It came slowly, like a bright morning sunrise flashing into being. He felt the valves open high up and the rush of the fluids down the pipes and then the primal driving thrusts that lasted for ten strokes before he gushed his last and fell on top of her, panting like a steam engine.

Morgan wasn't sure if she'd climaxed again or not in the fury of his own completion. He panted and marveled at the wonder of woman. At the same time he remembered a dead detective with a Chicago ice pick through his side.

Remembering all that, he checked the door and saw it was still closed and locked. Smart move. He felt the woman under him and knew she was helpless.

Relieved, he relaxed again and heard the woman under him even her breathing out. For a moment he thought she had dropped off to sleep. Then she purred like a contented kitten and turned to try to see him.

He reached down and kissed her nose. "Great. That was fantastic. Are you always so wild and wonderful this way?"

She moved and he lifted away and sat on the bed. She rolled over and sat beside him.

"Not always." She grinned and he saw something there he had missed before: a little girl shyness and a vulnerability. For all of her bravado and taking what she wanted, she really must be alone and afraid and worried.

He bent and kissed her breasts, then her lips. It was a soft, gentle show of affection. She flashed him a smile.

"That's some of the best part so far," she said. Her eyes went wistful for a moment. Then the snap came back and the green glint and she frowned.

"Damn, I should have brought some booze and cookies or a cake or something. You big ones always want to eat afterward."

"Eat or sleep, the nature of the man beast."

"Yeah, tell me about men." She shook her head sending the red cascade of hair into a dither. "No, don't tell me. Best man I ever knew was my pa."

"He dead?"

"Not exactly. In his prime he was a pistol. Had a ranch. Ran it like a clock. Everything just so. Barn, sheds, ranch house. My mother took real sick in the big pox outbreak of 'sixty. That near done my pa in. She got better slow, but for a while Pa had three kids to raise, and by damn, he did it all."

Morgan sat there without touching her. She was in a mood to talk and he listened.

"Damn, should have brought some booze. Don't know what I was thinking of." She looked up. "Not that I always drink a lot or that I need a drink to get my clothes off. Fuck, that should be obvious by now."

"You been working at Hannah's Place long?"

She squinted a bit when she looked at him. Then she grinned. "Long enough. I got a good deal there. Why should I quit?"

"Noticed a little different feeling to the place when I was in there. I don't know, quieter, not so much yelling and swearing, no fights."

"Anybody starts a fight in there, Hannah has friends who hustle them both out the door quick. She don't allow them back in for a couple of weeks. Some say it hurts business, but the doors are still open."

"No girls there, I'd guess. Didn't see any around."

"Don't go along with whoring around. Not natural for the girls, damn bad for most of them. Hannah says if they want to whore they got to go do it somewhere else."

Buckskin nodded. "Commendable. This Hannah—she must own the place. How did she come to own it?"

"Some say she fucked the owner, got him drunk and made him sign it over or she'd tell his wife. Not so. Some say she worked the whore trade for long enough in another town to blackmail half the town's leading citizens, left with her money and bought out the saloon. Also not so. Some say she played cards for it and won it in a poker game. That is so. Hannah is good at poker. Better than most men. Good enough to go on the road as a gambler, if she could get enough games. Men just naturally don't like losing to a woman."

She turned and pushed him down on the bed and snuggled against his chest. "One more little rest. Then we get serious about fucking up a storm. You be thinking about your favorite position for number two and I get to pick out the one for number three. Okay?"

He couldn't see her face but he agreed. He wasn't at all sleepy.

For ten minutes he watched her resting against him. She had dropped off to sleep at once just after she last spoke. That was total trust. How could she do it? It could be absolute confidence in her own abilities. He tickled her under the chin lightly with his finger. She brushed it away. The second time he tried it, she caught his finger.

"Gotcha," she said, turned over then leaned close to him. Her face was serious.

"Why do men like tits so much? You know what I mean. They gawk at my blouse, try to see down the front of a low cut dress, try for a touch and a feel when they can. Men just seem crazy over tits."

Morgan laughed and reached up and petted both of hers.

"That's about it. Men are crazy over tits. I can't tell you about other men, but for me, a woman's breasts are magical, delightful, amazing, beautiful. Have a friend who gets in trouble taking pictures of nude women. They aren't erotic or sexy. They're artistic. So beautiful it brings tears to your eyes. The sculptured shape of a woman's naked breast, the right angle, of arm and her face in profile maybe and darkly lit. He's good. Tits are just wonderful. Maybe that's because that's the part of woman that's easiest to see. You know, tight blouses, sweaters, fancy gowns with the tops showing. Enticing."

"But not the best part?"

"Not by far the best part once you have her undressed and in bed with you. Why do women like men's cocks so much?"

She giggled. It had been a long time since Morgan had heard a woman who must be nearly 30 giggle.

"Cocks are just delightful. Now let's see about what we can do for number two. I've got me an itch way down deep that needs you to scratch it."

It turned out to be a long, wonderful, exhausting night. They didn't wake up until almost ten the next morning, which wasn't surprising since they didn't get to sleep until nearly four in the morning.

Morgan got up without waking her, used some of the pitcher water and started shaving. When he looked at her, she was sitting up in bed, still naked and smiling at him.

"Good morning," she said.

"Yes, a fine morning, but it'll be noon soon."

"Good, I like noon. Can we have breakfast over at the saloon?"

Shotgun!

"Is it any good?"

"Top-notch bacon and hot cakes."

"I better pass. I'm supposed to be working."

She eyed him with a question on her face. "Work? I thought you were rich. What kind of work?"

He sensed his mistake as soon as she spoke. He fell back to his usual story to cover up his real work.

"Property. I'm looking for some property to buy for a client. Hush-hush stuff."

"Sounds exciting."

"It would be if everyone knew who I'm working for. So I'd better pass on breakfast."

"No fair."

"Life isn't fair. By now you know that." He put on a clean shirt, yesterday's dark pants and his black leather vest, and he eased the gunbelt around his hips.

She snuggled on the bed, then sat up and went on hands and knees. "This position remind you of anything?" she asked.

"Yes, of marvelous things." He walked over and petted both her hanging breasts and pulled her up. "Dressing time. No room for slackers. You might lose your cushy job over at Hannah's."

She grinned and slipped into her bloomers, then lifted the dress on over her head. "No chance I'll lose my job. I know too much about the boss. You come past and say hello today."

"I'll do that."

She combed her hair with his comb, pinched her cheeks and put on her shoes. Then they walked out. He let her go down the back steps first and he went out the front. No time for breakfast was right. He had planned today to see Josh at Lord Willy's Saloon. He hoped it opened early. Some of the drinking emporiums didn't unlock their doors until high noon.

He was in luck. Lord Willy's Saloon was open and already had two arguments going and a dozen drinkers at the bar. Josh wasn't behind it.

"Josh around?" Morgan asked the apron when he came up looking for an order.

"Nope."

"He coming on duty today?"

"No."

"Where can I find him?"

"You can't. He said he was going out of town for a while. All I know. You want any more answers, you go see the boss."

Morgan scowled at the apron, who said, "Hey, ain't my doing. Just telling you what he said."

"Yeah, I hear you, but I don't have to like it."

The apron went down the bar to a customer and Morgan left. Another dead end. First the derby man, now Josh the cattle buyer. Evidently he was the only man the stockyards dealt with. So how could he run down the buying setup if the man who evidently had purchased the rustled steers was not around anymore.

Morgan thought about the situation as he

walked the street. They wouldn't kill Josh off unless their operation was over. They needed him for the cash payout. Maybe he got scared and ran. Not likely if he was making lots of money on the rustling. Maybe he was afraid of getting hung. Many juries would consider such a man a part of the smuggling operation and nail him with a hanging offense if convicted. He could be scared. Or the big shots of the smuggling cartel could have simply put him under wraps. They would run him out when they needed him to buy cattle and pay for them. Lots of good food, whiskey and a woman would keep Josh happy for some time.

Damn it.

Moving on. Next problem. The derby man. Where in a town this size did a man get a British derby? At a men's clothing store. Was there one in town? Morgan stopped a well-dressed man on the boardwalk and asked the question.

"Yes, Philip's, down a block on the other side of the street. Quite a good selection."

Morgan thanked the man and walked to the store. The clerk was surprised at Morgan's question.

"We only have one man in town I know of who wears a derby. He gets a new one each year."

"Would that be Selby Holt?"

"Exactly. You know Selby?"

"Trying to find him. Old friend. Know where he lives?"

"Sorry, I don't know him that well. But he is

here in town. Not sure exactly what he does. Seems to have quite a bit of spare time. Gambles some, I'm told."

Buckskin headed back to the hotel. He hadn't checked his box that morning. He didn't expect any messages but sometimes they came. He walked up to the clerk behind the desk and asked about his room. The key boxes were partly shielded so he couldn't see his own.

The clerk handed him a sealed envelope. He thanked the man, went to a soft chair in the lobby and tore open the envelope. The note was short and direct.

Tuesday morning. At daybreak one of our line riders spotted four men where they shouldn't be. Might be planning a rustling operation. We will track them today. Usually they move out any cattle at night. Hope you can come with us to our little party tonight.

It was signed by Isaiah Roundtree. Buckskin checked the hotel clock. Slightly after noon. He'd grab some food and ride for the Bar B Ranch. It was about seven miles outside of town. Now maybe at last they would get a good strong lead to these rustlers.

Chapter Four

It took Morgan two hours to ride to the Bar B,
which Isaiah Roundtree owned. The Bar B ranch
house had been built on a little rise just off the
Yellowstone River, downstream from Miles City.
That put it west of town. The spread looked better than most. A three-story ranch house with at
least 12 rooms. The bunkhouse had a screened
area to one end and a kitchen beyond that with
a pair of chimneys.

Two big barns could hold a lot of hay for winter
feed in case of a snowstorm. Everything looked in
top condition. Some of the cowboys on this spread
knew how to use a hammer and saw. A rider met
him close to the house, took his name and rode
hard for the ranch house's back door.

By the time Morgan had tied his rented mount
at the hitching rail outside the big house, Isaiah
Roundtree came striding out the door to meet
him.

"Morgan, glad you got my note. Had a man ride it in first thing I heard. Looks like we got a rustler crew in the making. Can't figure out why they would come out a day early and take the chance to get caught. But we spotted them.

"Come in and have some coffee. Cook just made some gooseberry pie I want you to sample. We won't be moving out until about two hours before dark. Got two men watching this bunch. Five rustlers now. They're hiding in a little splash of cottonwoods just off the river about three miles downstream."

"They close to any steers?"

"Two weeks ago, we brought down about five hundred head into some low land near the river to fatten them up before we sell them. All steers and market ready. I'd kinda hoped the bastards would see the steers and not be able to resist. We've had one man watching them ever since."

The coffee proved hot and the gooseberry pie delicious. Morgan took a second piece and the cook beamed his approval.

Roundtree picked up a big yellow cat that rubbed around his ankles. The cat purred, glared at Morgan, then settled down on the rancher's lap, his tail curved gracefully around his feet.

"We plan on taking ten men. Like to circle these bastards and blast them all out of the saddle or catch them and hang them within an hour. Damn this makes me mad."

54

Shotgun!

Buckskin finished chewing a bite of the gooseberry pie and nodded. "Let's be sure to save one of them if we catch them. Want one to question. Might not get much out of any of the riders. My guess is that the brains behind this rustling picks up cowboys on the grubstake trail or loafers in the saloons, gives them a week's work for maybe thirty dollars, then boots them on down the line to get rid of them. That way there's nobody to testify against them."

"Might work that way," Roundtree said. "Still we'd have the contact man who hired them. The big money we're spending on you buying us anything?" He belched and the cat jumped, looked up at the man, blinked, then settled down again on his lap.

"Making some contacts, but nothing solid yet. You ever hear of a man named Josh Eagleston?"

The rancher wrinkled his brow and frowned for a moment. "Josh? Yeah, we used to have a Josh work for us. No, his name was Josh Randal. Not the same man."

"I might have something going with him. Not sure yet. Right now I'm running down every lead I can find. If we can capture one of the riders, it'll be a big help."

"You got a rifle?"

"No, just my Colt."

"Provide you one. We'll eat supper early. Don't get dark this time of year here until about eight o'clock. We'll push off at six and have lots of time to slip up on this pasture and circle it if we can without anyone spotting us."

The cat sat up and yawned, glared with slitted eyes at Morgan, jumped off Roundtree's lap and stalked toward the outside screen door. The cook let the cat out.

"You don't like cats, do you, Morgan?" Roundtree said.

"Not my favorite pet."

"Yaller there knew it the minute you came in. Don't know how he does it. Must be some kind of faint smell. Some damned thing. You want to take a nap? We'll probably be up most of the night if all goes well."

Buckskin did have a nap in a chair under a pair of pines outside the front door. Supper was meat and potatoes and lots of coffee, bread and vegetables with rice pudding for dessert.

They kicked out of the ranch yard promptly at six p.m., with Roundtree leading on a big black that looked 16 hands. He had to have some Arabian in him somewhere.

They rode generally west and then climbed into some low hills with scatterings of pine until they were a mile away from the river. Below, the land eased downward toward the river in a sea of shimmering grass that hadn't been grazed yet this year. Morgan saw the beef, a brown mass working slowly up from the river chomping on the grass as they moved.

The riders kept to the breaks and the scattering

of pine ridges and a few scrub oak. It was enough to keep them under cover from anyone watching below.

Roundtree pointed to a stand of cottonwood a quarter of a mile from the Yellowstone and almost in the center of the three mile long pasture. "They were in there. We didn't see any smoke before or now, so if they're there, they'll have a cold supper. Might make them a little testy."

"Remember. We need at least one of them alive to question," Morgan said. "I'd like to talk to all five or six of them one at a time, but that probably won't happen."

"Not a chance. We need to kill some of these rustlers to send a signal. Get a big story in the paper in town. Warn the riders it ain't no picnic out there. I've decided to pull in the sentries I've got scattered around this side of my place and put out about twice that number of range guards. Have them visible and each one armed with two rifles. A show of force and these fuckers just might leave me alone."

It was still an hour from dark as they waited in the pines. Ten minutes later somebody called out and they all saw the smoke filter through the tops of the cottonwoods below. The rustlers would have a hot meal after all. That might make them fat and happy and groggy and slow on the trigger. That was what Morgan hoped.

A half hour before dusk, they saw riders move out from the grove below. Roundtree had spread his ten men out in a long line through the trees. They covered the central half mile of the pasture where the market-ready steers grazed. He'd told the two men on each end of the line to wait for the signal, then to ride forward hard, bend around when they came to the river and close the ring from the back side.

Morgan waited with Roundtree at the center of the line and watched. The rustlers below worked the steers slowly, moving them into a compact herd. They took the bulk of the animals, but didn't waste time with those that had grazed outward too far or too far on each end. They wanted the most, the quickest.

"Where will they cross the river?" Morgan asked.

"Most of the stolen steers have been moved downstream. Any number of places within ten miles of here where they can cross. We don't want to let them get that far. Soon as they have them bunched and start moving them west, I'll fire one shot and we'll close in."

"It'll be a cavalry charge to get there," Morgan said. "We're half a mile from the beef."

"We'll be galloping. Them steers will be walking. Don't know what the hell the five rustlers will be doing or how long they'll stay with the herd."

"Some will cut and run as soon as they see your riders," Morgan said.

"Yeah, and we hope they ride right at one of our men who has his rifle up and ready to fire."

Shotgun!

Morgan figured it was about ten minutes to heavy dusk when Roundtree lifted his rifle. He fired one shot and he and Morgan kicked their mounts into motion and rode down the slope toward the bunched steers below.

Buckskin couldn't follow what happened after that. He saw one cowboy on the far side of the herd stop, look at the riders coming and turn his mount for the river. He splashed in and went into the water, letting the horse swim for the other side as he held on to the saddle.

One of the rustlers angled east and took fire from two Bar B riders coming hard at him. He went out of the saddle but Morgan didn't know if he had been shot or not.

Then Morgan was pounding for the herd. One rider on their side paused, saw the men coming and rode hard downstream.

More rifle shots sounded and the rider had his horse shot out from under him. He kicked out of the saddle, hit the dirt and rolled twice. Then he got up and kept on running the same direction.

Morgan angled after him, but heard a thundering ground swell of sound come from behind him. He was close to the herd by that time, and when he looked back, he saw 200 or 300 of the steers charging toward him. The shooting had spooked them and they were in a flat-out stampede, running for their lives.

Morgan pulled his mount to the right and rode out of the way of the charging critters. He thought of the man on foot and knew he couldn't outrun the steers.

Morgan spotted the grounded cowboy less than 20 yards ahead of the lead steers. Not a chance he could ride in and pick up the man up even if the cowboy could do a galloping pickup.

Morgan spurred his horse to keep up with the edge of the herd for a minute. Then he saw the cowboy get hit by one of the lead steers and stumble and go down. Morgan winced, pulled over to the side and waited for the thundering hooves to go past him. He heard some more shots and then a fading of the stampede until there was only a faint rumble in the distance.

Roundtree pulled up beside Morgan and shook his head. "Two of the bastards went into the river. Maybe they'll drown. What happened to that rustler who got his horse shot out from under him?"

"Just about to go look," Morgan said.

It was full dark by then, dusk suddenly ending and a half-moon settled in.

"The stampede caught him," Morgan said and the rancher swore. They found the cowboy in the faint light. His hat, boots and shirt had been ripped off him. One arm was missing. His torso and legs were masses of bloody flesh where the hooves of part of the 300 steers had slashed into him as they charged past. His head was smashed and battered so severely that not even his mother would have known him.

Shotgun!

Roundtree fired three shots in the air and lit a small fire from dried sage and waited for his men to assemble. They came in quickly. One had a dead rustler tied down across the rump of his horse. The mare he rode didn't like it and pranced around skitterish as a virgin at a cowboy dance.

"Two got away across the river," one rider said.

"Two dead, two got away," Roundtree said. "What about the other one?"

Nobody knew. They decided he must have slipped past them in the dark. Morgan lit a match and snaked a purse out of one of the dead man's pockets. It held ten dollars, an IOU for five dollars. He couldn't read the name of the man who signed the IOU. There was no name and no address of the owner to the purse. The mutilated body also had no identification.

"We brung in the one horse we caught," one of the cowboys said. "Should we look for a brand?"

Roundtree said they should. They walked the animal near the fire and used matches and checked him.

"Just a hair brand up on the shoulder," one of the cowboys said.

It was a temporary brand that would last until the new hair grew out. When a livery stable man sold a horse he'd shave off the hair brand and the new owner could use his own brand. They checked the hair brand. It was MCL.

"That's the Miles City Livery," Roundtree said. "Which means the cowboy was probably a drifter

61

without a horse. He rented one from the livery. You should check that out, Morgan."

"Sounds like a good idea," he said.

"We'll take both bodies back into town in a wagon," the ranch owner said. "They'll be waiting for the people of Miles City in the morning with a sign over them reminding cowboys about what happens to rustlers. Back at the ranch we'll heat up one of our Bar B irons and brand both of them on the chest. Give a little emphasis to the whole affair."

When they rode in at the ranch, Morgan decided to wait for the wagon for company into town. Riding alone at night out here could turn into real trouble. Two or more riders together were much safer. As Buckskin waited for the wagon to be readied, Roundtree gave him coffee and another piece of pie and they talked.

His wife and two daughters came in to say hello. The girls were 17 and 18 or so, both plump like their mother and both kept looking at his crotch. He'd seen ranch girls like these before. They were usually kept on a tight rein by their parents, and although they routinely saw dogs and cattle and horses breeding, they never had the chance to try it themselves. They had hollow eyes and didn't know what to do with their hands and their blouses were open one button more than their mother would approve if she'd seen. They said hello, nodded, blushed and looked at the lump in his pants behind his fly before they hurried out of the room with their mother.

Roundtree said he had two sons as well. One was away at college and the other one had been on the ride with them that night.

"Gonna break this rustling ring if it's the last damn thing I do on this earth," he said. "Damned if I won't."

Morgan said the bodies might stir up someone in town. He'd watch the people who came to look at them. Maybe someone could identify them and that could lead somewhere.

They shook hands and Morgan went out and stepped into the rented saddle. In town Morgan helped the wagon driver and the other man lay out the corpses in front of the sheriff's office. One of the women had made a sign at the ranch. It was stood up just behind their heads.

> *Two Rustlers Killed on the Bar B. Death to All Rustlers!*

No deputy came out to see what they were doing. It was 11 o'clock and a light still burned inside the jail. Morgan headed for his room. There would be time enough tomorrow to check with the livery. The man there just might remember something strange about the horse and saddle rental. He remembered the horses and made a detour with the two mounts and tied them outside the livery, then walked on to the Cattleman's Hotel. It had been a long day without a lot of sleep the night before.

The next morning, Morgan had finished breakfast by 6:30 and checked out the sheriff's office. A deputy stood outside looking at the two bodies, which hadn't been moved. The sign stood in place. Several men and one woman stopped by, looked at the corpses and hurried on.

"Anybody know who either of these men were?" Morgan asked the deputy.

The lawman shook his head. "Nobody can identify that one. He get under a stampede?"

"Looks like it."

"Sheriff asked me last night who pays for the burial?"

"Charge the Bar B. Roundtree is loaded with money. I'll check back with you later."

The man at the livery had just struggled out of his bed in the small office. He poured a cup of coffee for himself, didn't offer Morgan any and squinted at his visitor.

"Yeah, my horse. Got my hair brand on it. I rent to anybody who pays in advance. I keep records. Good records. Let's see. That's Marjorie. Yep, I rented her two days ago to a kid by name of Charlie Smith. Said he'd need it for three days. Tried to pay me with a brand-new twenty-dollar bill. I can't make change for those big bills. He came back with three singles for the three-day rental and I let him ride."

"Anybody with the kid?"

Shotgun!

"Not that I saw."

"Where did he say he got the twenty?"

"Didn't. I didn't ask."

"Guess I should tell you that your horse was used in a rustling try last night on the Bar B spread. Two men died, including the one who rode this mount."

"I didn't ride with them."

"Didn't expect you did. Did any other young cowboys rent horses the same day that Marjorie here went out?"

He looked at his book. "Yep, three more, all in the morning, all for three days."

"Seem a little strange to you?"

"Not especially. I rent lots of horses."

"The next time this happens, young cowboys without horses who need one for three days, you get in touch with me. Could be worth a five-dollar bill if you contact me at the Cattleman's Hotel quick enough. Can you do that?"

"For a fiver? You bet."

"I don't want any singles, but if a pair or three young cowboys rent horses on the same day, I want to know about it."

"Deal," the livery man said, and Morgan gave him a twice folded dollar bill and headed back up town. He remembered that he'd said he'd stop in at Hannah's Place. What an interesting lady that waitress was. One he'd be happy to see again.

Yes, why not stop by. He could even have lunch there. He thought about the word. Most Western towns didn't know what a lunch was. The word was quickly spreading through the country. In San Francisco everyone had lunch instead of dinner. But in the towns, people still ate three square meals a day: breakfast, dinner and supper.

He had just passed the hardware store when a display in the Howard General Store next door caught his attention. In the window was a stuffed bald eagle. It made an arresting picture, hanging in the air on thin wire that could hardly be seen. The taxidermist had done a fine job.

Morgan was about ready to move when someone bumped him in the side. He turned and looked down to see a small lady dressed all in white, including a frilly little white hat. She was young, close to 30, he decided.

"Excuse me," he said and a delightful smile blossomed on her face. She squealed.

"Oh, oh, don't tell me. I know who you are. We come from the same town. I knew you just slightly when I was in school up in Boise, Idaho. I know your name so well. Let's see now. How do I remember your name. Your pa's name was Buckskin Frank Leslie, and for years he ran a ranch. The Spade Bit Ranch. You raised horses outside of town and you came to school."

Morgan caught her elbow and moved her down the boardwalk.

She looked up at him again. "Yes, now it's coming back to me. You had a name different from your pa's. We always thought that strange. It was

66

Lee Morgan. You always said you wanted to be called Buckskin Lee Morgan."

"Yes, yes, you're right. We should talk, but somewhere not quite so public." He shook his head. "For the life of me, I can't remember your name."

Chapter Five

The small woman with straight black hair smiled at Buckskin. "Lordy, I'm so surprised to see you. No reason you should remember me at all. My name is Teressa—"

Buckskin pointed his finger at her "Yardley. Yes, now I remember. Teressa Yardley."

She smiled and Morgan grinned right back at her. She motioned. "Come in. My shop is just next door. I was on my way there when I saw you." She shook her head at the wonder of it. "Lee Morgan right here in our little town."

She led the way to the store and they stepped inside. Morgan found himself in a seamstress shop filled with cloth and patterns and dress dummies sporting half-finished dresses.

"Now I remember. Your father was a banker."

She laughed. "Actually he worked at the First Boise Bank as a teller. But he learned the business. Four years ago he came into a good inheritance from a aunt, and he took the money and opened his own bank here in Miles City. The Northern Pacific had just arrived and he figured it was a town with great growth potential."

She put her hands over her face. "Goodness, where in the world are my manners. Please sit down. Would you like some tea? I could boil some water in a minute."

Buckskin nodded. "Tea. Yes, I think I'd like that. Been some time since I've had a proper cup of tea."

The sight of the woman took him back a long way to his early days in Boise and outside of town on the Spade Bit Ranch. He didn't remember going to school all that much but he must have. He watched her move to a small kitchen area in back of the shop. She waved.

"Come on back and we can talk while the water heats." She lit an already set fire. "My father taught me always to set a fire in a fireplace or the kitchen stove when you're through with it. That way you can get a fire going quickly when you need it." She blushed. "I declare, I don't know what I'm yammering on about here. You're not interested in what my father taught me."

He sat on a straight-backed wooden chair in the kitchen. He didn't understand why, but he was strangely fascinated by this small lady. She stood barely five feet tall and couldn't weigh more than 90 pounds with her shoes on. She was slender with few womanly curves. She showed almost no breasts at all under the white lace dress she wore.

He stood and moved closer to the stove. "Do you remember if I went to school back there a lot?"

"You didn't. You came mostly in the winter when not much happened out at the ranch. I had an enormous crush on you. Since I was two years behind you, you didn't know that I existed. Now that I think of it, it didn't seem that you were all that much interested in girls."

"Horses were my true love back then," he said. They both laughed.

She watched him from soft brown eyes and he wondered what she could be thinking.

"How did you recognize me? It's been years?"

"Probably." She hurried on. "But you haven't changed that much. You were almost as tall then as you are now, and you had that same dark brown hair and rather stern features. As I remember you didn't smile a lot back in Boise."

Buckskin lifted his brows in surprise. "Seems you remember a lot more about those days than I do."

"Your brown eyes. That was what interested me the most since I had brown eyes, too." She turned away, color seeping up her neck. "Lordy, I'm carrying on again. Sorry." She pushed the tea pot on the stove, then used a lid lifter and took off the lid above the fire and placed the kettle directly over the flames now showing bright in the small stove.

She looked up at him, then away. With a little frown of determination she plunged ahead. "I do hope I haven't embarrassed you by remembering all of this."

"Not at all. Sometimes it's good to think back and remember how things were."

"I heard about your father. I'm sorry."

"I was gone from the ranch by that time. I've finally decided that the way he died was probably the way he would have wanted it."

"Still it was unusual," she said frowning. "I don't think I've ever heard of two men shooting each other in a call out that way when both of the men died."

"Unusual to say the least. I've never heard of it happening before or since."

She used a cloth holder and took the teapot off the fire, pushed the lid back in place on the stove, then dropped a spoonful of dark dried tea leaves into the teapot.

"Be ready in sixty seconds. That's my best tea steeping time." She shivered. "I don't know why I'm so nervous. Recognizing you is the nicest thing to happen to me in a long time. Will you be in town for long?"

"No. I'll have to ask you a favor. Don't use my real name when we're out in public. I'm here looking for some rustlers. I want to stay Buck Leslie for as long as I can."

She lifted her brows. "Leslie—your father's last name. That will be easy to remember." Then she looked at the tea and poured the steaming drink into two cups she had readied.

"Cream or sugar?" she asked.

"Some sweetness would be fine."

She provided sugar and set all the things on the small kitchen table, which had two chairs beside it. They moved to the table.

"How did you get started in the seamstress business?"

"I've always liked sewing. Mother helps me some days. We needed something to do, and I didn't want to teach school. Father loaned me money to start the business and now I've paid him back and I'm making enough to live on."

She put out cookies and he sampled one.

"Peanut butter cookies—they're good."

She smiled and nodded. The pink flush began again and he realized she wasn't used to being complimented by a man. He smiled. No wonder she was still unmarried.

When he finished his tea, a bell tinkled over the front door and she excused herself and hurried into the shop.

Morgan stood when she went into the shop. Fascinating. That was twice he'd thought of that word about her. He couldn't understand his feelings. She was tiny and slender and flat and opposite of the type of woman he usually felt attracted to. But something about this small lady reached out and grabbed him.

Shotgun!

The woman in the shop bought some thread and a package of medium needles. She looked to be in her late fifties and had spread somewhat around her middle.

"Dear, would you thread them for me? If you could put about three feet of white thread on each one I'd appreciate it. My old eyes just won't let me get the thread through the eye anymore."

"Of course, Martha. I'll be glad to thread your needles all the time. Here, let me show you a little trick my mother uses. She threads three or four needles onto the same spool of thread one after another one. When she needs a threaded needle, she pulls it out, breaks off the thread and leaves the rest of the needles threaded. I'll do that for you next time."

"Bless you, Teressa. I don't know what I'd do without you." The woman paid for the goods and hurried outside.

"Lunch, dinner—whatever you call it," Morgan said in a rush. For just a moment he felt tongue-tied. He hadn't felt that way around a female since the first time he and Linda Sue had an educational experience behind the schoolhouse one night. They had touched and fondled and kissed and learned about each other's bodies in a way that made them both feel a lot better.

He jerked his mind back to the present. "What I mean is, I'd like to have dinner with you this noon, if it would be all right."

"What? Oh, my. Well, yes, I'm sure. I don't have

anything pressing here at the shop. Why don't we go about eleven-thirty and beat the rush. Not that the places I eat are ever full. Mostly I eat here at the shop, but I do go out now and then. Could I pick out the eatery?"

"Be glad to have you do so. I don't know much about Miles City yet."

He said he'd pick her up at the right time, bid her good-bye and left for the boardwalk.

He paused a minute just past her shop and tried to remember where he had been going. Finding a person he knew from the old days was quite a surprise. It didn't happen often. He grinned. He was glad she'd spotted him. He frowned in wonder about the strange way she had made him feel like he was 15 and never had touched a girl's body anywhere.

He shook his head remembering how he felt when Teressa had turned and smiled at him. Remarkable. It was as if someone had hit him in the stomach.

Someone on the boardwalk brushed past him and he shook his head. Now, there was one little lady who he would not forget overnight. Not a chance. He remembered the curious way she had smiled, how her eyes lit up when he had said her name, how she had blushed so easily. Yes, he would remember Teressa Yardley for a long time.

Now where was he going before he stopped to look at that bald eagle in the window?

Shotgun!

Uh-huh. The waitress at Hannah's Place. He didn't even know her name. Buckskin shook his head. He'd never been with a woman all night and not even know her name. Somehow that night it just never came up. It had been pure passion—wild, animal sex, nothing more.

He checked his watch. Not yet nine o'clock. He'd rolled out of bed too early. Morgan found a pair of chairs outside a store and eased into one of them. He liked the custom of putting chairs in front of some stores so people could sit and talk, just contemplate, wait for somebody or take a nap.

The derby man wasn't missing. He did seem hard to find. Why was Josh suddenly out of circulation, out of business? Was he still on the team as a buyer for the St. Paul's stockyard? Had he cashed any checks lately at the bank? If the rustlers were using him for their payoff, he'd have to have cash money on the cracker barrel for them. Where else than from the local bank?

Buckskin came down from his chair with a thump and lifted off in a rush heading for the Miles City Bank. Most bankers were close about money matters of their customers, but with the pressure of the 23 ranchers of the Miles City district of the Montana Stockgrowers Association, Morgan figured he could find out what he needed to know.

He stepped into the bank, which he found almost straight across the street from Hannah's

75

Place. It was like most, with a generous lobby in front, a counter with steel cages fronting the tellers. There were spots for three but only one place occupied. He looked at the other side of the bank and found two desks in the front and two offices with closed doors.

One of the doors opened and a man came out. Buckskin was surprised. He recognized Mr. Yardley at once. He walked toward the banker, and when the man looked up, Morgan spoke.

"Mr. Yardley, I wondered if I could have a few minutes of your time?"

Yardley stopped and nodded. He frowned slightly, then waved Morgan into his office, letting him go in first. He closed the door and then frowned at Morgan. Slowly he began to nod; then he smiled.

"Yes, I have it. I do know you. When I first saw you I thought your face had a familiar look. You're Frank Leslie's boy. You lived out on the Spade Bit up in Idaho."

Morgan held out his hand. "Yes, sir, Mr. Yardley. Guilty. It's been some time."

Yardley waved at a chair across a desk that had three stacks of papers on top. Paperweights held down two of the stacks, a third evidently was the at work pile. Morgan sat in the chair and Yardley sank down himself in a high-backed chair behind the desk.

"Well, now don't tell me. I'm clawing at my memory trying to remember your name. Not right at the tip of my tongue but I'm getting there. Your name was different from your father's. Something about your mother. Morgan. Yes, you were Lee Morgan. Now I remember. That last year you were in town my daughter had quite a crush on you."

"Right, Mr. Yardley. I ran into Teressa about ten minutes ago. We're going to have lunch together and talk over old times."

"So, Mr. Morgan, what brings you into our small town?"

He explained his job and the banker nodded.

"Three of the small ranchers are almost at the end of their credit. They've been working hard, but if you lose half of your years's cash crop of steers, it makes it almost impossible to stay in business."

"I'm trying to stop all of that. I'd guess that all of the twenty-three ranchers in this area bank with you?"

"Yes, they do, from the largest to the smallest."

"Good, I'm hoping that will be a factor in your telling me what I want to know. I've been trying to figure out how they do it, and the only thing I can figure is that there is a lot of collusion and bribery along the way. Somehow they sell the stolen cattle to the stockyards and get the train to stop to pick them up at a siding on one or the other side of town. Just how they do it, I'm not sure yet."

Morgan watched the banker, who had leaned back and followed the logic of it all the way.

"What somebody needs is money to pay for the stolen cattle. These men won't take even the best cashier's check or bank draft. They will deal only in cash."

The banker shifted in his chair. "I'm afraid I see where you're leading."

"No way around it, Mr. Yardley. I have to ask you if one of your customers has withdrawn large sums of cash at various times over the past two months."

"I can say yes to that without violating any confidential customer information," the banker said.

"Good. So the money has been available. Now I want to ask you the tough question. Was the money withdrawn from a St. Paul Stockyard account by a local man named Josh Eagleston."

Buckskin watched Yardley closely. His left eye twitched and his lips tightened just a bit.

"I can't tell you that, Morgan."

"Mr. Yardley, you need to tell me so I can get about stopping this illegal rustling. We have to stop it before they drive three or four or six of your customers out of business."

"Business ethics, Mr. Morgan. I'm sure you understand."

Buckskin stood and walked around the room, went to the window and peered out. Then he came back.

"I'm having a talk with the county sheriff later on today. I'm sure that he'll tell me that everyone knowingly associated with the rustling in any capacity can and will be charged in these rustling arrest warrants. That will include the railroad men who stop the train and load the stolen cattle, the cattle buyer who pays for them and the banker who supplies the cattle buyer with the money. That is you, Mr. Yardley. Rustling in Montana is a hanging offense, Mr. Yardley."

The banker held his head in his hands. He shook his head, then moved his hands. "The first two or three times I couldn't figure out what he was doing with the money. It came in by wire from the stockyard's bank in St. Paul. A day or two later it would be withdrawn. Then I heard about the rustling. I guess I knew it all tied together. But business is business."

"Josh is in hiding somewhere. He doesn't tend bar anymore at that saloon. I don't know where he is. I would say that if you cooperate with us from now on, Mr. Yardley, that your name would never come up as a defendant in any criminal charges that are brought. How many accounts does the stockyard company have with you?"

"Three. They use various ones. Never the same one twice."

"Good. I'll get a court order instructing you to put a freeze on those accounts. No money may be put in them or taken out of them without permission of the court. Can you accept that, Mr. Yardley?"

"I can. I didn't know for sure what he was doing with the money."

"No problem. We'll go at them another way. This won't stop them, but it will slow them down a little. Josh or a new buyer will have to have the cash ready. Where's the next closest bank he could use?"

"Not much between here and Billings?" Yardley said.

"What about Glendive to the east?"

"Closer. Yes, old man Fogarty has a bank there. He probably would do business with the stock-yards in St. Paul."

"At least I'll know where to look." Morgan stood and held out his hand. "Mr. Yardley, I'm sorry I had to come with such bad news, but my guess is that you're glad to be out from under the trouble you thought you might be a part of."

Yardley took his hand and smiled. "I am relieved. Let me get you those names and account numbers so you can get your restraining order from the court. The circuit judge is in town during this month, so you shouldn't have any trouble."

"Oh, I'd like the balances on each of those three accounts as well."

A half hour later, Morgan walked into the county sheriff's office and told him the story of the rustling and the money that supported it.

"Yep," the sheriff said. He was in his sixties and moved slowly but with a determined fierceness that boded no refusal of an arm or a leg to obey his command.

Shotgun!

"You want to put a freeze on those accounts? You think that will help?"

"Sheriff, if the man who is paying for the cattle can't get any money out of the bank, it will grind things to a stop at least for a week or so. Also it will tell me for sure who is doing the buying and who should be on the list of men to hang."

"Right. I'd give a lot to get this rustling thing settled. Been friends with most of the big ranchers for years. Right now I just don't have the men to do a good study on it. Glad you're here."

Another half hour passed before Morgan and the sheriff went to the courtroom upstairs and then to the judge's chambers and presented the request for the freezing of assets in the three accounts.

Morgan had only started to explain when the judge nodded. "Got it, boy. No money, no pay for the critters and no more rustling. Until they figure a new way to get the money. Like Billings or Glendive."

"At least we can slow them down a little, your honor."

The judge signed the court orders and the sheriff walked them over to the bank. Then the sheriff and the banker went out for coffee and chocolate cake.

Morgan checked his pocket watch. He snapped the cover open. No time now to go see the waitress at Hannah's Place. After lunch.

He walked back toward the seamstress's shop.

One thing that Miles City had over Denver. He could walk to any spot in town in five minutes. Denver had grown too big for her britches. He might just relocate to Colorado Springs or Boulder. He'd heard a lot of good things about Colorado Springs.

Teressa came out from behind a curtain with pins in her mouth. When she saw him, she let the pins fall into her hand and smiled.

"Oh, yes, lunch. How exciting. Be ready in just a minute."

Morgan smiled at her as she vanished behind the curtain. Then he looked out the front window. He was just in time to see a man in a black derby walk by. Morgan surged toward the front door, determined that this time he wouldn't lose the derby man in the crowd.

Chapter Six

Once out of the dress shop, Morgan spotted the black derby bouncing along 30 feet in front of him. The man wore a dark suit and walked rapidly, moving past some people going the same way, crowding others, and pushing one youth to the side roughly.

Morgan gained on him and kept ten feet to the rear. The man in the derby made no move to slow down or to look behind him. Morgan got a look at the side of his face and decided the man under the derby was the same one who had hired him to do a cowboy job when he was pretending to be a down-and-out cowpuncher in Big Bend.

They walked rapidly down Main, across Third Street, then on past the Cattleman's Hotel at the corner of Main and Second Street. Between Second and Third Street the pedestrians thinned out considerably and Morgan dropped back another

20 feet, ready to turn or shield his face if the other man stopped.

The derby man fairly marched straight ahead. Past Second and toward First Street, there were only three stores and a few houses. Then the business section ended and only houses remained, except for the Miles City Livery at the corner of Main and extending down First Street all the way to the railroad tracks, where they curved away from the town.

The livery had to be his destination. Morgan sat down behind a stunted willow tree and watched the marcher. He never faltered and, with measured strides, soon vanished inside the livery's big door.

Ten minutes later he came out. He had a rifle in the boot and a sack tied on behind his saddle. He wore a black, broad-brimmed cowboy hat and range clothes.

Morgan gave him five minutes; then he jogged down to the livery, asked for a good horse with some depth and speed, got her saddled and angled out the door with not more than an extra word exchanged with the stable man.

The derby man had angled away from town, away from the river. He was barely still in sight as Morgan topped a small rise to the south of town and spotted him moving his mount at a fast walk generally toward the south and west.

Morgan remembered his ranch map and figured the other man was angling toward the

Dempsy spread, which was mostly west and south of town. Morgan hadn't been there, so he had no idea where the ranch buildings were, but it was a bet they were located somewhere close to the Yellowstone River, which was the dividing line between a lot of ranches.

Tailing a rider in open country wasn't the easiest of tasks. Morgan had done it dozens of times before, but never through country like that. In places it was bare, wide-open prairie with hardly a rock or a tree, but plenty of early spring grass.

In other spots there were stunted pines and cottonwoods along the draws and now and then small streams heading for the Yellowstone. Morgan worked draws and what few trees there were and figured, if the derby man hadn't looked behind him walking to the livery, he had no reason to watch behind him now.

Morgan knew Teressa would be pissed at him for ducking out on their lunch date, but he'd be able to explain. Teressa seemed as if she would be the most reasonable female in the world. A good, logical reason would get him off her pitchfork list.

He lifted over a gentle rise expecting to see the black form a half mile ahead, but when he stared at every possible point, the horse and rider did not show up. Where could they have gone?

Morgan searched the area again. Near where he had seen the rider at the last sighting, he spotted the faint impression of a draw that sloped away sharply to the north. It would be the start of a small feeder stream taking runoff to the Yellowstone.

He saw a scattering of trees in that area and kept looking. He had seen a few beef at a distance during most of his ride, and he figured he was on DD range. His watch showed a short few minutes after two o'clock. They had been riding about two hours, that would put them some eight miles from Miles City, and in the heart of the DD-brand range belonging to Lorne Dempsy.

With no one in sight, Morgan angled directly at the last sighting and kicked his mount into a gallop. He kept her at it for a quarter of a mile, then eased off. Now he could see the gully better; it spread out into a respectable valley with the stream reaching good size and breeding a swatch of green with brush and trees for five miles into the distant haze.

Somewhere close to halfway he thought he could make out a distinct increase in the haze and studied it closer. About two miles ahead someone had a fire going, hoping that the trees above it would conceal it.

Morgan scowled. What the hell was the derby man doing out here on Dempsy range unless he had come to ramrod a rustling attempt? He was dressed for cowboy work. He had supplies that could feed some troops he'd stashed out here.

The last few days he could have been back in Big Bend or down the tracks the other way whipping up a crew of five or six cowboys not particular about who they threw a wild loop for.

But why was the recruiter out here working the rustling himself? Did he play it both ways? The range clothes could be a disguise so he would fit in if anyone saw him. He could be out to supply food and to give orders. That made more sense.

So where did that leave Morgan? He wondered how close he should go, but he knew before the question fully formed. He had to go down and confirm that it was a team of cowboys, that the derby man was there as one of them or as a messenger and that they were there with the purpose of rustling cattle. Only then could he ride for the DD spread buildings and get some help to watch the group.

His practiced eye surveyed the area. Plenty of cover for him to ride to within a quarter of a mile, then move up on foot to check the layout. It couldn't be legitimate. Any group of DD riders out here would be supplied and instructed from the DD home place, wherever it was.

Morgan angled to the left, reached the line of trees and worked slowly ahead through them. The banker, Yardley, had told Morgan there had been no large cash withdrawals for at least a week from the stockyard accounts and no deposits for more than that time. If Josh needed cash money to pay off this rustling run, he wouldn't be able to get it.

Kit Dalton

This could be the start of a drive that Josh would watch. He wouldn't have to go get the money he needed until the critters hit the loading chutes. Only this time the cupboard would be bare.

It took Morgan a half hour to ride the mile and a half through the brush. When he stepped down from the saddle, he could smell the wood smoke. He didn't want to take any chances of blundering in so close the rustlers could see him.

He tied the mare in a grassy place where she could graze. Then he lifted the rented Remington repeating rifle from the saddle boot and started his hike through the woods to the rustler's camp.

The sharp smell of the wood smoke in the pure clean air led him forward like a beacon. That meant he would come into camp on the downwind side; he could hear voices carried on the breeze. He couldn't make out any words, but it was happy talk, not arguments.

Morgan moved ahead slowly through the brush and trees. He didn't recognize much of the vegetation. They weren't into the mountains of western Montana, where the pines and firs and hemlocks grew. This was brush and small hardwoods and a few cottonwoods and willow.

He edged around a good-size cottonwood and could see the campsite ahead through some screening brush. He counted six men sitting around the campfire eating. Without making a sound or breaking a dry stick, he moved forward

88

another 20 feet to a fallen log and eased up to look over the top.

Now he had a better view of the camp 40 feet ahead of him. The words of the men came through clearly, but in a jumble of overlapping talk.

"So I told this whore I wouldn't pay her no two dollars. It was the damn fifty-cent floor and she gets all mad and starts to scream."

Morgan spotted the derby man talking to another man in a red shirt. Maybe the other guy was the rustler honcho.

"Getting damn tired of lying around here."

"Yeah, Holt, when the hell we see a little action? This waiting is boring as hell."

The derby man turned and stared hard at the speaker. "You're getting paid, aren't you? So shut up and do what you're told. Tonight or tomorrow night, depending how fast they move that herd. I told you that twice already."

"Hell, won't be tonight, or we'd have heard something," another man said.

The derby man continued talking to the older man with the tan hat and red shirt. Morgan wondered how long the cowboys had been camping out here in the back side of the DD range. Even two or three days would make the chance of being spotted high. Maybe this was to be a bigger strike than usual.

Morgan hesitated. Should he ride for the DD ranch or try to take care of the problem himself?

Slowly he began to grin; then he chuckled sound-lessly and began to pull back.

He'd take care of the problem himself. He wanted a little space between him and the men below. He'd seen the horses picketed around the small opening where spring grass had started coming up. Yes, he'd take care of this little band himself.

Morgan wished that he'd brought some food with him. He found a small feeder creek that emptied into the larger stream and drank his fill. He didn't even have some jerky to chew on. He knew he could find something to eat in the woodsy place, but he couldn't take time to hunt for it. Instead he watched the camp through the rest of the afternoon.

Just after five o'clock he heard a horse coming fast up the valley. A rider charged into the camp and asked the closest man something, then rode over to where Selby Holt and the man in the red shirt sat in the grass. The rider sat a big rugged gray that seemed tired from the hard ride.

The interchange went quickly. It didn't seem to be very friendly. Soon the messenger stepped into the saddle, pulled the mount's head around and trotted out of the clearing heading downstream.

Selby Holt went over toward the men. They were scattered so he had to talk loud, and Morgan could hear him.

"That was the word. We won't work until late tomorrow afternoon. Only be one man on guard

90

duty and we take him out, then have our way. I've decided to stay and work the job with you. This is a big one, and when it's completed, you each get a fifty dollar bonus. So remember that and don't give me any trouble."

"Hey, for fifty bucks I don't give anyone any trouble," a man called and they all laughed.

Morgan grinned and faded deeper into the brush and trees. He had a few preparations to make. With Selby Holt staying, it made things that much better. He sharpened the six-inch blade of his boot knife on a piece of fine-grained rock he had found near the stream; then he checked his six-gun and the rifle. It was a Winchester five-round repeater. He had a box of 20 extra rounds in the saddlebag. He wouldn't need them.

What he needed most was darkness. He moved up again to watch the camp. The five riders had bunched to one side of the fire, and the derby man and the red shirt were on the other side. They had eaten an evening meal that one of the men fixed from the sack that Holt had brought.

Morgan memorized where the men spread out their blankets. The horses had been moved back a ways in the edge of the valley. Morgan grinned, then took a quick nap. He ordered himself to wake up just before midnight.

Later he stirred and came awake. He had no idea what time it was but the darkness was deep. He adjusted his revolver in leather, picked up his rifle and worked his way forward. Morgan went silently around the sleeping men and toward their horses. All had been unsaddled.

He'd always been good with horses. He found the first saddle and took off the lariat from it, then moved to the next saddle and did the same thing. He carried the ropes and worked up slowly to the first horse and rubbed her nose and head, then her flanks and undid the picket rope and moved her gently back to the next horse.

In ten minutes he had all seven of the horses formed into a line using the lariats and their reins. Slowly he led them upstream across an open stretch of 100 yards of moonless semidarkness.

He kept going for another half mile until the woods closed in and made the going tougher. There he tied the lead line to a sturdy tree and went into the brush and found his horse. It took him a half hour but there was no real rush. Next he led his mount back down the valley near the camp and tied her.

It took him ten minutes to make sure he found the man he wanted. Selby Holt lay rolled in his blanket to keep out the evening chill. Morgan drew his Colt and brought it down sharply on the side of Holt's head. He groaned, tried to sit up, then fell back unconscious.

Morgan holstered the Colt, hoisted Holt over his shoulder and walked out of camp with the recruiter. Back at his horse, Morgan draped Holt over the saddle and balanced him there as he walked the mare upstream to where he'd left the other horses. There he used some of the lead line to tie Holt's hands and feet together under the belly of one of the barebacked horses.

Then Morgan rode. It took him a half hour to get out of the trees and brush; then he cut due north, hoping it would put him somewhere near the DD-brand ranch buildings.

Two hours later he and the string of seven horses came to the Northern Pacific tracks and he knew he'd come far enough north. Which way—east or west to find the double D?

Holt became conscious a half hour before and begun shouting and wailing. Twice Morgan had stopped and talked to him.

"Holt, I know who you are and what you do. Right now we're going to the Double D ranch, where I'll turn you over to Lorne Dempsy to do with you as he wants. Now keep quiet or I'll gag you."

That shut Holt up.

Morgan turned west and came to the dark Dempsy spread within two miles. He banged on the ranch house kitchen door with his six-gun butt until somebody stomped to the door. It turned out to be the cook.

It took Morgan ten minutes to explain to Dempsy what he'd found in his back country. Then almost a half hour to roust out of bed a dozen riders, get them awake and dressed and on their mounts. Dempsy sent his foreman, Ward Trask, to help round up the horseless rustlers.

"Hang every one of the bastards that you catch," Dempsy thundered.

Morgan shook his head in the kitchen lamp-light. "Can't do that, Mr. Dempsy. They haven't rustled any cattle yet. You can't hang a man for what he might do."

"Damn it, should be able to. What about this worm, this Holt?"

"Same thing with him. You could take him to the sheriff and charge him with conspiracy to rustle cattle, but no good judge would give him more than sixty days in the county jail. I've got some ideas for him when we get back. You have a lockup where we can leave him?"

They put him in the meat house, which had enough air circulation so he wouldn't die.

When the riders left, somebody said it was nearly three o'clock. They had an hour's ride. One of the men on the jaunt rode a big gray, and the closer Morgan got to him, the more certain he was he had been the messenger.

Morgan rode up beside the foreman in the darkness. "Trask, who's the man on the gray gelding?"

"New man I hired on for the upcoming roundup. Think he said his name was Cavanaugh."

Morgan rode back by the young cowboy and started talking. "Understand your name is Cavanaugh. Any relation to the Cavanaughs in Billings?

Shotgun!

The cowboy shook his head. "Not that I know of. I'm from farther south in Wyoming."

Morgan moved over close so his leg almost brushed the other rider's. "Cavanaugh, I want you to lead me back to that valley where you were just before dark. You rode in and told Holt that tonight wasn't right for the rustling."

The kid moved away from Morgan. "No damn such thing."

"You want me to blow you out of the saddle right now, Cavanaugh?"

"You got no cause—"

"Shut up. I saw you up the creek, talking to Holt. You came in fast and you talked and you left fast. I don't know this ranch. You do or you couldn't have found the rustlers. Now, you lead this crew up there fast, with no detours, and I might forget I saw you up here. Otherwise, you'll hang with the rest of them. Understood?"

"Yeah, okay. I didn't rustle no damn cattle."

"You tried to help. That's the same thing under the law. Now let's get out front. I'll do the talking. You do the leading."

With that help, they found the campsite just before dawn. Morgan went around the sleepers, gathering up six-guns and rifles. He had all but one, when one of the man reared up and fired a shot at him. Morgan drew and fired before the man could get off another shot. The round missed dead center, but caught the rustler in the shoulder, slamming him to the ground.

Then the other DD riders swarmed in with guns out and the rustlers held their hands up in surprise. The man in the red shirt made a break for it in the trees, but Morgan rode after him, fired twice in front of him and brought him back.

They waited until daylight. The six men were roped together with lariats and forced to walk back to the ranch, nearly six miles away.

All the cowboys hated to walk. The idea of going even six miles on foot turned out to be severe punishment for the men. The DD riders kept jawing at the walkers, figuring out how they could hang them.

"I say we put a pole between the cookshack and the bunkhouse," one cowboy called out. "That way we can drop three of them at a time."

There were a dozen other suggestions and the rustlers dropped their heads more and more as they walked. By the time they got to the ranch buildings, all were sure that they would be hung.

Morgan kept his word to Cavanaugh. He said nothing about his being in on the plot. Buckskin talked to him as the DD men ate a late breakfast.

"Holt recruit you?"

"Yes, in Big Bend."

"Your job was to keep him and the rustlers up to date about where the best herd was?"

"Right. I contacted him once in town and twice at the camp."

"How long the men been out there?"

"Three days."

Shotgun!

"Cavanaugh, if I was you, I'd draw my pay and high-tail it down the trail fast as I could ride. You want to keep a rope off your neck you best get moving before Holt is brought out. He'll give you up to us quick to save his hide. If you're gone, he can't. Now go draw your wages and pack your kit."

Cavanaugh rode out of the ranch 20 minutes later.

Lorne Dempsy sat in his oversize chair in the ranch house kitchen and pounded a big table with his fist. "You mean I can't hang these bastards. What can I do?"

"Scare the shit out of them. Make them think you're going to hang them. Then kick them off your ranch. How about without their horses and without their boots."

A gleam came in the nearly 300-pound rancher. "Yeah, without their boots, their shirts, their hats and their pants. Leave 'em in their long underwear and run them for town."

Dempsy laughed until tears came down his cheeks. He wiped them away and turned back to Morgan. "Let's do it now. Trask, you heard it. Get those cowboys stripped down to their long handled underwear and boot them off the place. Make sure they keep walking. Send out a couple of riders to nudge them toward town."

Ten minutes later the neophyte and unsuccessful rustlers took tentative steps along the trail toward Miles City. Two of them had full set of long underwear. Three had only the bottoms, and one man had Eastern-style underwear. They bellowed in rage and shook their fists at Dempsy, but the obese man fired his six-gun in the air and laughed at them.

"Now, what about this damn Holt? He's been in on the rustling from the first, you think?"

"Yes, he recruits the men. I tried to get recruited in Big Bend and he took me. He told me it was a week-long job and then I had to get on the train or the trail and get out of the county fast."

"Can we hang him?"

"We don't have any proof. The court wants proof."

"Hell, we can hang him right here on the ranch. I've got all the proof I want."

Morgan shook his head. "That would have worked twenty years ago. Now it won't. We've got more law than that now. Somebody would file charges and you'd get convicted of murder. Not a good plan."

"So what the hell?"

"So we make him talk. We keep him here on bread and water and we make him spell out the whole damn plan of the smugglers."

Dempsy laughed and it came out vicious and cruel. "Yeah, now you're talking. I know exactly how we can make the fancy bastard talk."

An hour later Morgan watched as they led Holt out of the meat house. He blinked at the

Shotgun!

light, looked around confused for a moment, then dropped to his knees.

"Gonna hang your ass, Holt," Dempsy said. He'd struggled out of the house and sat on a sturdy bench in the middle of the ranch yard. A fire had been started and burned brightly to one side.

"I don't understand what's going on," Holt said.

"You brought food and instructions to your six rustlers in the hills out here on the Double D spread," Morgan said. "I followed you and brought you back here last night. Looks like they're going to hang you for rustling."

"No cattle were touched or moved," Holt said. "You have no grounds to even hold me, let alone hang me. I want to talk to my lawyer."

Dempsy laughed, spittle drooled out the corner of his mouth and his small eyes shrank even smaller. "Not a chance. You'll hang. First, we want to talk with you. You're going to spell out exactly who is doing the smuggling, who the real brain is behind it, how it works, who gets the money—the whole damn thing."

"I don't know what you're talking about. I'm not a rustler."

"You keep saying that." Dempsy turned and looked at the fire. "Are they hot yet?"

"Damn near, Mr. Dempsy. Another minute or two." The words came from a man with heavy leather gloves who turned over two branding irons in the fire. They both were the DD brand.

"Strip off his shirt and bring him over by the

99

fire. Probably need two men on each leg to hold the bastard and two on each arm. Put him facedown in the dirt there and we'll get a good brand on his back."

The cowboys pulled off Holt's shirt, ripping it in half in the process, and dragged him up near the fire. The iron man nodded.

"Two irons ready, Mr. Dempsy."

They flopped Holt down in the dirt and four men held him there, one with his boot in the middle of Holt's back. Holt screamed in rage and fury. Another man grabbed one of the branding irons and lifted it from the fire. It glowed red-hot as he carried it to the victim.

"Show it to him!" Dempsy said. "Show the bastard what's gonna brand his back for all goddamned time."

The branding man held the red-hot iron a foot from the Holt's face and he screamed.

"No, no. I'll tell you everything. Keep that thing away from me." Holt began sobbing and looked up at Dempsy.

The fat man motioned with his head and the brander took the iron back to the fire. "Let him sit up," Dempsy said. "Now you sneaky bastard, you tell us everything about this rustling scheme."

Holt wiped his hands over his face. The dirt on his hands streaked his face. Tears still came down his cheeks. He took a deep breath.

"Yes." He gasped twice, then went on. "Yes. I'll tell you anything you want to know."

Shotgun!

"Names?" Morgan asked.

"Oh, yes, any names I know and you want."

"All right, all right. Enough of this blubbering," Dempsy growled. "Let's get at it."

Holt swallowed, wiped his face again. "I first heard about it nearly six months ago. The plan was spelled out to me by a man I hardly knew."

Before he could continue, a rifle boomed from somewhere behind them and the heavy slug caught Holt in his left eye and blew half his skull off.

Chapter Seven

The shot that splattered half of Holt's skull all over the far side of the Dempsy ranch yard came from behind Morgan. He whirled, his six-gun out, but he had no target. The ranch house showed behind them. No windows were open. He saw no puff of white smoke from the black powder.

Just to the side of the house stood the crew cookshack and beyond that the bunkhouse. Morgan sprinted to the edge of the cookshack, but saw no one. He ran to the side of the bunkhouse and circled it with his Colt ready, but he saw no shooter.

"What the hell?" Dempsy bellowed. "Who shot Holt?"

Morgan charged into the bunkhouse. Only one man inside, and he lay stretched on a bunk face-down snoring. Morgan looked under the bunk and found a rifle, but when he smelled it, he could tell it hadn't been fired recently. He checked every other rifle he could find in the bunkhouse but none had been fired.

Outside again, Morgan scowled at the body sprawled in the dirt. He turned to the ranch owner. "Who could have done this?"

The ranch owner scowled right back at Morgan. "Damn it to hell, I wanted you to tell me. I got me twelve riders, and they all went on the run with you guys except Zeek who's been skunk drunk for three days now. He's still sleeping it off in the bunkhouse."

"Anybody else around?" Morgan asked.

"Sure. Fatboy, the cook. My wife, Marjorie, and my daughter, Tina. You want to question them, too?"

Morgan shook his head. "Damn it. We were so close. We had a talker here. He could have blown this whole thing wide open to breakfast."

"Could don't put no beef in the stockyards," Dempsy said. He sighed and shook his head. "Okay, you loafers. Pick up what's left of this man and bury him. I'll send a report to the sheriff. Not much more we can do now."

"Damn it!" Morgan said again. He shook his head. "It's like starting all over again."

He walked around in a small circle, then stared at the angle the shot must have taken. Casually he walked back to where the body still lay and stared at it a moment, then lined it up with where he had been sitting in the dirt and upward to where the shot must have come from. He turned and wandered out the other way, then went and found his horse tied to the side of the corral.

He knew one thing for sure. Holt would have spilled his guts right out on the dirt for them. He was ready to tell them everything he knew. Somebody didn't want him to. Somebody shot him dead. When he lined up the body where Holt had sat, it was easy to see that the shot that had killed Holt had come not from between the ranch house and the cookshack, but from the kitchen door that led into the main ranch house. Someone inside the ranch house had killed Holt.

Morgan talked with the ranch owner before he left. Dempsy had gone back inside the kitchen, and Morgan found him in his oversize chair near the varnished plank table.

"Thanks for saving my beef," Dempsy said. "In the bustle I forgot to say that. If you hadn't followed Holt out of town, I'd be out about four hundred head of beef. Heard they were going to go after the critters tonight."

"You're welcome. I wish I had stopped on the way here with Holt and made him tell me everything. No chance to do that part over again."

"Next time," Dempsy said. "The sons of bitches can't be lucky all the time. We're bound to grab them one of these times."

"I'll be in touch," Morgan said. "Oh, is the committee going to meet again this Friday?"

"Did mention something about it. We'll let you

know with a note in your hotel box if it's to happen. Most of us ranchers are starting to get busy, so it just depends."

Morgan waved and rode out of the DD-brand yard. On a little rise to the side of the house, he saw two men with shovels digging into the earth near a number of gravestones. Holt would rest through the ages near strangers.

It was near noon when Morgan rode back into Miles City. He went straight to the seamstress shop, but found it closed and locked. Out to lunch again. He had turned the horse in at the livery and continued up the boardwalk past the real-estate office to Hannah's Place Saloon.

He had whacked the dust off his clothes and hat at the livery, then did a quick washup in a pewter bowl set out for that purpose and even combed his hair before he slid back on the brown Stetson with the black-and-white-diamond headband.

Now he stepped into Hannah's Place and went directly to the second table on the lunch side and looked around. It took a minute or two before the redhead came forward with a cup of coffee and silverware and put them in front of him.

"Hello. Sorry I haven't been in before but I've been busy," he said.

She lifted her brows.

"No, I mean really busy." He grinned. "I never did catch your name."

"Red. Call me Red, half the people in town do.

What'll you have? The lunch special?"

"What is it?"

"Bowl of soup, beef barbecue sandwich and a piece of pie. Coffee, of course."

"Done. Only bring two of those barbecues. I could eat half a grizzly bear."

She smiled. "You have been busy." She left and he watched her tight little rear end twitching across the way under her skirt. She wore another one of those white blouses. He grinned. Red was put together exactly right with everything going for her, while poor Teressa Yardley had almost nothing going for her.

Well, Teressa had that smile, that little half grin that did him in. Then there was the gentle way she spoke and those soft brown eyes that he wanted to dive right into. Even without trying, Teressa gave a man a lot to remember.

Morgan contrasted that with Red's surging bare breasts and the way they swayed and then heated up so fast when he chewed on them and licked her nipples. Oh, yes, and her soft, silky inner thighs.

Morgan shifted his thoughts to something else. He had to find Josh Eagleston. So far he hadn't had time to look for him. He would this afternoon. If Josh wasn't at that saloon, someone might know where he lived. There was always the postmistress in the Howard General Store. But sometimes the post office folks got a little hesitant about giving out addresses. He knew they wouldn't do it in a big town. Still, that idea might work here. This was Miles City.

The soup came a moment later. Red set it down and left at once. Crackers filled another bowl on the table. When Morgan had started to say something, Red had held up one finger and hurried away. She'd be back so he could finish the idea. Whatever it was. She was one amazing lady: attractive, pleasant, full bodied and so damn much fun in bed.

Morgan closed his eyes and concentrated on getting back to thinking about work. So how would he find Josh? It wouldn't be easy.

Red brought the sandwiches. Each was six inches square and looked as if it had half a steer barbecued and sliced between the large square bun that resembled a thin loaf of bread.

"Wow, you didn't say they were this big."

She grinned. "You didn't ask."

She pulled out the chair opposite him and sat down. "You've been buying a lot of property?"

For a moment he didn't connect. Then he remembered his cover-up story.

"Looking mostly. Only the big boss can buy. I make recommendations."

He had a few bites of his sandwich and she produced a cup of coffee for herself. Then he said, "About the other night—"

She looked up, her face neutral. Then she smiled. "I loved it." Their voices were low, but still she looked around to see if anyone was close.

The little saloon was almost deserted. "Tonight I want you to come to my place. Meet me here at eight and I'll take you there."

"At eight. I think that might be arranged. This sandwich is good."

"I'm glad." She stood and he admired her body in the white blouse and tight skirt that came to the floor. "See you tonight. I have some work to do."

Morgan finished the soup and the second sandwich, but had no room for pie. He paid 65 cents for the meal and went out to find the saloon where he had first talked to Josh Eagleston. The man behind the bar shook his head when Morgan asked about Josh.

"I'm new on the job. I don't know no Josh. If he was here, he's gone and I don't know where."

"What about the boss? Is he around?"

"Not more than he has to be. Right now, he ain't here."

"Great. I owed Josh twenty bucks. Guess he won't get it."

The bar man shrugged, evidently really not knowing what had happened to Josh.

That killed Morgan's search for the moment. He left the saloon and walked across the dirt street to the Howard General Store on the other corner. The store held the usual trade goods. A little of everything from women's clothes to nails, roofing, pliers and horse collars. As more specialty stores opened in town, the general store would be frozen out of business, but not yet. Business looked good.

Morgan went past horse blankets and canned goods, a cracker barrel and candy in a two-gallon glass bottle to a small counter at the side marked as the post office.

No one stood waiting behind the counter. Morgan shifted his weight from one foot to the other and soon a woman came up. She had a bad limp but a big smile.

"G'day," she said. "Could I be helping you now?"

She had one eye nearly closed and a nose far too large for her face. Her hair hung in black strands cut short off her neck. Her lopsided smile made Morgan return a smile.

"You sure can. Hunting a guy I can't find. Said he lived in town but he quit where he's working and I promised to meet him today. Suppose you can help me?"

She looked over the way he had come and lifted her brows. "Ain't supposed to, but I might if'n I know who the gent or lady is?"

"Oh, yeah. Josh Eagleston. Used to tend bar at one of the saloons."

"Yep, recollect the gent. He used to come get his mail. Then he had them put an address on it. 'Course we don't got no home delivery here yet, but I got a box for him. Still in town, I guess."

"Could I ask for the address?"

She hesitated, looked to her left, then grinned.

"For such a nice smile from a handsome lad like you, anything." She looked at the box and nodded.

"Yep, 144 B Street. That'd be down toward First Street on B, which is two blocks behind Main."

"Thanks. Oh, I should have three of those three-cent stamps."

She nodded, gave him the small squares and he paid her for them and ambled out of the store.

The address turned out to be Maud Christian's Board & Room. No one answered the door when he knocked. He opened it as most folks do at a board & room and called out.

"Mrs. Christian?"

"In a minute, damn it."

Morgan grinned and waited. The woman who came around the corner three minutes later was tall and slender. "So?"

"Looking for Mr. Eagleston. Does he still live here?"

She cackled, her soaring laugh piercing through the three-story house like lightning. "Live here? He never more than hung his hat here. If you find him, you pry three weeks room and board money out of him for me. The little sidewinder. Money he has for the whores and the gambling, but not for his rooming house. He'll never stay here again—that I kin tell you certain. He's no good."

"If I can find him, I'll try to collect."

After that, Morgan checked every bar in town.

Shotgun!

He figured there were seven or eight, but he lost track. At each one other than Hannah's Place, he asked the barkeep if he knew Josh and if he had a notion where he was. Three of the aprons knew of Josh, three said they didn't and one man said he figured Josh had moved on down the rail line to greener pastures.

Morgan gave up and walked back toward his hotel. He passed the seamstress and saw that she had a sign advertising dressmaking and tailoring. He went in and she came to the front at once. There were no customers in the small store.

Teressa had both small fists on her hips as she frowned at him. "A gentleman would at least have excused himself and not flown out the front door and never returned. I waited for you for an hour yesterday. What in the world happened?"

He explained to her that it had been urgent business that couldn't be put off. "Acutally I saw someone go past on the boardwalk I had to talk to right then and there. I almost lost him, but at last we talked. Then one thing led to another and I couldn't get back here. I'm sorry. It was important to my work or I wouldn't have left."

She seemed satisfied. Her hands slowly unclenched and she dropped her hands to her side. It took longer for the slow smile to work across her thin face.

"Well, I guess it's all right. I really don't enjoy waiting for someone who never comes."

"Never happen again. I can guarantee it."

"Unless some important business deal comes up."

"It won't. Why don't I take you to dinner tonight to make up for yesterday?"

Her face lit up like a new sun had just hit it. Then she frowned. "Oh, dear. This is the night Mother has her guest dinner at our house. She invites four others and me to come and have dinner. I really—no, I just can't have dinner with you tonight."

"Maybe lunch tomorrow?"

She brightened. "Oh, yes, I'd like that. We'll go to the same place we were going to go to yesterday."

"Good. Oh, I'm trying to find Josh Eagleston. Have you heard of him?"

"Josh. No, I'm sure I haven't. I have a cousin named Josh and it's always been a favorite name. If I knew one in town I surely would remember it."

"Thanks, anyway. I better be looking some more."

Morgan started to turn but she stepped closer, reached out and touched his arm. "I'm glad you stopped by, just ever so glad." He saw the emotion in her eyes and realized this was as forward as she had ever been in her life with a man.

Morgan smiled and caught her hand. He lifted it to his lips and kissed it gently. "Teressa, I'm glad I stopped in, too. I'm looking forward to more talk about Boise at our lunch tomorrow."

Shotgun!

Then he let go of her hand and went to the door. When he closed the door, he saw her still standing where he had left her, wearing that curious smile as she watched him.

Good, one small fence mended. He stepped up to the next level of the boardwalk in front of the real-estate offices. Each business had built the boardwalk in front of its location. Sometimes it was level, sometimes it went up or down a step, depending where the merchant wanted to situate it. Some towns had passed laws that the boardwalks had to be level, but evidently there was no such edict in Miles City.

Morgan was about to take his next step on the boardwalk when someone bumped into him and he staggered forward. At that point the boardwalk took a ten-inch drop to the next level in front of Hannah's Place, and Morgan didn't see the drop off. When his foot dropped farther than he figured it would as he half stumbled, he lost his balance and lunged forward.

At that precise moment a six-gun blasted from directly in front of him and not more than 20 feet away. The slug intended for his heart nipped the top of his shirt and skittered into the side of the real-estate office.

Morgan caught his balance, drew his Colt and surged forward. When the gunman realized he'd missed the easy shot, he darted past Hannah's Place into an empty lot and raced away.

Morgan had trouble getting past two elderly

ladies on the boardwalk, and by the time he got to the corner of the saloon and looked to the left, the attacker vanished around the side of the saloon.

Morgan pounded after him, his long legs chewing up the ground in huge chunks, but he knew the other man had too big a head start. In the alley behind the businesses there were dozens of places to hide, to lie in wait, to set up an ambush that wouldn't fail.

Morgan got to the back of the saloon and he peered around the side of the wooden building. He saw only trash, a barrel smoking, a stray cat and a painfully thin dog digging through some garbage.

Morgan was angry about being shot at, more angry still that he had let the bushwhacker get away. There was nothing he could do about it now. Who had set the man on him? Was this a sign that he was hurting the men who had set up the rustling ring? It must be.

Morgan scowled down the alley, but still saw no one. He went back to the street and down Main to the Cattleman's Hotel. In his room, he laid out a pad of paper, a pen and an inkwell, and he began writing up a report on the chase of Holt. He wanted it down in writing before anyone could change the facts. He wanted the sheriff to have it in case any problems came up about the death of Holt and what had happened to the other rustlers.

Morgan didn't have the names of all the men and he wasn't sure that Dempsy did either. At least he'd have it in writing for the sheriff about how Holt had died. He made no speculation about who fired the fatal shot at the Dempsy ranch.

Morgan also put in the report that he figured the fatal shot came from inside the kitchen of the Dempsy ranch house. He signed the report and sealed it in an envelope that he'd take to the sheriff the next morning.

He had an early supper at a different cafe this time, took care of the steak, potatoes and gravy and walked three blocks to Hannah's Place shortly before seven. As soon as he stepped up to the bar, the redhead came up, smiled sweetly at him and served him a draft beer.

"Early."

"Couldn't wait to get here."

"Good. In five minutes come through that door there at the end of the bar and up the first steps you see."

She vanished and Morgan wondered what she was up to. He didn't mind. Almost anything other than murder would probably be all right with him.

After he finished his beer, he pushed through the door and found one flight of steps and two rooms on each side. He went up the stairs, and at the top, he heard music. Strange. He went toward the music and realized it came from the only door down the small hallway. He hesitated at the

115

door, then took one more step and looked in.

Red, the waitress, sat on an elegantly draped four-poster bed. The music came from a phonograph at one side where a wind-up spring turned a needle against a wax cylinder and produced music of popular ballads. The song, "Oh, Dem Golden Slippers," finished and before he could move, "My Darling Clementine" began.

Morgan looked up at Red, who grinned. "Welcome to my web, you great big fly," she said.

He realized it all at once. Red, here smiling at him, had been toying with him all along. She didn't work at Hannah's Place. She owned the saloon, and she was Hannah. He should have figured that out.

"Hello, Hannah. Nice to make your acquaintance. Why didn't you tell me?"

"Would it have made any difference? I like what I like and I go after what I like. I told you that on the first night we met."

"That you did." The song finished and she turned off the phonograph.

"Nice," he said. "You have a lot of those cylinders?"

"Enough to play them all night and not repeat. What would you like to hear?"

"Anything. I don't get to hear much music."

She put on another wax cylinder and before it finished they had heard "The Flying Trapeze," "Silver Threads Among the Gold" and "I'll Take You Home Again, Kathleen."

Shotgun!

He sat down on the bed beside her and she pushed over so her thigh pressed against his. That was when he realized she wore only a thin robe.

"Aren't you going to be cold in just that?" he asked.

She grinned and reached for the buttons on his brown shirt. "Oh, my. I certainly hope not."

Chapter Eight

They lay side by side in the bed, staring up at the canopy overhead attached to the four-poster. In the light from three coal-oil lamps, the cloth seemed to be constantly changing colors. Hannah reached over and rubbed his chest. It was nearly midnight. They had made love three times. The first time wild and demanding, then slow and loving.

As they rested she began telling him the story of her life and how her father had lost his cattle ranch about 20 miles from Miles City.

"So that was the beginning of the end. It seemed like we had more sick animals and lost more cattle in the breaks than was normal. At last pa realized what had been happening. The bastards on both sides of us had been stealing the calves, taking them away from their mothers as soon as the young ones were able to graze on their own.

"You know a ranch lives or dies on the number

118

of calves that can be produced every year. If you get a ninety-percent drop from the brood cows, all is fine. If half of those are steers you can cut them and feed them out for market. That way, after the first three years, you'll be having some income from the market-ready steers each year down the line.

"We went for three years and had less than ten percent drop on our cows. Pa couldn't believe it. But by then it was too late to prove to anybody what had been happening. That last spring, Pa went out and watched his cows calve. He counted them and put a man out there to guard them. He figured we got over ninety percent live calves.

"When he knew they were old enough to free feed on the range grass, he put a cowboy out there with a rifle as a guard. One night he went out and checked and he stayed four days. When he came back, he had lost his horse and had a rifle slug through his right shoulder.

"He said his rider had quit and thrown in with the rustlers, who had rode in and carried off over two hundred calves. He sat at the kitchen table and cried while Ma tied up his shoulder. He swore he was going to get his rifle and go kill himself a half-dozen rustlers. He didn't because he was too weak to ride.

"Two days later, while Pa's shoulder hurt him like hell, the bank manager came out and said he'd have to foreclose if Pa didn't come up with fifteen hundred dollars to make the two years in back payments on his ranch loan."

"Pa said he'd wire his brother in Kansas City and get the money. Pa didn't have no brother in Kansas City. That night Pa got his first attack. He sat in the chair shaking and shivering and then he screamed. We couldn't figure out how to make him stop screaming.

"That was the last day he went out of the house. He kept screaming and crying and nobody could help him. The doctor came out and tried, but he said it wasn't anything physical. Pa had just given up. He didn't want to live anymore but his body was still strong and refused to die.

"Ma took sick and died a month after that. She died a week before the sheriff came out and ordered us to move off the ranch. The bank took everything that was left and we settled into a small house in town that Pa had paid for when things were good. It was all he had left. Pa didn't talk to no one. He ate only when he was told to. After a while, he couldn't even get out of bed."

Hannah rolled over and there were tears in her eyes. "I ain't told nobody this before. I wanted you to know, just wanted you to know."

"The ranchers—are they some of the ones in business around Miles City now?"

"Most of them, the biggest ones. I don't name names, but the biggest ones almost never get that way by being honest and hardworking."

She changed her mood, rolled on top of Morgan and slid one breast into his mouth.

Shotgun!

"Now how about something a little more enjoyable. I didn't mean to spread out all my troubles for you that way. Really I didn't. Sometimes I just want to talk about it."

He chewed on her breast until she rumbled deep in her throat and he felt the hot blood coursing into his crotch.

"My, my. It seems the man here is not completely worn-out after all. This is going to take some serious planning."

Morgan rolled her over and lay on top of her naked form. "Woman, we don't need any planning. What we need is action." He spread her legs, lifted them, put them on his shoulders, then drove into her hard and fast.

She bellowed in delight and tried to stroke with him, but he was far ahead of her and climaxed with a roar. He quickly let her legs off his shoulders and draped over her, panting as if he'd just finished running a mile.

"You didn't wait for me," she said.

"Damn right," Morgan growled. "My turn."

She laughed. "Good for you. Sometimes I dominate a man without trying. I shouldn't do that. Maybe someday men and women will be equals, but not yet. It's still a man's damn world and I should remember that. Here in my place I get used to ordering men around. Yeah, I like the feeling. Not many women get to do what I do. I love it."

Morgan roused from his recovery and eased off

her. He still wondered about her father.

"Your dad just willed himself to die?"

She blinked and tears welled up and she brushed them away. "No, he retreated into a world of his own. He's still alive. He doesn't know me. Doesn't know who he is or where he is. I hire a woman to feed him and take care of him. He lives up here, down the hall the other way. I try to give him anything he wants. Mostly he sits in a chair and looks out at the prairie and the far-off hills. I think, in his own world of fantasy, he's still running the JC Ranch."

"I'm sorry."

"Yeah, thanks. I've survived. I've learned that a person does what she has to do. Sometimes it hurts and sometimes its better. At least once a week he asks me for his .45 revolver so he can kill himself. I never give it to him."

"Who bought your ranch from the bank?"

"Isaiah Roundtree. Oh, it was all perfectly legal. Three outfits were at the auction. They paid nearly what it was worth, maybe five thousand less. We got forty thousand dollars for it, and that was after the bank loan was paid off. I used half of it to buy the saloon. Yeah, I tell everyone I won it in a poker game, but that was just a little show we staged one night after the cash had changed hands."

"You're quite a woman, Hannah."

She snorted. "Yeah, that's what the banker and half the men I know tell me. Right now I want to make enough money to buy one of the smaller spreads up country and get Dad back on a ranch again. He's only 53. He might snap out of it if he could ride a horse again."

"Possibly. I've seen that kind of thing happen."

They talked again. Then Morgan let Hannah seduce him, and before the night was over, they had made love six times. Morgan wasn't sure just when he would wake up the next morning.

By six a.m., he was wide awake and getting up. He moved slowly so he wouldn't disturb Hannah. As he dressed, he sensed her watching him.

"I always have been an early riser. You snuggle back down and have another nap. No sense in your getting up."

"Breakfast?" she asked.

"Your place isn't open yet. I'll get something across the street. Now have a nap."

She grinned, shook her wild red hair at him and dropped back on the pillow.

Morgan went to three small cafes before he found one open. He slid into a chair at a table halfway back and checked the other early risers. Only three: a couple in their forties and a 30-yr-old man. Morgan looked at the man again. He left the chair, moved over to the counter and looked back at the single man working on bacon and eggs. Then Morgan walked over to the man, who had just stabbed a piece of toast into the yolk of an egg, and sat down across the small table.

"What in the—"

"Don't be alarmed. I've never killed anyone

when he was eating breakfast. I'll wait until I can get you outside where there'll be no witnesses."

"What the hell?"

"That's about as close as you'll come to heaven, Josh. I've been looking all over for you."

The man winced. "Got the wrong man, mister. I'm Larry Lawrence, a drummer out of Omaha. You want some good kitchen knives and meat saws?"

"Forget it, Josh. You're the cattle buyer who lately has been buying rustled cattle with three or four brands and rushing them right through into cattle cars before anyone can find them."

Josh put his fork down. He adjusted his black tie and straightened his dark jacket. "I don't know what you're talking about."

"Five thousand head of prime beef. That's over two hundred thousand dollars worth. That jog your memory?"

"Last year I bought ten times that number of cattle. The cattle shipping season hasn't started yet."

"No, but the rustling season is in full swing. That's the part you know about. You're the only cattle buyer in town, so you have to be buying the rustled stock and putting them on the train to the St. Paul stockyards."

"Speculation. Scurrilous unfounded charges that could get you in real trouble if you repeat them in the presence of more than three other persons. It's called slander, and I'll sue you at the

drop of a branding iron. So watch your mouth."
Josh stood, the rest of his breakfast forgotten.

Morgan stood as well and loomed over the
shorter man. "I won't deal in the law, little
man. First time I catch you with rustled cattle
on your sales receipt or your bill of lading, I'll start
shooting as I would with any other rustler. You
remember that rustling is a hanging offense in
Montana. You better remember it good, because
I'm in town and I'm gonna nail your worthless
hide and watch it cure into leather. Do we
understand each other?"

Josh spun around, too angry to talk. He grabbed
his hat and stalked to the door. Morgan hurried
past him, pushed him to the side and marched
out heading north on Main. Josh came out after
him, stared hard at Morgan for a moment, then
turned south. Morgan stepped into a storefront's
doorway and paused. When he saw Josh striding
away determinedly, he came out and followed
him. It would be interesting to see just where
the angry cattle buyer would go to blow off some
steam.

Josh looked behind him twice on his walk. Both
times Morgan had time enough to slip into a store
or hide behind some people on the boardwalk.
Josh walked quickly past Third Street and turned
in at the bank. It wasn't open yet. He knocked
on the door until someone unlocked it and let
him in. Small-town banks had to be flexible,
Morgan knew.

Josh came out two or three minutes later and even from half a block away, Morgan could see he was angry. He paced up and down for a moment, then walked back along Main half a block to the Northern Pacific train station. He went into the telegraph office.

Morgan grinned. Josh would be asking his company to send money to another bank where he could pick it up. Which way would he go?

Morgan waited in the end of the railway depot while the cattle buyer sent his wires. Then Josh bought a ticket at the counter and went out to wait for the train. When Josh walked out of sight, Morgan went to the ticket window.

"Next train through is eastbound," the agent said. "Should be in here in about half an hour. She's due in at eight-thirty-nine."

Morgan folded a five dollar bill in his hand and showed it to the agent. "That last gent who bought a ticket. How far did he went to go?"

The man's hand moved out, covered Morgan's and came away with the folded bill palmed neatly. "His ticket went to Glendive, about eighty miles up the way. Scheduled to arrive there in three hours."

Morgan nodded and paid for a ticket. Then he faded around the corner from the waiting room and did his time outside, but he kept an eye on Josh.

The cattle buyer rushed on the train before

anyone else. Morgan stepped on the second passenger car and stayed out of Josh's sight for the three-hour ride north and east. There were several stops, but Josh didn't get off at any of them.

Morgan settled down in the passenger car for the rest of the ride. The fabric on the seats had been well used and stained. The front of the seat would still swing either way to form a double seat with passengers facing each other. He caught a small nap.

At Glendive, Morgan watched the cattle buyer leave the train. Then he tailed Josh by half a block to the Merchant's Bank of Glendive. If all went well with Josh's telegram, he should be picking up a large amount of cash wired to the bank from the St. Paul stockyards people.

Morgan had a cup of coffee and a doughnut across the street and watched the bank's front door. Fifteen minutes later, Josh left the bank, followed closely by a man well over six feet tall and favored with bulging muscles. Morgan grinned. How better to advertise that the case you carried held close to your body was filled with thousands and thousands of dollars in greenbacks than to hire a bodyguard?

The wait for the westbound was a little over an hour. On the way back, in the afternoon sunshine, Morgan checked the spots that had sidings and sidings with cattle pens. He found four that looked as if they could load a respectable number of cattle. He wrote down the names in the small notebook he carried in his pocket: Kinsey, Terry, Fallon and Slow Bend.

So Josh had his money. Now he needed a herd to buy. The rustlers had fallen on bad times lately. Morgan wondered if Josh would push them to get a herd ready.

When the train pulled into Miles City, Morgan held back again and followed Josh and his muscle man two blocks north on Main. Then they cut over to B street to the left and entered a house. The number read 316 in hand lettering. It was small and showed no board-and-room sign. Josh could have his own house. A few minutes later the bodyguard left the house and headed back down town. Morgan watched him go, then gave up on Josh leaving and ambled back down Main Street. It was a little after four. He stopped in at Teressa's shop when he saw it still open. He hoped she wasn't mad that he'd missed another lunch date.

She looked up and frowned. "I guess you had some more important business to tend to this afternoon."

"Yes," Morgan said. "But if you don't have to have dinner with your mother again, I'd be please to take you out tonight."

Morgan watched Teressa, amused. She was so open, so wanting, so hoping that he'd ask her again. Her beautiful smile held and he grinned. "I'm ready right now for an early dinner if you are."

Shotgun!

Teressa squealed in delight, leaned over, kissed his cheek, then jumped back, her hand to her mouth. "Oh, I'm sorry. I mean, I'm not sorry that I kissed you, but I didn't mean to be so forward. I mean, I wanted to but I didn't ask you and it's not ladylike to kiss a man in public and anyway I'm glad I kissed your cheek. I'm glad we're going out to dinner. Let me get the shop closed up and fix my hair."

Morgan's grin widened and he nodded. "Sure, go right ahead."

She vanished behind the screen that shut off most of the large back section from the store in front.

Morgan stood near two dress dummies. Both had partly finished dresses on them. The store was feminine, smelling of sachet and rose water. Morgan looked at the bolts of cloth, the treadle sewing machine and a cutting table where cloth had been laid out from one of the bolts and a pattern pinned to it.

Teressa came back a moment later. She wore a different blouse. This one looked fuller around the bodice and didn't emphasize the smallness of her breasts. Her hair shone as if it had been brushed 50 times.

"Ready," she said, her eyes sparkling with delight. She walked beside him to the door. Then outside she locked it and dropped the key in her reticule.

"Where are we eating?" Morgan asked.

"Right down this way. A friend of mine runs the cafe and it is delightful. All homelike and not fancy, and it has excellent food. I think you'll like it."

She walked closely beside him but he knew she would never take his arm without being prompted. He held his left elbow out near her.

"Latch on here so we don't get separated. I'm not used to all of this big-town traffic."

Teressa colored slightly, then put her hand through his arm and held it lightly. He didn't draw her up closer. The color quickly faded from her throat.

They met three women, whom Teressa spoke to. After the last one she glanced at him. "I'm going to be the talk of the town tomorrow. I can just imagine all of the things they will be saying about me."

Morgan chuckled. "My old pa used to tell me it doesn't matter one iota what folks are saying about you, as long as they don't know what they're talking about."

She watched him and nodded. "Yes, yes! Oh, I like that. Your pa must have been a fine man. I never met him but once, I don't think. Leastwise I saw him. I didn't actually speak with him since I was only about twelve at the time."

They came to a cafe with a sign outside advertising Violet's Fine Foods. Morgan held open the screen door and they went in. The first thing he smelled was the glorious scent of baking bread.

Shotgun!

"I'm going to like it here at Violet's," he said. "That bread smells wonderful. I'll have two loaves, a square of butter and a jar of jam."

Teressa believed him for a minute, then got in the spirit of it. "That will be just for your snack before supper. Let's sit over there by the window."

The window tables were for two. The frilly curtains masked much of the Main Street boardwalk traffic from looking in, but still gave the diners a look at the walkers outside.

The menu at each place setting had been handwritten on a square of colored paper. Morgan scanned his quickly—limited to be sure and one type of food in each class. The food was basic but he figured it would be delicious.

A waitress came up, grinned at Teressa and winked. "Made up your minds yet, folks?" she asked.

Teressa ordered the beef stew dinner, with coffee, and a fruit salad and cherry pie.

Morgan asked for the hot beef dinner with mashed potatoes, peas and carrots and a green salad. The salads came first accompanied by a small loaf of bread six inches long and four inches high with a bread knife, a tub of butter and a pot of strawberry jam.

Morgan grinned. "Why didn't I find this place before? I'll be eating most of my meals here from now on."

The food was delicious, and over second cups

131

of coffee, they talked about Boise. There wasn't a lot they didn't both know about. Teressa thought about two more kids they had been in school with.

"Remember Vince Barstow, the towheaded kid who always needed to blow his nose?"

Morgan furrowed his brow, then nodded. "Yes, he was one year behind me, but smarter than most of the kids two years ahead."

"He finished eighth grade and took a year of high school. Then one day he vanished and he came back to town about a year later with a gang of six men who robbed the Halverson State Bank. Three of the robbers got shot and killed including Vince. Nobody could figure him out."

"That blonde, tall teacher we had the last year I was there," Morgan said. "Did she stay around or get married?"

"Miss Nelson. Yes, she was our teacher for almost ten more years at the school. Then she married one of the merchants in town. He had lost his wife to diphtheria. She had three blonde kids and when we heard about her last she was happy as a grasshopper on a mulberry tree."

They went on talking. The waitress came and filled their coffee cups again and winked at Teressa. The pie came later and Morgan had a piece as well and by the time they finished it and talked some more it was almost eight o'clock.

Teressa giggled. "I haven't giggled in years. Nor have I spent hours eating supper."

Shotgun!

"I enjoyed it," Morgan said. They went outside and she turned back toward the shop.

"I do have a dress I have to finish tonight. I promised Mrs. MacEacherin I'd have it done for her tomorrow morning. She's entertaining tomorrow night and it has to be just right."

They walked back to her shop and he saw her inside. She touched his hand.

"Lee Morgan, I had a purely delightful time. I thank you. I hope we can do this again soon."

"Let's plan on it. I'll stop by again."

Then he walked down the boardwalk. For just a moment he wanted to retrace his steps and go back to Hannah's Place, but he figured tonight was a time for sleep.

At the Cattleman's Hotel he found a message in his box. He opened the sealed envelope, guessing it was from the Cattlemen's Committee. It wasn't.

Buck Leslie. Three young cowhands rented horses this afternoon for a week. Asked to leave them here until early tomorrow morning. They want to pick them up at 5 a.m. Came separately, but all said the same thing, and all paid me with a new twenty dollar bill. Made each one go to the bank for change. Figured you should know.

The note was not signed, but it had to have come from the owner at the Miles City Livery.

Morgan went up to his room. It was not 8:30

133

yet, but he would be at the livery before five the next morning to check out the cowhands. This time he'd have some cooking gear with him and a sack of food. He spun on his heel, left the hotel and found the general store not quite closed. He bought what he needed. He'd be ready for an early morning ride and a stay in the brush for two to three days.

It had to be another rustling try. He'd be ready for them.

Chapter Nine

By 4:30 the next morning, Morgan had roused the stable man, and rented a horse. He loaded his sack of food and supplies on the back of his saddle, rode up the street and hid behind an empty house. He sat on his mount, watching the livery.

A little before five, three young cowboys straggled into the livery, picked out their horses from the stalls where they had been left, saddled up and rode out.

The three rode together. They moved along the Yellowstone River a quarter of a mile to the ford, walked the sleepy horses across the cold water, then moved out to the north at a little quicker pace than they had started.

Morgan held back a quarter mile, watching the men, judging where they were headed. There was little cover again for him to hide in. That difficulty pushed him back another quarter until he was a half mile behind them in the early morning darkness. He would take no chances on being spotted.

As it began to get light and dawn came, he caught sight of the riders plainly again. They moved almost due north. Morgan had memorized the map the association had drawn for him, showing where the nearby ranches were situated. Some were far to the east and north, some far to the west. From what he remembered, the Isaiah Roundtree spread was north of the river and slightly to the west of town.

This bunch rode along the eastern edge of the Bar B spread, but he had no idea where they were heading. From where he rode, he couldn't tell if they had checked their backs or not. If they stopped he stopped and remained as motionless as possible. The best way to be spotted in the open was to move. The speck on the landscape could have been a rock or a stump or even a cow. But if it started to move and looked like a horse and a man, they would discover him.

The three men rode for two hours almost due north and nothing happened. Morgan faded to the left or right of the line of march to hide in any of the small creeks or gullies that angled toward the Yellowstone. He figured the rustlers were at least eight miles from the river. The Roundtree spread would probably use the Old West method of establishing rights to land—by homesteading or buying river frontage and then claiming rightful use of one day's ride at right angles to the stream.

Shotgun!

This usually was considered to be 20 miles. In this case, if there were water somewhere north, some other rancher might be ensconced up there and cut down on the old 20-mile rule.

Morgan paused just before he crested a small rise and stared ahead with the binoculars he had brought from his luggage. He adjusted the lens for distance. The three cowboys had stopped and were discussing something. Then one pointed west and they rode that way. When Morgan was sure they were on a set course west, he turned at an angle to their new line of march and saved himself half a mile by cutting across the right angle of the trail they rode.

From the time he crossed the river, Morgan had seen clusters of cattle. Here and there he saw a cow and a calf, a marauding range bull and then a cluster of 15 or 20 mixed cows, calves and steers. As the men moved west, the number of cattle seemed to increase, with a heavy balance on the steer population. Many of them looked market ready to Morgan.

The land around him showed nothing but one huge sea of waving grass. Some rose a foot tall, in other places it hugged the ground where it had been grazed low. For as far as he could see in any direction his view showed only the grass and some rolling country that never turned into hills. He wondered if this soil was good enough to grow crops on if a farmer could get water to it. He had seen much of the wasteland of Nebraska and Kansas sprout with fertile fields once the sod had been broken and the soil worked.

The route of march turned north again, and for another hour they rode through the grass. More cattle were evident. Here and there he found small creeks that supported a smattering of brush and stunted trees.

Half an hour later the rustlers came to a slightly larger copse of trees and brush along a stream. Morgan paused at a small rise and watched the riders ahead of him move into the brush and trees. They did not continue on through.

Morgan wondered if there would be six hands again to rustle the beef. Six men could handle a thousand head of beef on a trail drive. Of course here they had to round them up first. He looked around for some cover of his own. There wasn't any.

Morgan slid off his mount, ground tied her on the reverse slope, crawled up to the crest of the rise and bellied down with the binoculars. First he checked the sun. No chance the sun could flash off his binocular lens and give away his presence.

He concentrated on the center of the brush, and through some sparse trees on one side, he saw where two horses had been tied. Through the lens he spotted smoke rising into the brush. Someone had made a nearly smokeless fire. Morgan lay a little over a quarter of a mile away and the smoke was almost undetectable. He wished he knew their plans.

An hour later Morgan saw a rider come in from the west. The man rode directly into the brush and disappeared. The cowhand could have been a scout out looking for the right place to start a gathering of steers. Or he could have been a spy from the ranch who wanted to let the rustlers know where the best spot to take the cattle would be.

The smoke increased and Morgan figured they were getting some food ready for a noon meal. He checked his railroad watch and saw that it was a little after ten o'clock.

Chances were this outfit wouldn't do any gathering during the day, unless they felt tremendously secure. Night would be their work time.

Morgan looked again for some concealment. A half mile off he saw a depression. At least it would keep him off the skyline and out of sight if any of the rustlers headed his way. He mounted up, rode to the spot and found it to be a small ravine with enough brush to hide him and his horse.

Morgan moved into it at once. He dismounted but left the horse saddled and broke out his sack of food and equipment. He'd had the idea before, but hadn't had the right equipment. Now he did. The best way to break up a rustling operation was to stampede the bunched cattle. On the trail, the hands guarded against a stampede in every way they could. Out here as a defensive tool, it would work wonders. The cowboys couldn't stop the charging cattle. They would have to start over again with a roundup. It would throw off their timing and ruin the whole drive.

The more Morgan thought about it, the more he considered waiting until the men had rounded up their herd and had driven it several miles. Then he'd stampede the cattle and the rustlers couldn't do a thing until the next night.

Morgan sat near a small trickle of water and worked on the material he had brought. He'd seen dynamite used before to spook cattle. It worked almost too easily. He made two bombs with some tape fastening the sticks together. Then he punched a hole in one of the sticks and inserted the long thin metal tube that contained the detonator on one end and a hollow area on the other end.

Into the hollow end he pushed a length of dynamite fuse. The fuse burned at a foot a minute. For a 30-second fuse he used six-inch fuses. That way if the fuse was bad and burned more quickly than the usual rate, he'd still have time to get rid of the bomb without blowing himself up.

He cut off a foot of fuse, took out his watch, then lit the fuse and timed it. The minute hand showed one minute and the second hand had eight seconds on it before the fuse burned out. Close enough.

Morgan made up six of the bombs from the

dozen lengths of 20-percent dynamite he had brought with him. He packed three of them carefully in the gunnysack with the rest of his food and slid three into the right-hand side of his saddlebags. He had a dozen matches in his pocket, so he was ready.

Food came next. He opened a container of canned peaches, ate a big cheese sandwich and finished his meal off by drinking the juice in the can of peaches. A meal fit for any cowboy.

The early morning rising took its toll and he soon stretched out in a patch of warm sun that filtered through the trees and had a short nap. The nap ended abruptly when he heard horse hooves pounding toward him. He grabbed his mount's muzzle so she could do no horse talking with the other animals. Then he peered out from his safe haven. Two cowboys rode past, 50 yards away. They checked the land as they went, and he saw one put a scratch on a pad of paper with a pencil. They were taking a tally to see which way to ride to get their steer, Morgan decided.

The cowhands rode on past and vanished over some small rises to the south. Morgan relaxed again but he couldn't sleep. Just knowing that there were riders out scouting kept him alert. This meant they would be doing their dirty work that night. There was no chance to ride to the Bar B ranch and let Roundtree know what was happening. He'd have to do it on his own.

With that decided, Morgan relaxed in the sun

as it moved over his patch of warmth and about 4:30, he dozed off. He figured the rustlers would be having a big meal to tide them over until tomorrow noon. They should have the cattle rustled and into a pen somewhere along the tracks or in a holding area.

Morgan had about decided that must be the way they worked. Small bunches of cattle were driven to some central holding location where the steers were grazed until they had enough for a load. Then the rustlers notified Josh and he talked to the train people to drop off up to 15 cattle cars at a specific location. Morgan wondered how many steer could be put in a cattle car.

Morgan ate again. He had a chunk of cheese and half an apple pie he'd brought along and all the water he could drink from the stream. Then he packed up and waited for darkness. Just before dusk settled in, he mounted and rode cautiously up to the same rise he had used before. His binoculars showed him that there were more horses in the brush. The cooking fire had probably burned up the dead wood, and it gave off more smoke.

Morgan watched as dusk fell, and just before it grew dark, the men lined up outside the brush on their mounts. There were eight men and a ramrod. That looked as if they wanted to be sure of getting a good herd tonight.

Morgan moved out when the riders below did. The nearly full moon looked three days away from

Shotgun!

total, and it provided enough light so Morgan could trail the sound of the riders and now and then get a glimpse of them from his position 200 yards behind. He used the binoculars, remembering that someone had told him that the glasses at night not only magnified the distance but also the amount of light that was available.

The rustlers rode two miles due west and Morgan saw there were more and more cattle. Someone barked an order into the night and the men spread out in a long line, sweeping everything before them. If they did it right the wings of the line would eventually swing around to the front and meet to trap the animals in the ring of riders.

Morgan sat off a ways and watched the operation. The rustlers circled the catch, cut out the cows and calves and heifers and drove the steers forward. He figured they caught about 20 steers in the try.

Three more times Morgan watched the process. The rustlers had over 100 steer. They shifted directions and worked more northwest, maybe to find more cattle, perhaps to keep farther away from the home place on the Roundtree spread. Morgan wasn't sure, but if it followed form, the home place buildings would be somewhere near the Yellowstone River. Morgan figured they were at least ten miles north of the Yellowstone.

By a little after two a.m., the rustlers had the steer they wanted or they had run out of time.

The critters were spread out in a line now about six wide and 100 yards long. Whips cracked and ropes flailed steer as the rustlers moved the line out in a march that went due west.

Where to? Morgan wished he knew. He tagged along behind until three in the morning. Then he rode around to the front of the steers, staying well away from the point riders. He took out the three bombs and rode slightly ahead and to the north of the critters. He lit the first fuse and threw it directly in the path of the plodding steers. It would go off while they were 30 or 40 yards from the bomb.

He rode to the side north of the line and threw the last two bombs to help push the stampede back into the Bar B range, where they belonged.

The first blast triggered screams from the horses of the two point men. One horse bucked and screamed. It threw the rider and charged away from the blast. The lead steer stopped and others jolted into them from behind.

Just then the second and third blasts thundered into the stillness and the steer, unhappy about having to walk when they wanted to lay down and sleep, tore off away from the blasts. The fear and panic thundered down the line like a chain of lightning, and soon the whole herd of some 500 steer charged across the range due south. There was nothing the cowboys could do to stop them.

Morgan saw one of the point men charge along with the steer, trying to turn them. The rustler fired his six-gun until it was empty, but the fear-crazed steer kept running south. The farther they ran, the more they fanned out, and as Morgan watched the last of the steer fade into the darkness, he saw that they were scattered a half mile wide. Most of them wouldn't stop running until they were exhausted and six or seven miles from their starting point.

Morgan hooked his leg over the saddle horn and grinned. Damn, but it was fun when a plan worked out right. He loved his work.

A half hour later, Morgan heard three pistol shots far to the south and figured the ramrod of the rustlers had called the troops together. The ramrod couldn't do anything with them. The cattle were spread out in three times the area they had been when he captured them. They were dangerously close to the ranch headquarters, and they must know that some of the ranchers had posted rifle guards. Morgan took off at a steady trot, angling back toward Miles City. He might meet a rider or two along the way.

If he got in before the three men who had rented horses, he'd wait for them. They might have an interesting story to tell as the sun came up over the prairie.

Morgan beat the other riders in, arriving a little after five. The sun was up and the town began to come alive. The first two riders who came in from the north were in their early twenties. Morgan tried to strike up a conversation with each one in turn. One would say no more than "Hi."

"Dead tired, mister," the second rider said. "If you want to sell that horse, see me later this afternoon."

The third man looked over the mare, said it might be a possibility and why didn't they talk it over as they had some breakfast. He said he'd been working all night, getting ready for a roundup, and he was starved.

Over breakfast at the only place open in town, Morgan got the kid to talking. "Yeah, I get this job riding, see. The ramrod who hired me said it was a small roundup and they needed three or four extra hands just for a week. Hell, I been on roundups like that before when I didn't have a regular spot riding for a big outfit.

"I figured it was all right. Then he told me he'd pay me ten dollars a day because it was a short job, and I should have been suspicious. But I rented a damn horse and went anyway.

"Soon I figured out it was a rustling try. They made us come in early morning from the backside. Two of the other guys said it was a rustling job. They'd worked for this guy twice before. I wanted out, but by then there was no way to do it. Besides, I could use the ten bucks a day.

"Well, we got maybe five hundred head and started them down a trail west. Went fine for an hour or so. Then all hell cut loose. I was riding drag and having my hands full when the whole sky exploded up near the head of the line. I figured lightning, but I never even saw a cloud in the sky. Then it happened twice more and I knew it had to be dynamite.

"Somebody had been waiting for us and he threw some bombs to spook his own cattle. Let me tell you, it worked. Them critters run seven or eight miles, I swear. No chance we could get them rounded up again. The ramrod was spitting shit, he was so mad. He got us together, paid us off our ten dollars and told us all to get out of Miles City as soon as we could."

"How would you like to stay in town?"

The kid swallowed a gulp of coffee and shook his head, his eyes looking a little wild. "Lefty be damn mad if I did that."

"Lefty won't know. I want you to stay and be ready to testify against Lefty in his trial for rustling."

The kid tensed and he started to rise, but Morgan said, "My Colt is aimed at your belly, kid. You move another inch and you die. Now settle down and smile. I'm saving your ass here from a rustling charge that could get you hung. Smarten up. I don't want you. I want Lefty and the others running this operation. They've been doing this now for two months."

The kid looked scared. He shifted back and forth on the chair. "Lefty said he had two hired guns who would come after anybody who stayed in town after he paid us off."

147

"He's bluffing you, kid. You've played poker. He's got no hired guns. What's Lefty's last name?"

The cowboy shook his head. "Never heard it. He talked to me and a buddy in a saloon one night and signed us on. We both thought it was a real job."

"It was—a real rustling job. I'll pay you a dollar a day until time for the trial. All you have to do is stay in a room at the Cattleman's Hotel until you're needed. Might have you sign some statements about what you did, who hired you and all that. You won't be charged with anything."

It took Morgan another half hour to convince the cowboy to stay in town and cooperate with the county sheriff. At least he had one witness. The kid didn't know much, but at this point any witness was a golden one.

All Morgan had to do was find Lefty and get him arrested on rustling charges. The sheriff would cooperate anyway he could. But finding this Lefty might be a tougher job than it seemed.

Chapter Ten

Hannah Johnson sat at one of the tables on the cafe side of Hannah's Place and scowled at anyone who looked at her. She was as angry as she had ever been and today she would see some of the fruits of her labor. She sipped the whiskey and branch water and nodded. Yes, today she would start the evening-up process.

She had dressed in a tight white blouse that had three buttons open in front, showing just a trace of the cleavage between her breasts. The skirt she wore was close fitting around her hips and hugged her thighs. Then it flared in a wider flounce to the floor. She sat up and stretched her arms upward, and she could feel the blouse stretch tight across her breasts. He wouldn't last five minutes.

She looked at the Seth Thomas clock over the bar. Almost five o'clock. She was to meet him in half an hour on First Street, a half block down from the livery stable. No one would be around there that time of day and no one lived on that block. She found her thin dark coat and slipped into it. Upstairs in her apartment she put on the new black hat with the heavy veil and slipped out the back door. No one was in the alley.

A cat yowled and startled her. She felt in the pockets of the coat and found everything there she would need. She had let the veil down so no one would recognize her. At the end of the alley on Third Street, she turned right and went down Third until she came to A Street, which paralleled Main. From there it was only another two blocks to the spot she would meet him.

He had not wanted to come. Only her threat of telling his wife about his trips to Matilda Jones's whore house had made him agree. She had talked with him on the street two days earlier with another veil so she wouldn't be recognized.

The plan was set. All she had to do was carry it out and strike one blow for her poor father. She had no thought at all about the right or wrong of it all. She had been planning and waiting for so long. She had watched her father grow worse and worse, and she knew without a conscious thought who to blame.

A rider came down the street in front of her and he moved his horse closer to the dirt path alongside the street. He said nothing and she ignored him and walked on.

Then she saw that she was passing Matilda

Shotgun!

Jones's, the biggest and only pure whorehouse in Miles City. Matilda had forced two other madams out of business before the girls could fairly get established. Matilda was said to be a fine business woman who knew how to make money and how to please her clients.

Hannah checked her pockets to be sure everything was in place. Then she turned the corner on First and saw the black buggy with the side curtains sitting where he said it would be under the elm tree.

She walked directly to it, opened the side door and stepped inside the buggy.

The man there grunted. "So you came," Isaiah Roundtree said, a frown pulling down the corners of his mouth in his suntanned face. He shifted on the buggy seat, then moved again and fumbled with the reins. "I never really expected you to be here when I arrived. I figured I'd give you a half hour, and if you didn't show up, I would leave."

"But I'm not late, Isaiah. You're early. I'd say that you're curious and a little excited meeting me on the quiet this way."

"Not at all. It's business. You said you could tell me who has been masterminding the rustling of stock from the ranges around here. That's why I came. I was curious how you knew and who is doing it. But that's about it."

"You're prepared to pay for the information?"

"Of course. The rustling is costing every rancher in the area a lot of money. If a little money will help us stop it, I'll foot that bill myself."

"I thought you might be difficult. I want fifteen thousand dollars."

"Fifteen thousand." He frowned and stared at her. "Even on a pro-rata basis that would cost each rancher a lot."

"How much did you lose last week to the rustlers? Four hundred head? That's sixteen thousand dollars worth of prime beef at the loading pens."

He scowled. "You know a lot about ranching."

"I grew up on a ranch."

"Fifteen thousand. I'll have to think about it and talk to the rancher's committee."

"Good, you do that and next week the ranchers will probably lose another five or six hundred steers from what I hear."

"You said you know who is doing it."

"Yes, but I'm feeling exposed here." She glanced out the small window. "Let's drive out in the country a little ways. I'm worried that someone will come bursting through these flimsy curtains at any minute."

Roundtree never questioned her. He just slapped the reins on the fine black mare and they moved out First Street past four houses, then to the end of the street, which ended in a lane and meandered a mile to a picnic area near a tributary that ran into the Yellowstone River.

Halfway there Hannah touched his hand. "This is far enough. Now here is what I have for you." She opened the last four buttons on her white blouse and spread the sides of it and the black coat back to reveal her surging pink-tipped breasts.

"My God—"

"I hear you're a tit man, Isaiah. You like big tits you can get your face in. Try this pair on for size." She caught his hand and pulled it over her breasts.

"Hannah, you didn't say anything about—"

She shushed him. "We're friends. We share. You like big tits and I've got some so we share. Go ahead. Play with them. Kiss them. I like that."

He tried to pull his hand back. "No, Hannah. I can't do this. I swore to my wife I never would again be with anyone else."

"For God's sakes, Isaiah. We're just messing around a little bit." She put both his hands on her breasts, and he moaned, then fondled them. She reached over and worked on his fly.

"No. Oh, no."

"Yes. I get to have some fun, too. I like to see him get hard. Oh, damn, he's hard already. I think you like my boobies, Isaiah."

She opened his fly and pulled out his erection. "My, what a dandy." She opened his belt and unbuttoned the top button and pulled his pants open. Then she eased away from him. She pulled his face down to her bosom.

"Kiss my ladies, Isaiah. You know you want it. It's all right."

He grinned and kissed her breasts, then nibbled on her nipples. As he did, she took an over-and-under derringer from her coat pocket with her right hand, and before he knew what happened, she pushed the muzzle against his belly and pulled the trigger.

Hannah pushed him roughly away from her, jolting him against the side of the buggy. Isaiah Roundtree's eyes went glassy for a moment. Then he roared and started to reach out for her, but the small movement brought to him made him stop. The pain came at once—searing, knifing through his intestines like a white-hot sword. Sweat beaded his forehead. He gasped for breath. His heart raced and brought a quick flush to his face. Slowly he turned his head, and when he discovered that didn't hurt, he looked at her squarely.

"Why in heaven's name?" he asked, his voice shrill with the pain and the shock.

"You might not know exactly who I am. My last name is Johnson. I haven't made a big thing of last names around town. My father is Ralph Johnson, who ran the JC ranch about twenty miles north and west of here. You must remember him."

"Johnson. The JC ranch. Been a long time."

"It's been exactly five years, Isaiah. Five years ago you and a few other ranchers ruined my father by rustling the calves. You cut him down and wrung him out and stole so many calves that the bank foreclosed on the ranch."

Shotgun!

"Can't remember. Don't know your father. Sorry he lost his ranch. Not my doing."

"Oh, but it was. You bought it at the sheriff's sale for half what it was worth. You don't remember that either. You must have gobbled up a dozen smaller ranchers in that area north of the Yellowstone.

"You ruined my father and sent him into a sickness of the soul that he'll never recover from. You know where my father is right now, Isaiah? He's in a room upstairs over my saloon, drooling like a crazy man, banging his dishes together, staring out the window for hours at a time without moving or saying a word. When he's not doing that, he's pissing in his pants and shitting all over his bedclothes. That's what you did to my father, you son of a bitch."

Isaiah moved his right hand carefully over the wound on his stomach. It didn't bleed outwardly. The big-caliber round had not penetrated his back, but it had lodged somewhere in his intestines. Any movement of his torso sent him into screams of terror and disbelief.

"How could you shoot me this way?"

"You shouldn't have to ask. I've been telling you. You sentenced my father to a lifetime of sickness and terror and failure, making him so crazy he doesn't even know his name any more. You should have put a bullet through his brain out on the range somewhere. It would have been better for all of us. That's why you're going to sit here screaming for no one to hear when you try to move an inch. You'll scream until your voice gives out and then I'll be laughing at you."

"A belly shot. No doctor can save me. Why did you shoot me?"

"I just told you twice. You deserve to die. I deserve to kill you for what you did to my family. You as good as killed my mother when she saw what happened to her husband. Then you left my pa in a state worse than death. You left him in a living hell. You have two hours to live, more or less. Two hours of the worst pain that you've ever imagined. You'll probably faint from the terrible intensity of the pain, but I'll bring you back to consciousness again so I can enjoy your terror."

"Good Lord, woman, you're mad."

"No, my father is the crazy one in our family. I'm the smart one. Smart enough to figure out how to get back at you and the other ranchers for what you did to my pa."

She fell quiet then and watched him. The pain came in surging waves, washing over him until he shivered, and then his hands shook and his body vibrated and at last he screamed. They were a half mile beyond the nearest house and no one could hear the screaming.

Hannah sat beside him in the buggy. She looked at a small watch from her reticule. "Well, a half hour gone already. You still have an hour and a half to live. How are you going to spend your last hour and a half on this earth?"

156

Shotgun!

Roundtree screamed again, tried to lunge toward her but movement brought such pain that he dropped his hands and slumped against the far side of the buggy.

Hannah took the reins and tied them to the front of the buggy frame and stared at the rancher. "You'll never know how much I'm enjoying this, Isaiah. I've dreamed of it for so long, and now it's happening."

His pale face turned slightly toward her and he looked at her through drooping lids. "You'll fry in hell for this, woman. You'll burn—" The pain hit him again and he bent over, screamed in protest and sat back up, his face livid with anger and pain, his hands helpless in his lap.

The horse nickered. Hannah pulled gently on the reins and the black settled down.

"No one is going to rescue you, Isaiah. That's why I set this up so secretly. No one will know or even suspect. It will be a fine mystery. Out here no one can hear you screaming, and I can enjoy your pain and agony and terror to the fullest."

She watched him. His head sagged forward. She punched him in the belly and he bellowed in fury and came back to consciousness.

"Stay with me on this, Isaiah. I want you to savor every second of your pain. It wouldn't be fair to my father otherwise. Do you think you've suffered much here today? Think what it would be like wallowing in your own puke, pissing your pants and your bed, being fed when you didn't

157

want to eat, and all the time not even knowing who you were, where you were, or even who your own daughter was. That's what you're missing. I'd arrange it if I could, but I don't know how. This I can do."

Hannah reached in her other coat pocket and took out a ten-inch-long knife. She showed it to him. "It will start to get dark soon. Then I can walk away and no one will see me. But I don't want to leave you to die alone. I want to make sure no one rescues you."

She placed the tip of the knife under his rib cage on his left side and stabbed it through flesh an inch, watching his expression. He must have hardly noticed the pain. His eyes stared vacantly at the roof of the buggy. His hands balled into tight fists. She pushed one hand out of the way and angled the handle of the knife down so the blade pointed upward and across his chest.

"Good-bye, Isaiah Roundtree. May you roast in the undying flames of hell!" She rammed the knife upward. Her aim was precise. The point and four inches of the Chicago ice pick sliced into his heart.

Isaiah Roundtree gasped once. His eyes went wide, closed and then slowly opened. His mouth came open and one long gush of air came out of it, escaping from his lungs. Then his head rolled slightly to the left and rested against the side of the buggy.

Shotgun!

"Good-bye, Isaiah," Hannah said again.

Then she pulled the long knife out of the corpse, wiped it off on his shirt and put it back in her coat pocket. She took one last look at Isaiah, tied the reins tightly to the front of the rig so the horse wouldn't move, then stepped down from the buggy to the ground.

Dusk had just fallen. It would be dark in ten minutes. Hannah let the veil down over her face again, adjusted her hat and turned toward town. She made sure that her shoes left no impressions in any dust around the buggy, and she stepped into the weeds at the side of the trail so no footprints would show there. Then she walked quickly. She hummed a little tune that she used to hear when she was a child. She had never known a name for it or the words, but she could remember her mother singing it when she had put Hannah to bed every night.

Slowly tears came to Hannah's eyes. She missed her mother so much. Those had been fine years when she grew up. If only she could have her mother and her father back with her for just a few hours. She blinked away the tears and lifted the veil to wipe the moisture off her cheeks.

She had done it. She had evened one score. But there were more to take care of, more to settle with. She hadn't decided just how she would do it, but the day would come. Yes, the day would come.

Hannah smiled and took a wayward route back

to the alley behind her saloon, being careful that as few people saw her as possible. Even if they did see her, what connection could a lady in a black coat and black hat have with some poor soul who was found dead at the far edge of town?

Hannah went in the back door to the saloon and up the stairs. She quickly changed her skirt to a bright red one with a little matching jacket over the white blouse. She put away the hat and dark coat and combed her hair in the mirror.

Downstairs in the saloon that night, several remarked that Hannah seemed in an extremely good mood, laughing and joking with the bar customers and even watching the poker games and making funny comments. Hannah smiled at the men gambling. All in all, it had been a good day.

Chapter Eleven

Two 12-year-old boys found the body early the next morning when they went fishing at the creek. They called out to the buggy, and when no one responded, they went up and opened the side curtain. Neither one had ever seen a dead man before. They both screamed, dropped their fishing poles and ran back to town.

A woman who lived on that side of town heard them and went out and talked to them. They told her about the dead man in the buggy down the lane. She didn't believe them and told them to go straight home. She checked the buggy and went directly to the sheriff's office, which hadn't opened yet, but the deputy on duty listened to her story.

The whole town knew that one of the biggest ranchers in the area had been murdered before breakfast had ended.

Morgan heard about the murder when he had

his morning meal a little after seven. He hurried out to the spot and found Sheriff Attucks going over the death scene. Morgan called to the law-man from well back and asked if he could take a look around.

Sheriff Attucks nodded. "Yep. Just tell us if you find anything we don't. Looks like Roundtree was shot in the belly with a close-up gun. Powder burns all over his pants where the bullet went in. Then there's blood on his side under his ribs."

"A long knife into his heart the same way that the detective got himself killed in his hotel a couple of weeks ago?"

The sheriff nodded. "Yeah, about the same thing could have happened here. Don't let it get around, but the rancher's pants were open and his dick hanging out."

Morgan nodded. "The bullet wound wouldn't have bled any if the knife in the heart had killed him first. A slug in the gut will put any man down. The pain is tremendous."

"Yeah, pain. I had to hold a friend's hand while he died from being shot that way."

A deputy came up where Morgan and the sher-iff stood. "We found quite a few footprints near the buggy, but most are from the two kids who found him and the woman who reported him dead."

"Okay, keep looking. Spent rounds, bits of cloth, somebody's name and address."

The deputy grinned and hurried away.

Shotgun!

Sheriff Attucks scowled at Morgan. "You saying there could be a connection between this killing and that private detective who came to town?"

"Looks reasonable," Morgan said. "I'll bet the doctor will tell us this man died with a long, thin blade through his side and into his heart. Same way that detective died. The detective came to town to work for Roundtree and the committee. About as close a tie-in as you could want."

"A woman killer in both cases?" the sheriff asked.

"Could be. The detective was naked when they found him in his hotel room. He could have been an easy death after being seduced by a woman. I've heard of the shot in the belly before. It puts a grown man down and a little guy or a woman is then in control of the man for whatever devilment that's played out."

"A lot of pain and then the final thrust to be sure the victim is dead." The sheriff hooked his thumbs in his belt and scowled again. "Sounds like revenge. But what revenge would a local person have against a newcomer to town like that detective?"

"Maybe that one had something to do with the Stockgrowers Association trying to stop the smuggling."

"Could be, but you're still alive. You're here on the same job he was."

"Yeah, but not a lot of people know that. Maybe I'm still alive because I'm more careful."

"Better stay careful. Didn't I hear about somebody taking a shot at you on the street the other day?"

"Yeah, he missed and got away. Hardly seemed worthwhile reporting to you."

"It is. Next time, report it."

"I hope there won't be a next time."

Morgan waved at the sheriff and walked a 30 yard circle around the death scene. About 20 yards down the way, he found a set of footprints off the regular roadway. They paralleled the road and some of the weeds that had been crushed by hard soles, some had been snapped off and others hadn't sprung up to vertical. He checked where one shoe had left a plain print on a section of damp sand. It was no longer than the span of his hand from spread thumb to little finger. A woman's shoe. He called the sheriff over and showed him the print. It was aimed back toward town. There was a slight pattern of a sole on the sand.

"Going to make a plaster cast of it?" Morgan asked.

"What's that?"

"A cast of the print. Just mix up patching plaster and spread it on the shoe track there in the damp sand. When it hardens you have an exact impression of the track in the sand that the shoe or boot made."

The sheriff nodded. "Then if we get a suspect we can check her shoes and boots for a match."

Morgan nodded, left the plaster detail to a deputy and did another circle, but found nothing else of value.

He headed back to town on foot. Killing the rancher didn't make sense. Why kill the goose that laid the golden egg? He figured the first killing was simply a try to protect the rustling. The gentleman detective from the big city could probably have been frightened off, which would have given the same results.

Dead then didn't make any sense. Dead now on Roundtree made no more sense—unless Roundtree was in on the rustling and somebody found out. Nope, that didn't hold water either. If somebody figured out the rustling he could simply lay out his proof for the rustlers and join them, not fight them. That way the newcomer could demand a share of the profits.

Maybe this killing had no connection with the rustling. Maybe—but that was not high on the list of good explanations either.

Back in town, Morgan checked his box at the hotel. A long, thin envelope held a note that asked him to meet the Stockgrowers Association the next day at noon, same hotel room as last time.

So, he had all day to track down something on his own. He could tail Josh Eagleston. Morgan still figured the man had to be the weak link in the chain. The railroad men were another breed. He didn't know how to talk to them. They stuck together, and even if one train crew had made arrangements with Josh to pick up cars and load cattle, how in the world could he prove that it wasn't a part of their regular job?

He needed some coffee. He headed for Hannah's Place, but saw the dressmaker's door open and stopped there first. A woman came out with packages and he held the door for her. Inside he saw another woman near the front of the store and Teressa working away on one of the dress dummies. She looked up and her face blossomed.

"Hello, glad you stopped by." He walked back near the dummy and saw the pins, needles and scissors. She put down a paper of pins and grinned. "I've thought of three more people you might remember—kids who were in school when we were."

"Hope that I know them. What's the talk around town this morning about Isaiah Roundtree?"

Teressa lost the smile and frowned. "Oh, dear. That's such a tragedy. I always thought he was a nice man. He even came to church, which most of the ranchers don't. He helped buy books for the first grade one year when the ones they had got all ruined in a snowstorm."

"What are people saying?"

"About him being shot to death that way? I haven't heard much. I heard a couple of men snickering about it, and I don't know what for."

"Have you chanced on any theories about who shot him or why it was done?"

She shook her head of dark hair so it waggled

back and forth on her shoulders and down her back. "No, not a single one. Oh, one woman said her husband heard someone say that he must have a mistress here in town. Maybe she got mad at him. Isn't that a terrible thing to say about a fine man like Mr. Roundtree?"

Morgan agreed that it was terrible. The woman from the front of the store came back as if pulled in by the juicy gossip. She sniffed and waited until there was a pause.

"Well, I heard that Mr. Roundtree had been fooling around over at that place run by Matilda Jones. Then I guess his wife found out."

"So his wife shot him to death and left him out in the fields?" Morgan asked.

"Well, I don't know about that, but if she didn't, then she was entitled to. What's good for the goose is good for the gander I always say."

Teressa looked up at Morgan with a big question on her face, but he didn't let her ask it.

"Ladies, I have to go. I'll stop by at another time."

Morgan waved from the door. Teressa waved back plainly not pleased that he left so quickly. She looked up at the woman near her, who was still venting her ideas about what happened to Isaiah Roundtree.

Morgan felt lucky to escape and moved quickly down the boardwalk, checking both ways, watching for anyone who seemed to be staring at him. He took the step up to the walk in front of Hannah's Place and pushed in through the batwing doors. The place looked as if it had just opened.

Three men stood at the bar. He eased up beside the last one in line, signaled for a brew and listened to the men.

"Has to be a woman," the first drinker said. "I mean, what man would gut shot a guy like Roundtree and then put a blade into him? Had to be a woman. A man would call the sucker out man to man and shoot it out. Give him a fair chance. Maybe one of the floozies from Matilda Jones's house."

"Not a chance," the next man said. "Why should a whore cut off a customer? That don't make no sense."

"His wife has to be the killer," the third man said. "I've seen her. She's a dozen years younger than he is, with a little Mex blood in her. A spitfire. I've heard she has a wicked temper. She'd be mad as hell if old Roundtree was stepping out on her. I mean, why else were his pants down and his prick hanging out?"

The talk eased off as Hannah came around the bar, waved at Morgan and pointed to a table in the back. He joined her. She had a cup of coffee.

"So everyone has an opinion of what happened to poor Mr. Roundtree. What's yours?"

"Can't offer one. I don't know his wife. Don't know if he had a mistress. Can't say if he'd been a customer over at Matilda Jane's fancy house. Seemed like a fairly respectable man for a rancher, from what I saw of him."

"You met Roundtree? Where?"

"Here in town about a week ago now. Just in passing in the dining room at the hotel."

"Oh." She wore a bright red blouse that was tight as her white ones. A red kerchief tied her hair back and to one side. All the reds matched or complemented one another and her red hair.

"I never thought redheads looked good in red, but you are ravishing this morning."

She smiled. "Thank you. You hard at work?"

"Not really." He tried to remember if it was Hannah or Teressa he had told he was a real-estate buyer. He couldn't remember. That was one of the problems with telling so many lies about his job. Maybe that was a mistake. Hannah must have heard a lot of men talking in her saloon. Should he tell her he was a detective working on the rustling. Then maybe she could help. He wasn't sure, so he put it off.

"What does a guy have to do to get a cold beer around here?" Morgan asked.

"Most people I know simply ask for one." Hannah waggled a finger at the barman. He brought over two cold beers, set them down on the table and left without a word.

"Thanks. Your finger signal works. I'm still caught up in this killing, I guess. Mysteries always have intrigued me, kind of a hobby, especially ones where there's been a murder."

"I thought that's what we had the sheriff for."

Morgan laughed. "This country-boy sheriff, who would rather give speeches and ask for votes than run the law apparatus of the county? He's a desk sheriff, probably never solved three crimes in his life."

"I voted for him last time."

"Good for you. The county probably got about what it deserved." He frowned. "Strange. That buggy way out there in the prairie and not a footprint around it. I'd think, if the killer rode out there with the rancher, he'd have to walk back somehow after he pulled the trigger."

"Flew, maybe," Hannah said with a grin.

"Probably." Morgan tilted the cold bottle, trying to remember exactly why he had come in here. Maybe it was just to get away from that harpie in the dress shop. Yeah, that was it. No special reason. He drained the beer and put it down gently on the table.

"I've got to go see a man about a store," Morgan said. "He should be back by now."

"What store?"

"Sorry, can't tell you that. You might swoop in and buy it right out from under my boss."

"Not with the current size of my bank account." Hannah smiled one of her best and touched his hand. Her voice came low and throaty. "You tired of sleeping alone? I am. If you're not busy tonight, I'll buy some wine and cheese and some crackers. About eight?"

Shotgun!

"Not sure. I'll have to let you know later. Still early in the day and I do have some more work to do."

Morgan stood, winked at Hannah and walked out of the saloon. He wondered if she watched him from the door. If she did, he decided to confuse her and stopped in at the real-estate office. Then he went into the dressmaker's shop.

Teressa waved a swatch of cloth at him and took the pins out of her mouth.

"You're going to swallow a few of those pins one of these days," he said.

"Never have, never will. Hey, it's almost noon. How about if I fix you lunch in back. I'm living here now. I moved out of my folk's place a month ago. Decided it was time I did things on my own for a change."

"Lunch sounds fine," Morgan said. This would let him have some time to think through the Roundtree death. It had to have a direct tie to the rustling, but he hadn't figured out what it was.

Teressa smiled, hurried to the front door and turned around the sign so it said closed. She snapped the lock and pulled down the door blind. Then she walked slowly back to Morgan. She looked up and grinned.

"Trying to figure out what to give you for lunch. I don't have much left. How about a peanut butter and honey sandwich? Bet you haven't had one of them in a long time."

"I happen to love peanut butter. You make your

bread or buy loaves down at your friend's cafe?"

"I buy it down there. They make it a lot better than I can."

Ten minutes later they settled down to peanut butter sandwiches and steaming cups of coffee.

"I remembered those other kids we used to know. Do you recall a redheaded kid a year behind you in school called Rusty Smith?"

Morgan shook his head. "I remember Rat-face Smith."

Teressa laughed. "Same one. He wound up going through high school and to some college and now he's one of the important lawyers in the legislature in Boise. He's a real power around there."

"Making all the kids pay for it who made fun of him in school. Who else?"

"Bertha somebody. Can't remember her last name. She's a teacher and professor at some college there in Boise and highly respected."

"Didn't anybody we know turn out bad, like us?"

Teressa laughed and her big brown eyes swallowed him. He struggled to the surface to see her nod.

"Yep, Clarence Hempstead, the smartest guy in my class. You must remember him. Always studying. No sports or games or play, out of school and home to study. He started to go to college, flunked out and took off for Alaska with some Indian woman twice his age. Nobody could figure out what happened to Clarence the bookworm."

The sandwiches were gone. She stood and leaned across him to get his plate. Their faces came remarkably close together. Morgan reached up on an impulse, caught her face and held it as he kissed her lips.

Her eyes closed the moment he kissed her, then popped open in surprise. When he let go of her, she lost her balance and fell with her shoulder in his lap. He looked down at her.

"Hey," she said surprised. "You kissed me."

"Did you mind?"

She frowned for a minute, then shook her head. "I liked it," she said. He bent and kissed her again. She put her arms around his neck and let the kiss last a long time. When she let him lean up, he grinned at her.

"You've been practicing," he said with a grin.

"No such thing. Just a natural thing to do." She lay there a minute, then squirmed off his lap and stood.

She stared at him and nodded. "Yes, that was warm and friendly and just a little bit sexy. I liked it."

"Want to try it again," he asked.

"Oh, yes!" she said. She put her arms around him and bent enough to kiss him hard on the mouth. The kiss lasted longer that time, and when she at last eased away, she was breathing heavily.

"That kind of thing could get a girl just a little bit excited."

"You're already excited. Anyone would be."

She beamed at him, then nodded. "Yes, I agree, we should get married. I can move where you live if you want me to. After all, I can start a dress-making shop anywhere. Mother will be crushed, but she'll just have to endure. I think I'll tell my parents tonight. Could you come to their house and we'll tell them together. It always makes it so much nicer that way. Don't you agree?"

Chapter Twelve

When Morgan stood, Teressa caught him around the middle and hugged him, snuggling her head against his chest.

"Yes, yes, yes. I love the sound of that. We'll go tell my folks and then we can figure out just when and where we'll get married. I think a church ceremony—"

Morgan unwrapped the girl from around him and frowned. "I didn't say anything about getting married."

Teressa looked at him, her face changing from a contented, knowing smile to surprise and then worry.

"But you kissed me four times. Isn't that enough for a girl to expect? I mean, I've always said that I wouldn't kiss a man that way unless he wanted to marry me, and you did kiss me that way, hard and with your mouth open and all. And I just figured— oh, have I done it again?"

Morgan smiled and held her tight for a moment. Then he let her go and helped her to sit down in her chair.

"I shouldn't have kissed you in the first place. It was just a spur of the moment thing. I'm sorry. I had no idea you would react that way. I admit that I enjoy kissing pretty girls. You are an extremely good-looking woman. So what could I do? It was my fault and I apologize. My work takes me all over the country and there's no chance that I can get married."

"Oh, damn," Teressa said softly. "Looks like I've done it again. When am I going to learn about men and kissing and courting and all of that?"

"You'll learn. It's not all that hard. Just be yourself—that's the important part."

She sighed and looked away. "Sometimes I'm afraid that I don't even know who the real me is." A tear seeped down her cheek and she brushed at it. He kissed her cheek and held her again. She closed her eyes reveling in the contact.

When Morgan stepped away, he smiled. "Hey, you're going to be just fine. One of these days the right man will come along and you'll know it. You'll know in your heart and in your mind that this is the man to spend the rest of your life with. I guarantee it."

"Honest?"

"Honest. Now I better get moving. Work to do. Thanks for the lunch. I've been missing my peanut butter and honey sandwiches. I'll stop by again."

Teressa waved, but she looked so alone and forlorn that Morgan almost hugged her again. But he knew he shouldn't. She had jumped to such a huge conclusion from a few kisses. Some girls were still that innocent, thank goodness. That could have been a close encounter with marriage if he hadn't straightened her out fast enough. He thought of a shotgun in Pa Yardley's hands and he shivered.

He toured a pair of saloons, but didn't see Josh Eagleston, the cattle buyer. He walked back to 316 B Street and watched it from cover for two hours. No one went in or came out.

Morgan settled down beside the weed-filled empty lot half a block from the target, and he decided to give Josh another hour. Josh had to be the center of this whole affair. If Morgan could get some evidence on Josh and get him arrested, it would put a crimp in the whole rustling operation.

About four o'clock, Josh walked down the street and went in his front door. Soon smoke plumed up from the brick chimney. Could be fixing an early supper. Why?

Morgan timed Josh. The man stayed inside his house for 46 minutes, then came out in a different set of clothes. When Josh moved down the street, Morgan tailed him. Josh walked straight to Hannah's Place and pushed inside. Morgan stopped two doors down. He didn't want to go in because Hannah would want to talk, and then he couldn't tail Josh if he went anywhere else. He waited near the general store. There were no chairs out front, so he leaned against the wood structure and waited.

Morgan pulled his brown Stetson down over his eyes a little to help conceal his identity in case the gunman who had tried to kill him once was looking for him again. Nothing happened for ten minutes. Then Josh came out the batwing doors and headed the other way toward First Street. The cattle buyer walked right past the depot. Farther down the street were a barbershop, some more stores and the Cattleman's Hotel at Second. Between Second Street and First Street were only two business firms—a printer and a real-estate office and then the Miles City Livery on First and Main. Maybe Josh was riding out of town to meet some rustlers or to inspect some rustled cattle.

Instead, Josh turned right on Second and went past the hotel on the corner and down to A Street, where he cut back the way he had come. Then Morgan knew. Josh was heading for Matilda Jones's fancy whorehouse.

Morgan made a quick evaluation. Josh wasn't going to buy any cattle or meet any rustlers in Matilda Jones's place. Was he a one-shot man or an all nighter? Morgan decided that Josh would be there for some time, perhaps all night. That established, there was no point in waiting.

Shotgun!

Morgan suddenly gained a fondness for wine and cheese. He'd go to Hannah's Place for an early supper and then see what the young lady had to offer in her upstairs bedroom besides the wine and cheese. It could prove interesting—and did.

The next morning, Morgan was up early. He left Hannah's bed at 6:30 and had a quick breakfast. He was in position to watch Josh's house by seven o'clock. Smoke trailed up from the chimney at the back of the house a half hour later.

Another half hour and the front door came open, and Josh walked out in his cattleman's working clothes: jeans, a light blue plaid shirt with long sleeves and a black leather vest. He topped it with a black Stetson.

This time the cattle buyer walked up Main and to a law office two doors down from the barbershop just below the depot. Why would Josh need a lawyer? Maybe to get the court order rescinded from his cattle-buying accounts?

The rest of the morning proved unproductive as well. Josh left the law office after an hour. He hit three saloons and had a beer at each one, but talked to no one except the apron. Morgan surveyed the crowd in each place because Josh could have been hunting someone.

Morgan made it right on time for the noon meeting of the Stockgrowers Association in the Cattleman's Hotel. Only four ranchers sat around the table this time. The leadership evidently had fallen to Lorne Dempsy. At each place was a chicken dinner and two bottles of cold beer. The men ate first. Talk would come later.

After they finished eating, they pushed the plates and bottles to the center of the big conference table and stared at each other.

"All right, he's dead and gone," Dempsy said, breaking the silence that had started to stretch out. "Not a damn thing we can do about that except try to find out who killed him. Better we try to find out if Isaiah's murder had anything to do with the rustling. Any ideas?"

Harry Nelson, the rancher with the smallest spread of any in the committee, shook his head. "Not a one here. The very idea of Isaiah getting done in by some harlot right there in his buggy is almost too much for me to believe."

"That part could be false evidence somebody planted to throw off the sheriff," Dempsy said. "I've heard of it happening before. Point the evidence at someone else, so the real killer has a chance to get away free and clear."

They all looked at Morgan, who said, "Yes, that has been known to happen in a big city somewhere. Out here in the country, that would be less likely."

He looked from one face to the next. "My job here is to stop the rustling. I've done some of that already, working from the inside out. I don't know who's behind the rustling yet, but we're chopping off some of the arms of the monster.

Shotgun!

With no arms, it can't function, just as it can't operate if it has no head.

"My job is not to catch Isaiah Roundtree's killer. The only way I'm interested is if the killing is somehow tied in with the rustling. For example if Isaiah was a partner in the rustling and his partner killed him to take it all."

"Not possible," Harry Nelson said. "Isaiah was an honest man."

"Good. Now you know what I've done so far. With your help, we've stopped some attempted rustling operations and scattered the rustlers. So far, we haven't caught any of them alive. I think we know who it is who is buying the rustled stock and getting them the train, but we have to catch him in the act for enough evidence to hang him. Have any of you experienced any losses to rustlers this past week?"

"Not us, and I haven't heard of any of the other ranchers who have had any losses," Lorne Dempsy said. He sighed and shifted his bulk.

Morgan suggested that the men post two or three night guards at the most probable route that rustlers could drive cattle off their property. "That way you'll have a chance to challenge them and shoot them off their horses if they press on with your beef. This range guard idea should have been put into practice the minute you discovered your losses. Yes, go ahead and hire new hands, give them rifles and send them out as guards. If you can save ten steers from your spread, you'll be money ahead."

The men nodded. Morgan hoped that they would follow through on the plan.

"Don't know much else we can do this time," Dempsy said. "Let's try to keep tabs on what's going on. Meet in two weeks?"

It was decided and the group broke up. Again they left the hotel at different times and by different doors.

The word would be spread about progress in the fight against the rustlers and the need to put out range guards. Each of the four ranchers would send riders to contact the two ranches closest to them or nearby. Those eight ranchers would each send out riders to contact one other ranch and all the ranches in the group would be covered. Anyone missed would find out quickly about what had transpired.

Morgan knew that he should wait a day and then ride out to each ranch and check on their range guards. He should, but he didn't want to. It would take three days at least and he wanted to be in town if something happened.

An idea popped into his head and he walked up to the train depot and wrote out a telegram.

Manager, Northern Pacific Division Point, Minneapolis, Minnesota. Now and then, a Northern Pacific train passing eastbound through the Miles City area, stops along the route and picks up a string of loaded cattle cars. These steers have been rustled from nearby ranches and are not legitimate freight.

No regular ranch in this area will be ready to ship steer toward St. Paul stockyards for at last another six weeks. Could you check on arriving trains with steer during the past month and see who shipped them and from where? It is believed that this rustling on a grand scale could be done only with the collusion of employees of the stockyards and Northern Pacific trainmen. I'll await your reply. Lee Morgan.

Morgan gave his message to the telegraph man, who frowned. "Cost you more than ten dollars to send this."

"I figured." Morgan put 20 dollars on the counter and the clerk began tapping out the message.

When he finished, Morgan said, "When you get a reply, keep it here. If I hear that anybody else in town knows this message went out, I'll chop off your ears and stuff them down your throat and laugh when you choke to death. You hear me plain and simple?"

"Yes, sir. Against policy to reveal any—"

"Always has been. I'm talking to you, not to policy. Be damn sure you forget this."

Morgan could see the man sweating. He left

the depot and wondered what Minneapolis would have to say. Maybe nothing. Maybe some smoke and fast shuffling. He'd find out probably tomorrow.

Outside again, he walked toward Hannah's Place. He had a different slant on her since he'd found out about her father. What a strain, what a financial drain. She'd have to hire someone almost around the clock to take care of the man. He agreed with her. It would have been kinder if the ranchers had just blown her father apart with gunfire on the range, rather than to reduce him to the helpless creature he had turned into.

Morgan made an abrupt change of direction and cut over toward B Street to see what was going on at Josh Eagleston's place. Sooner or later Josh had to make some kind of a move.

Hannah had tired of watching the drunks and gamblers in her saloon. It was between times when men came in for food. She went upstairs to her apartment, carefully avoiding the two rooms she had set aside for her father. Some days she couldn't bare to look at him, let alone spend any time with him.

Often she wished that he could die and be at peace. Why did a loving god let a man go through so much pain and torture? She couldn't understand it.

She sat in her living room, which looked over the row of houses behind her and at the far off ranges of the mountains. Usually they were too far away to be seen, or clouds or haze obscured them. Now and then, on a sparkling new day, they rose as towering peaks covered with snow. Today she couldn't see them.

She took out a book she had been reading. It was *The Wide, Wide World* by Elizabeth Wetherell, which had been published nearly 30 years earlier, but was still fascinating. It told the story of Ellen Montgomery from childhood to marriage. It had been a popular woman's novel since it was published in 1851.

Hannah read a few pages and stared out the window. She had to even the score. It would happen eventually, but she was impatient. How could she speed things up?

The third largest rancher in the area was Mike Corrigan. He was in his early forties and a solid family man. He loved to hit the gaming tables now and again, especially in the winter when the ranching demands were fewer.

Yes, Corrigan would be the man. She'd talk to the photographer in town and borrow some of his equipment. She'd tell the photographer that she wanted to play a trick on a friend. She was sure he'd set up the camera for her and fix the right amount of flash powder. All she needed was a long release device. It would set off the flash powder and release the camera lens's shutter at the same time.

She brightened. She had thought of Corrigan

because he was downstairs in a small game of poker at a back table. She hurried downstairs and walked up to the table.

"Mr. Corrigan, could I have a word with you please."

He looked up, surprise showing on his face. She was sure he remembered being in some vicious poker games with her. He stood and they went off a ways.

"I'm having a high-stakes game in my living room tonight if you'd care to stay around a while."

Corrigan was sandy haired, five eight and on the heavy frame side. He worked his cattle with his men, and he was as tough and strong as Isaiah Roundtree had been. He wore a short, well-trimmed beard, and he calculated her from behind thin green eyes.

"How high?" he asked.

"Name the stakes when we get there. Just four of us. I know it's better for good poker with six, but all I've found so far are four. Can you make it?"

He grinned. "I brought some pocket change. What time?"

"Nine o'clock, so we don't attract any pinch-penny players."

"Nine o'clock, it is."

"Mike, it's your bet. We're waiting on you," someone called from the table.

"I'll be there," Mike Corrigan said and went back to the table, spreading his hand and checking the five pasteboards there.

Hannah hurried upstairs, took her reticule and put on a fancy hat to match her blue dress. She went out the front door of the saloon, angled across the street and down to the photographer's studio just below the law office on Main and this side of the hotel.

There she talked with Wild Charley. Charley came from Chicago and said he'd photographed many of the country's most beautiful women in the nude. Everytime he saw Hannah he asked the same question: "Can I take some fine photographs of you soon?"

They both knew he meant nude pictures and she always put him off. This time she surprised him when he asked his question.

"Yes, next Tuesday night. Here in your studio."

"Really? Fine. I'm thrilled. You know I always go naked as well, so it's all fair."

"You told me. First, there's a favor I need you to do for me tonight. I'm playing a joke on an old friend in my rooms, and I need you to set up your camera and flash powder so I can take a picture of the two of us. You said you had some kind of a long release cable that would snap the picture and set off the flash powder."

"Yes, simple. No problem at all."

"I want you to be most secretive about it. Come in the back door and up the steps to my quarters. Sometime after six tonight if you can."

"To photograph you in the buff, I'd climb Pike's Peak in my underwear."

187

Hannah laughed. "Now that would get your little bottom frozen right off."

They both laughed. She told him she would be waiting for him. One picture would be all she wanted.

"No problem, I'll be there at six-thirty."

Hannah left smiling. One more settled score for what those ranchers had done to her father five years ago. It would be tonight!

Chapter Thirteen

Hannah met Wild Charley that night a little after six when he came to the back door of the saloon. She carried a box for him and they hurried up the steps before anyone happened out the back door. He had arrived with everything they needed.

"You want me to take the shot for you?" Wild Charley asked.

"Not this time. That's next week. Bring the things into the bedroom. I want to set up the picture there."

She nodded. She would get Corrigan half drunk, lead him on, get him to the bedroom with everything arranged and take the photo. Yes, it would be worth its weight in diamonds and rubies!

She showed Charley where she wanted him to focus the camera and lay down the way she would be.

Charley grinned. "Hey, I know what you're

doing here. Now you got to come through for me and pose."

Hannah laughed softly. "Charley, I'll do that next week like I promised, and I'll give you a little preview tonight as soon as we get this set up."

He put the camera on some boxes on a table and taped it down so it wouldn't move. Then he focused on the exact spot and set up the plate. He judged the amount of flash powder, put it on the flat holder and taped it to the side of the dresser. Then he fixed the long release cable that she could push from the bed to set off the flash and the shutter at the same time.

"Okay, it's all set. All you have to do is push this release here and it'll work. I've done this a thousand times with a shorter lead."

"Just so it works."

"It'll work. Photography has come a long way since the old wet plates. They used an older process back then. Hey, we're way past that now. I've got the latest plates. Now I can have them shipped from Chicago and they last for six or eight months. A lot easier than lugging those old plates around. We had to put the emulsion on them ourselves just before we used them. Glad those days are gone forever."

"You sure it's going to work?" Hannah asked. As she did, she unbuttoned the first two fasteners on the white blouse she wore and Charley watched her in amazement.

"I told you I'd give you a preview," Hannah

Shotgun!

said. She took off the blouse and dropped it on the bed, then lifted a chemise over her head to show her breasts.

"My God. Wish I had brought some extra plates. Beautiful—just amazing and beautiful. You know you've got big breasts, but do you know how perfectly formed they are. Still slightly upthrust and their weight—my God, they're beautiful." He took a step toward her and she put out both hands.

"Hey, just a little look and certainly no touching. Those are the rules." She lowered her hands and turned around slowly. He asked her to stop on the side view, then move just a little.

"Oh, damn, but the pictures I'm going to get of you. I could take twenty shots just of your breasts. No face, no legs. Oh, damn."

She slipped the chemise back on, then her blouse. "You promise, Charley, that you won't tell a soul about bringing your equipment up here tonight, right?"

"Oh, damn right. We shoot you nude next Tuesday at my place."

She nodded. "Right. Now let me get you out of here without any one seeing you."

They made it all right and she went back upstairs grinning. Was she going to have a surprise for Mike Corrigan later that night. She went ahead and set up a poker table with five chairs, put out the chips and cards. It had to look good. They'd drink waiting for the others. Yes, it would work. She'd pretend to get a little drunk.

She was in the saloon that night at 8:30 when Corrigan arrived. He found her at her table in back and grinned.

"Had me a little nap, a big supper, and I'm raring to play some big-stakes poker. You ready?"

"Anytime you are, cowboy." She downed the rest of her drink, which was actually tea, and reached for his hand to get up. She was a little unsteady on her feet, but she straightened up and walked with elaborate care to the door to the stairs. Corrigan came beside her, ready to help her if she slipped. She didn't. She showed him the card table and sat down. He sat beside her.

"Hey, where are the others?"

"You're way early," Hannah said with just a slight slur. "We need something to drink." She brought a bottle of whiskey, two glasses and a pitcher of cold water from her ice box.

"Wanna start?" she asked again, slurring the words just a tinge.

Corrigan grinned. He'd had a bath and a haircut since she saw him last. The man was ready.

She laughed. "You want to know a secret?" she asked leaning toward him. She didn't stop leaning until her head almost touched his and came down on his shoulder. She sat up and grinned. "Oops. Sorry. Wanna know a secret?"

"Sure. A secret from a beautiful woman is a pleasure."

"This is a small poker party. I lied about six players. Guess how many?"

192

He shook his head. She held up two fingers. "Just us three. You and me and the whiskey bottle." She reached for it again, then stopped and stared at him.

"Hey, you're pretty. Good-looking hunk of man. Know what I mean? Good shoulders and arms, almost a flat belly."

He downed his whiskey and pushed his chair closer to hers. "Hey, what do you mean an almost flat belly? Bet my belly is flatter than yours."

"Is not. Silly. Now don't be naughty. Cards. We was gonna play some poker."

"Strip poker," he asked with a grin.

She shook her head. "Hell, no. It's too damn slow. Whoops. A lady don't say that." She covered her face with her hands and peeked out. "Even if it's true." She undid two buttons on her flame red blouse and he watched.

"Too damn hot in here. Hey, you wanna see a pretty room? Just fixed up my room so it looks classy. You wanna see it?"

He shook his head. "Rather play strip poker."

"Too damn slow." She stood, weaving on her feet. He was up in an instant, holding her. She leaned heavily against him so her breasts pressed against his arm.

"Oh, damn. The room is moving on me."

"Steady. You'll be all right. You were going to show me a room."

"Oh, damn. Forgot. Yeah, back here." She was unsteady as she led him to her bedroom. She stepped inside and his brows went up in surprise.

"My room. Ain't it nice? New bedspread and pillows. New wallpaper. All nice and cozy." She stumbled and almost fell and sat down hard on the bed. She shook her head. "Damn whiskey. Musta got a bad batch."

She rubbed her hand over her face and shook her head. When she looked up, it was with surprise. "Hey, you're in my bedroom."

"Looks that way."

"Can't play poker in here."

"Damn straight," he said.

"Hell, guess not. What game you wanta play?"

"There's the old poking game."

Hannah scowled and looked at him. "That's not nice thing to say to a lady in her bedroom." She grinned and giggled. "Poking—you mean like fucking?"

"About the same thing."

Corrigan reached for her blouse and undid the rest of the buttons. She hadn't worn her chemise this time, so her breasts swung out, pink tipped with her nipples throbbing already.

"Oh, damn!" Corrigan said. "What great tits."

"Oh, I got two of them."

Hannah giggled and pulled his head down to her breasts. As he sucked and nibbled at her breasts, her eyes took on a deep green fire. She looked at the camera mostly hidden behind some pillows. She had it all worked out.

Shotgun!

She pulled him away from her breasts and fell backward on the bed. "Oh, Lordy, I got me that feeling again that a big strong man like you could do just about anything he wanted to with me." Her words were plain, but tinged with the liquor.

He lay gently on top of her, his hips pushing against hers. "I don't reckon you'd mind a little poking, then, would you?"

She grinned. "Wouldn't mind a fuck of a lot. You think you're man enough to satisfy a woman like me?"

"Hell, I can try."

He pulled her skirt off and saw she wore nothing under it. In a few moments he stood and undressed. She giggled.

"Look, your belly isn't as flat as mine."

"Took lots of your beer to grow that belly," he said, dropping on top of her again.

"On your back," she said. "The first time I want to be on top." She had worked it out so his face would be easy to see in the picture that showed them together.

Corrigan grumbled a little, then rolled over on his back. She lay on top of him, then lifted and let him position himself so he could lance upward into her as she lowered herself. A moment later they were together.

"Yes, I like it up here," she said. Then she leaned away from him, found the release cable and laughed. "You could at least look like you're enjoying fucking me," she said crossly.

"I am, but I don't like being on the damn bottom."

"I'll make you like it," she said.

She ground her hips at him and he grinned. When he did, she pushed the release and the blinding flash of the flash powder ignited. She came off him like a coiled spring and caught up a .32 revolver from where it had been hidden under a scarf on the dresser.

"What the hell?" Corrigan asked, sitting up.

"You've been fucked good and proper, and it's going to cost you one hell of a lot," Hannah said. She swung her long red hair back out of her eyes and held the revolver pointing at Corrigan.

"A picture? You took a picture of us?"

"I did. Now get your clothes on and get out of here. I'm going to make a dozen prints of the picture. I'll give you one each time you give me a thousand dollars in cash. Otherwise I'll send the pictures to your wife. If she saw this picture of you fucking some strange woman in a strange bed, she'd tear your eyes out and then eat your heart. You know she would."

Corrigan growled and started toward her. "You fucking bitch."

She waved the gun at him and he stopped. "Yes. Nice doggie. Now how much cash you have on you?"

Corrigan sat down on the bed, his sudden anger subsiding. "You don't have the picture yet. All I have to do is smash the camera and ruin the plate.

Shotgun!

Easy." He came off the bed toward the camera.

Hannah fired one shot from the .32 into the floor a foot in front of his bare toes. He stopped.

"God, woman, you're serious. The drunk act was just all pretend? Damn, I don't believe this."

"You will tomorrow morning when you think about it. Your ranch is worth more than losing your wife. Of course, if you don't play it right, you could lose both your ranch and your wife. Now how much cash did you bring with you?"

"A hundred and fifty dollars. I was supposed to buy some special medicine for my stock."

"Give me the cash as your first down payment. After you pay me twelve thousand dollars, you get the plate back and all the pictures."

"You fucking bitch!"

Hannah laughed. "About right, you womanizing, two-timing, unfaithful husband. Now give me the money. Then get your clothes on and get the hell out of my saloon. Once a week I want to see you with a thousand dollars in cash money in your hand. Get your fucking clothes on. I hate the very sight of you."

"Why, Hannah? What did I ever do to you?"

"You don't even remember."

She made him dress, took the money, then led him down the hall and showed him inside her father's room. The air stank of human waste and urine. Ralph Johnson lay on a bed with a rubber sheet over it. The dark stains of human feces covered half his body.

"His name is Ralph Johnson. He used to own a ranch six miles from yours. You and the rest of his neighbors ruined him, stole his calves and put him into foreclosure with the bank. He couldn't stand being a failure and lost his mind. This, Mike Corrigan, is what you did to me and mine. Now get the hell out of my saloon and don't come back without that thousand dollars in your fucking hand."

Corrigan shook his head at the ugly excuse for a man lying on the bed and hurried out.

Hannah had dressed as well before they came down the hall. Now she said, "Julie, come tend to Papa. He needs you again."

A half-Indian woman came from the adjoining room. She nodded and got a pail of water, brushes, cloths and towels, and she hurried up to tend to Mr. Johnson.

Hannah would have Wild Charley come get his photo gear the next day. She'd keep the plate. Charley said it would be good for six months without developing it. She'd see what Corrigan did. If he made his payments, fine.

Hannah sat in her living room a minute, remembering the shock the anger and despair on Corrigan's face when he realized he was being blackmailed. There was absolutely nothing he could do about it. She had him by his balls and he had to pay up or lose his wife. Hannah's grin was a bit grim. In cases like these she loved to be in the powerful position so she could dictate the terms.

Shotgun!

Unknown to Hannah, Mike Corrigan had saved two dollars when he gave Hannah his money. Down in the saloon, he decided at once what to do. It wasn't hard. Anything was better than facing Wanda.

He took his last two dollars, bought a bottle of whiskey and carried it outside. He found a chair along Main Street, tilted it back and had a drink of the raw whiskey. He could afford better. At least, he could have an hour ago. Not now. He took another slug of the booze and felt it start to warm him. He might need to use half the bottle.

No rush. He had all night. He drank and thought about his wife and family. The picture of him whoring would kill his wife and his mother, who lived at the ranch. His two sons and two daughters would never be able to understand what had happened. He had failed them. He had let them down. He had let a conniving whore trick him.

He drank again. A deputy sheriff came by. It was illegal to drink in a public place, but the deputy knew Corrigan as one of the big ranchers and looked the other way as he passed him on the boardwalk. Technically the deputy had not seen Corrigan breaking the law.

The rancher took another slug of the booze. Yes, the booze had worked. Corrigan sensed tears brimming his eyes. He hadn't cried in a long time. The tears came and flooded over his eyes and rolled down his cheeks.

"Damn, how did it happen so fast?" he whispered. He had no answer. Then he remembered the shell of a man lying on the bed in that upstairs room. He remembered Ralph Johnson as a good rancher. But Corrigan's ranch had needed more land, and Johnson had blocked a big section of range with his river-run homestead, which was laid out to include the Yellowstone and 50 yards of land on each side in parcels that ran downstream for seven miles.

The CR brand needed that river frontage. Corrigan had tried to buy the man out twice, then worked the plan to steal the new calves and deny Johnson any increase in his herds. It had taken three years before Johnson was down and out. The bank took over the ranch. At the sheriff's auction, Isaiah Roundtree had stepped in and given the winning bid, denying Corrigan again the rights to the river along the far side of his land.

He'd been working hard ever since. He had bought some more land, and his CR brand outfit was on firm ground at last.

Corrigan took another long pull at the whiskey. He wasn't drunk yet, but it was time. He took the six-gun from his holster, put the muzzle in his mouth and pulled the trigger.

The round exploded through his mouth and tore out the top of his skull, spraying brains, gray matter, blood and bone over a large section of the hardware store's front wall.

Shotgun!

The deputy sheriff, who had been checking doors on the far side of the street on his return trip, rushed over and looked at the body, which had been blasted out of the chair and lay on the boardwalk. The gun was still clamped tightly in the dead man's mouth.

"It's Corrigan," the deputy whispered. "God, Mike Corrigan just drank half a bottle of whiskey and blew his brains out." He ran for the office to see if Sheriff Attucks was still there.

Down the street in her saloon, Hannah did not hear the shot, and she didn't know about the suicide until more than a half hour later when somebody came in with all the details. She set up a beer for the man and nodded grimly.

"Would you mind going over that again. I didn't hear all of what you had to say." On the outside, she showed proper respect for the dead. Inside, she was shouting with joy and rapture. One more stroke in evening the score for the ruination of her father.

Chapter Fourteen

Morgan had tried working the saloons again, to see if he could find anyone hiring cowboys or talking about the rustling. He came up with absolutely zero. Most of the working cowhands were hard at it out on the prairie, getting ready for the spring roundups.

He found two young men who were asking about jobs, but no one knew any of the local ranches who were hiring. Morgan followed them to three different saloons but they had no luck getting any work.

He gave up and headed toward Hannah's. He'd been in there a while back, but she wasn't around. The barkeep said he wasn't sure where she was. She usually told him if she'd be gone for more than a few minutes.

Morgan went outside and found himself behind a deputy sheriff working up the street, checking doors to be sure they were locked. He heard a muffled shot and wasn't sure where it came from. He figured across the street somewhere.

The deputy swore loudly and ran across the street. In the dim moonlight, Morgan saw a man sprawled on the boardwalk near the hardware store. He ran that way and saw the tableau. The dead man lay crumpled on the rough boards with a six-gun still in his mouth, his teeth clamped in a death grip, the top of his head spread out in full color all over the hardware store's front wall.

The deputy shook his head. Then he ran off and Morgan crossed the street. By then, a dozen men and two dance-hall girls had crowded around.

"Holy Saint Christopher," a man said. "That's Mike Corrigan, rancher out south of town a ways. Has one of the three biggest spreads around here."

Morgan frowned. Another rancher murdered? Or had he eaten his revolver barrel all by himself?

The deputy came back with a blanket and spread it over the dead man. The lawman shook his head. "I saw him sitting here when I went down this side ten minutes ago. He had a bottle. Is it still here?"

Somebody found the half-empty bottle lying under the chair that had fallen over.

"Didn't look like he was in any trouble," the deputy said. "Just a little sitting and thinking."

"Then he didn't have his gun out when you went by?" Morgan asked.

"Hell, no, or I would have stopped. He was just sitting there, having a nip now and then. Had the chair leaned back against the wall like we've all done."

Sheriff Attucks came up, looked under the blanket and nodded.

"Yep, it's Corrigan, all right." He shooed everyone else away except Morgan.

"Another one of your employers dead, Morgan. You have a good alibi?"

"The best—my bartender. Is it murder or suicide?"

"Can't say yet."

He went across the street to the Northern Pacific depot and asked a new telegrapher if there was a message for him under the name of Buck Leslie.

"Yes, sir, Mr. Leslie. Came in not an hour ago. Had a note from the other operator to hold it here."

"Thanks." Morgan took the envelope and carried it out to the waiting room, where two lamps still burned. He tore open the envelope and read the wire.

Buck Leslie. Miles City, Montana Territory. Checked our records. Unusual activity in cattle shipments. Much too early for this many cattle coming from Miles City area. Deeply concerned there may be collusion

204

Shotgun!

between smugglers and at least one train crew. Am sending Special Railroad Detective Kay Butterfield. She left an hour after we received your wire. Butterfield should arrive Miles City about noon tomorrow. Butterfield is experienced, knows our routines and procedures and will be invaluable to you in tying down the rail end of the rustling operation. If you need any assistance, wire me direct. Richard Lawrence, Manager, Minneapolis-St. Paul Division Point, Northern Pacific Railroad.

By the time Morgan walked back to the blood-splattered wall, the body had been taken away and a man talked earnestly with Sheriff Attucks. Morgan drifted that way.

"So, Sheriff, that's about the way it happened," the man said. He was short and wore a white shirt with garters holding the cuffs away from his hands but no jacket. He could have been a merchant.

"Mr. Oakes, would you go over that again to be sure I have it right? You were closing up your store across the street and saw a man sitting over here in front of the hardware."

"Yep. I've been robbed once a couple of years ago, and I like to take a look around before I leave my store. This time I stopped when I saw the man across the street. Then I pulled back into my doorway when I saw him take out his revolver. Didn't know if he was gonna run over here and rob me or wait until I headed home and then catch me. So I waited. Not a minute later I saw him put the muzzle in his mouth. He didn't wait a second. It went inside his mouth and he pulled the trigger."

"No one else was anywhere around him?" Morgan asked.

"Oh, no, sir. He was all by himself. I didn't see the bottle. I guess he'd put it under the chair by then."

"Thanks, Mr. Oakes. I'd like you to write out exactly what you saw and bring it down to the office tomorrow. Or I'll have a deputy pick it up. Just write it on a piece of paper and sign and date it."

The citizen said he would and hurried off, late already for the supper that his wife must be holding for him at his house.

Sheriff Attucks looked at Morgan. "So, looks like that case is closed before it gets started. A suicide. Why he did it is probably another story, but not my worry."

Morgan had wondered the same thing. Why had Corrigan killed himself? He had a huge ranch if he was one of the three largest in the area. He was worth a lot of money. Morgan remembered the line he'd heard about suicide. Suicide was a permanent solution to a temporary problem. Usually it was tragically true.

He would have to check around, but he didn't

see how this suicide involved the rustling. It might tie in somehow, but right now he didn't see how. If it did, he had no idea how that could help him catch the rustlers in the act.

Morgan went back to the hotel, checked his box, which was empty, and went up to his room. No one waited for him in the hall. No one lurked inside his room and the window was down and locked.

He got into bed without lighting a lamp. No use advertising that he had returned to his room. Tomorrow he planned on tracking the movements of the late Isaiah Roundtree. There could be a connection here somewhere, and he wanted to find it if possible.

Morgan dropped off to sleep with his door locked. The key was in the keyhole and turned halfway so it couldn't be pushed out, and the straight-backed wooden chair was propped under the door handle. If anyone tried to get in his room, he would have to break the chair first, giving Morgan plenty of warning that guests were nearby.

As usual, Morgan's mental alarm clock awoke him promptly at 6:30 and he had breakfast at the cafe where they baked their own bread. He had a stack of toast, a three-egg cheese omelet and black coffee.

He checked at the bank well before it opened. Mr. Yardley saw him at the side door and let him in. When a rancher went to town he often had banking business to attend to. Yardley was positive.

"Yes, Mr. Roundtree came in just as we opened that day he died. We worked out two small problems he had with an account and he made a withdrawal and left here. I'd say about ten-thirty."

"Was it a large withdrawal—the size that some men would kill for?" Morgan asked.

"I wouldn't think so. I'm not sure of the exact amount now but it was less than two hundred dollars. For any large amounts he always took a bank draft or a cashier's check."

"Good. I'm trying to retrace his movement that day. Did he say where he would go from here?"

"Matter of fact we talked about that. I asked him about what kind of shoes I should use on my riding horse, and he said the small, thin ones to lighten the load. He said they used heavier ones on long drives. He mentioned that he was heading over to the blacksmith's place after he left here to pick up two dozen pair he'd ordered a week before. They were ready."

Morgan thanked him and went down to the blacksmith on the other corner across from the Livery Stable fronting on Main and First. Somebody said the same man owned both places.

The smithy was not a large man. He stood no more than five four and worked with his shirt and undershirt off in the morning warmth which was compounded by the heat of the forge that

Shotgun!

he pumped up from time to time. The smithy slammed the eight-pound hammer against the chunk of red-hot iron he held with black tongs and flattened it a little. Another jolt from the hammer turned the chunk of metal flat on one side. A dozen more blows and the hot metal took on the square shape of a rod half an inch square. It had been heated twice more and then straightened on the flat head of the anvil. When he finished with the foot-long rod and had pounded a rough point on the end, he looked up at Morgan.

"Don't like to bother a man at his trade," Morgan said.

The smith had shoulders and arms like a strong man in the circus. His hips and legs were normal size, but the continual lifting and flailing away with a six-, eight- and at times ten-pound hammer had built his whole upper body into a bulging muscled masterpiece.

"I could buy the rods preformed this way, but I like the feel of making my iron work fences myself. What can I do for you?"

"Isaiah Roundtree. I'm trying to follow his movements that last day of his life. I hear he stopped by here to see you."

"Roundtree. The Bar B. Yep, I made up ten or twelve sets of heavyweight horse shoes for him. He loaded them in a light rig he had in town."

"A black buggy?"

"No. That much weight would go right through the floorboards. He had a Democrat wagon, with one seat and room for plenty behind him. Loaded the shoes in myself."

"He here long?"

"A while. Isaiah used to work some iron himself at a forge he had out at his ranch in the early days. Then he tried to teach a cowhand how, and the first one quit and the second one got a bad arm and Roundtree gave it up. Roundtree pounded away on a piece I was working on that day. He worked up a sweat, thanked me and left."

"What time—eleven o'clock?"

"More or less. Couldn't have been here more than a half hour."

"He paid you for the shoes and you gave him a receipt?"

"Nope. we have a running account for the Bar B and most of the big outfits. Easier that way. They pay up once a month, regular."

"He mention where he was going from here?"

"Not directly. But usual after he works up a sweat he has a thirst, too, and he heads for the nearest saloon, which from here is two doors up from Second, there on Main."

"Thanks."

Morgan overcame the urge to pound some of that red-hot iron himself and moved on to the saloon. The apron remembered Roundtree. The day he had been found dead somebody recalled that the rancher had been in the saloon. He drank some beers and stayed till near noon. The guess then was that he'd headed for some food since

Shotgun!

Isaiah was not a man known to miss a meal.

From there on toward the middle of town there were five different eateries. All of them small to medium size, and nobody in any of them remembered Isaiah coming in that day he died.

"We get lots of people in and out all day," the owner of one of the places said. "Not a chance we can remember each one of them. Ones we remember do something outrageous or terribly kind. You kill somebody in our place and we'd remember you."

Morgan worked other stores and cafes until nearly noon, but no one else had remembered Isaiah in town that day he died. He had checked on arrivals at the station when he went by. A westbound would come in at 12:10 and she was on time, according to the latest telegraph message from down the tracks.

Morgan sighed and went back to the station. He heard the train whistle as it came around the near bend before it straightened out a quarter of a mile east of town. He and the train should make the station in a dead heat.

As it turned out, the train had some switching to do in the yards just to the east of the station and Morgan had to wait nearly five minutes for the passenger cars to arrive. More than 50 people hurried off the train, most lugging along cases and boxes and a carpetbag or two.

Morgan leaned against a baggage cart and waited. Two men loitered near the train a moment, then saw someone at the end of the platform and hurried that way. Soon there was only one person left looking around outside the station.

"Butterfield?" Morgan called from 40 feet away. The woman turned and nodded, picked up one small leather satchel and walked confidently toward him.

"Damn," Morgan said softly. She was tall, five eight at least and slender. She wore a pure white Stetson with a medium crown and a white blouse tucked inside a dark brown skirt. Woman's boots peeked out from under the nearly ground-level skirt when she walked.

As she came closer, Morgan saw short blonde hair under the edges of the hat, clear blue eyes, a shapely nose over a firm mouth and a delicate chin.

Kay held out her hand and dropped her bag at the same time. "You must be Buck Leslie. We got your wire and the chief is about wrung out of shape. He hates it when anything crooked happens by employees of the road. Oh, I'm Kay Butterfield. No, before you ask, I don't own part of the Butterfield Stage of recent history."

She paused and then grinned. "Do you talk, or are you the strong, silent type?"

"I usually can talk. It's just that—"

"I know. Stunned by my remarkably good looks, great figure and outstanding record as a detective. It happens."

Buckskin laughed. "Right. I can see that you've gone through this before."

"On over ninety percent of my cases. Now let's find me a hotel. I'd prefer to stay in the one you do. It will make coordinating things easier. Which way?"

"Let me have your bag and I'll be your native guide."

"I can carry it."

He pried it out of her hand. "I'm sure you can. But this is a small town in the West and it's expected that a man will carry a woman's bag. We're blending into the local scene here. So relax."

She frowned for a minute and sighed. "Yes, all right. But I'm not here to be waited on, put upon or left with nothing to do. The Northern Pacific is extremely interested in clearing up this problem as quickly as possible."

"Good. Tell them not to authorize leaving any cattle cars on sidings within one hundred miles of Miles City for the next two weeks. That would be a big help."

They walked to Main and down the boardwalk past the sheriff's office, the barbershop and a law office. The Cattleman's Hotel was on the other side of the street. Morgan led Kay into the dusty street and she barely missed stepping in a cow pie that had not had time to crust over yet.

"Yes, no cattle cars would be a help, but I'm not sure the road would do that. There might be

213

a legitimate early shipper out here."

"If there is, I'll know it far enough in advance. Few cattle are shipped before the big spring roundups, and they won't happen for two or three weeks yet. We need a good rain so the new grass will grow and bring the cattle out of the thickets into the open, where the cowboys can round them up."

"I'll wire them and see what they can do, but I can't promise anything."

"Who orders for the cattle cars from out here?"

"Usually the cattle buyer in each shipping point. Here it would be Josh Eagleston." She looked at Morgan. "Is he a suspect in this scheme?"

"He is."

At the hotel she registered, getting a room on the second floor, three doors down from his. They took her bag upstairs. Then he asked if she'd like a cup of coffee and they retreated to the dining room.

When they had been served, Kay took out a small notebook from her pocket and a pencil and looked up at him from huge blue eyes. "So, you must have been hired by the local cattlemen."

"True. They said they were losing up to five thousand head a week. At an average of forty dollars a head, that's two hundred thousand dollars a week. It can't continue."

"I would hope not. That's a terribly lot of money. Our figures don't add up quite that high on cattle shipped through Miles City to the stockyards in

St. Paul." She flipped back a page or two in the notebook.

"We show a total of two thousand four hundred and eighty four head that have come through Miles City over the past six weeks. Your owners have been exaggerating. That's still almost a hundred thousand dollars worth of cattle, so we understand why everyone is so upset. We want any possible trainman collusion stopped, which should solve the problem. Why rustle cattle if you can't ship them."

Morgan leaned back in his chair and sipped the coffee. "Good, I knew they were exaggerating. I just didn't know how much. Two of the ranchers in this area have died in the past two or three days. One last night—self-inflicted bullet wound. I'm not sure if this has any bearing. Just want to bring you up to date on the situation."

"Any other players in this game?" Kay asked, her blue eyes curious.

"Not many. A man by the name of Selby Holt had been hiring cowboys for a week's work, used them to rustle the cattle and sent the cowboys down the rails and out of the state. We captured Holt but he was shot dead by someone who didn't want him to talk. Not sure who it was. Now there's bound to be another man hiring the rustlers' cowhands.

"We broke up some rustling attempts by tracking certain people and rented horses from the livery. Now you're as up to date as you can be."

Kay nodded, made some notes in her small book and slipped it into a pocket in her skirt.

"Can you use a gun?" Morgan asked.

"If I need to." She made a small motion with her right hand and a second later a .32 revolver with a two-inch barrel appeared in her hand aimed at Morgan's chest. She put it away at once and he nodded.

"Good, you can draw it. This afternoon we'll go out of town a ways and check to see if you can shoot it. Nobody who works with me gets the time of day unless she can use that gun like a professional."

"Fair enough. I'd like to see if you can shoot as well. I also ride and I can take care of myself in a brawl. No, I'm not married. My parents live in Chicago and my father has worked for the road since it began. If you're not used to train talk, road means the railroad."

"Sounds reasonable. I'm not married either and have no intentions along that line. I grew up in Idaho and now work out of Denver. Yes, I'm getting paid a lot more for this job than you are and it doesn't bother me a bit because I didn't ask for any help. The road volunteered you, so I'll try to cooperate. Let's make the best of it."

Kay's eyes hardened as she stared at him. "You don't like me. Fine. That's not part of the job. I told my boss I can work with anyone and I'm not going to let you make a liar out of me. Ready for some shooting?" Morgan nodded. "Good. Let's go upstairs and get a box of thirty-two caliber rounds out of my bag and I'll be ready."

In her room she left the door halfway open as she unsnapped her fancy leather valise and dug around for the box of rounds. They vanished into a pocket in her skirt and she watched Morgan a moment.

"Look. I grew up with four brothers. They told me constantly about their conquests and their love life. I know men. I know how you think and what you want. Right about now you're wondering what it would be like to kiss me and if you can get me into bed. So let's get it straight from the start."

She pushed forward, caught his face with her hands and kissed him hotly. Then she stepped away.

"That's the first part. Now you know how it is to kiss me. The part about getting me into bed is only for your dreams. So let's move out and I'll show you how I can use this weapon. Will we ride or walk?"

Morgan grinned as he watched her. She was all business and in control. He knew it was mostly bluff. The kiss had been a surprise—a most pleasant surprise showing the fire that burned underneath all that talk.

"Hey, we'll walk. That was a good kiss, in case you keep score. There's a spot about two blocks down where the town runs out of houses and we can shoot all we want and not bother anyone."

Kay's expression hadn't changed but he saw some small softening around her eyes. Maybe there was hope for her yet.

"Good. Let's get started. I want to meet the next westbound train and see what crew they have onboard. I'll know some of them. It could help."

He held the door open for her. She hesitated, then walked through and led the way down the steps. Morgan sighed. This would take some time.

Chapter Fifteen

They put small rocks on top of large rocks 100 yards behind the blacksmith's shop and Morgan quickly saw that the lady knew how to use the little six-gun. He positioned her 20 feet from the rocks and had her fire at the first four rocks. She hit three of the four. He put new rocks on the spots and had her pull the weapon out of her skirt pocket and fire as quickly as she could.

He ran Kay through that one for each of the four rocks. She hit two of them but the rocks were less than three inches wide.

Morgan nodded. "I'm impressed. You use that like you've fired it before. Have you ever shot at a man or a woman?"

Kay looked away, her face suddenly slack, without the bravado and the confidence. She frowned, then lifted her brows. "No, I've never had to. I know some policemen who have carried revolvers for twenty years and never had to fire a shot."

Kit Dalton

"It's different out here. This isn't Chicago. It's one hell of a long way from Chicago. A man here in town tried to kill me three days ago. Fired so close to me I could see the color of his eyes. He was no more than fifteen feet away and had me cold. I stumbled on a drop off from one store to the next on the boardwalk or I'd be buried in the ground about six feet down right now. Out here that weapon is a necessity, not a show piece, not a toy to play with on the shooting range."

"Fine, I get the point. Now let's see you shoot." Kay was somewhat subdued as she put rocks on the same boulders and moved Morgan back 30 feet. "Draw and shoot two rocks. Then holster it and do the same thing again."

Morgan looked at the targets. Then his right hand snapped down and came upward against the butt of his .45, lifting it out of leather. At the same time, his thumb dragged back on the hammer, cocking the weapon. His trigger finger filled the hole, and a fraction of a second later, when his Colt muzzle cleared leather, he pushed it forward in an aim-and-shoot movement. His finger stroked the trigger. The first rock exploded as he hit it and the second one jolted off the boulder.

"Fair," Kay said, but her brows had arched upward as she saw the speed of his draw. "This time I'll give you the word draw and then you go for your Colt."

Morgan nodded and settled the iron in leather.

Shotgun!

He looked away and suddenly she said, "Draw!"

Again he drew in a split second and the third rock vanished with a lead assist and the fourth rock exploded as he hit it dead center.

Kay smiled. "You'll do," she said. Then she laughed a little self consciously. "You are fast on the draw, I'll give you that, Buck Leslie. Can I call you Buckskin Lee Morgan now? I know who you are. My guess is that a lot of people in town know, too."

"Let's keep it Buck Leslie. I'm still alive. It might be helping. I have enough old enemies who are on the lookout for me as it is. They couldn't miss me if they knew I was here."

"Fine. You can't help us if you're dead." Kay looked at him and a small grin showed. "Now what's next?"

"You wanted to meet the next westbound. You can be a big help if you work the train side. You must know what it takes to get empty cattle cars dropped off at a siding somewhere. Check the procedure and notify the division point, or wherever the order goes to, to tell you by wire whenever an order for empties comes from a siding within fifty miles of Miles City, either way. Can we find out that?"

"Easy. Sometimes cars are left on sidings and get lost. Any engineer who wanted to could hook on a dozen of them and dump them on the siding of his choice. That part we can't know about. Any legitimate request would go through our regular channels, and I'll have them notify me."

"You're saying that if the rustlers want empty cattle cars, they most likely won't go through channels."

"That's the general idea," Kay said.

"Then the division point won't be much help."

"I know some of these crews. The engineer, the conductor the brakemen—the whole crew would have to be in on the scheme to pick up rustled cattle. One or two of our engineers I wouldn't trust with a fresh cherry pie, let alone fifty thousand dollars worth of beef."

She thought for a moment as they walked back toward the Northern Pacific station. "I can wire for a crew schedule to be sent to me each day for the westbound trains through Miles City. They can do that easily. Then we'll have an idea which train might be the one."

"Good. Get that started. Are there any of the sidings down the tracks either way that could be used to load steers?"

"I'm not sure. I'll have to ride the rails and find out. I'll go all the way west to Custer and make a list of sidings that could be used for loading. Then tomorrow I'll go the other way out to Glendive and do the same thing. Give us something to work with. What? What are you grinning at?"

"Maybe I was wrong about you. Hell, you might even be some help before this thing is all wrapped up. I need to go watch Josh's house and see if he's doing anything unusual."

"Josh the cattle buyer for the stockyards in St. Paul?"

"Yeah. He's as crooked as a mulberry tree. I just have to catch him at it."

He dropped her off at the train station. By then it was almost two o'clock. She checked the clock in the waiting room.

"I won't be back until about eight or nine," Kay said. "I'll knock on your door when I get in and tell you what I've found. Maybe we could have a cup of coffee or something then."

Morgan agreed and headed up the street. As he passed Teressa's dressmaking shop he saw a flash of brown. Then the seamstress hurried out the door and caught his arm.

"Mr. Leslie, I need to talk to you for a minute." She tugged at his arm. "Come inside where you won't make a spectacle of yourself."

"Teressa, I have some business to take care of."

"This won't take but five minutes. I've got something to tell you that's important."

He knew he shouldn't, but he let her lead him into the shop. There were no customers.

She moved away from him and stared at him, her grim expression softening a little, then breaking into a smile. "You are just so handsome that I can't believe it. But I'll get used to you. This is the situation. Tonight I'm going to tell my mother that I think that I'm pregnant. That you did it to me three times and it was just long enough after my monthly so I would be most likely to get pregnant."

"Now wait just a minute."

"No, you wait, Buck Leslie. You came in here and seduced me and kissed me and made me like it. Mama will understand. We had a long talk one day. She'll go straight to Papa, who will be sure to see you tomorrow and he'll use a shotgun if he thinks he needs to. I'll swear on a stack of Bibles that you seduced me and had your way with me three or four times and I'm bound to be pregnant and you simply must do the right thing and make an honest woman of me."

Her grim expression turned into a touch of a smile, then a smirk. "Don't worry. It won't be so bad being married to me. I can even support you. Papa has always been protective of me. He knocked down a man in the street who made advances to me when I didn't want him to. Knowing you did it to me, he'll be furious. I might have to talk him out of killing you, telling him marrying me would be better."

Morgan shook his head. "Teressa, you really think this will work, don't you? Don't you think I've had a problem like this before? I have. Sometimes it's hard, but with you, it's easy. All I have to do is demand that a doctor examine you. He'll tell your parents that definitely you are still a virgin and cannot be pregnant."

Shotgun!

Teressa sucked in a breath and Morgan grinned. He watched her wilt. All of her bravado and steam and drive seeped out of her. She dropped into a chair and put her face in her hands.

Morgan knelt in front of her, lifted her head and moved her hands. He kissed her cheek and brushed away the tears.

"Hey, all is not lost. I can still be your friend. Just don't try anything like this again. I keep telling you that one of these days the right young man will come along and you'll fall head over heels in love with him. It will all work out well."

Teressa looked at him through tearstained eyes. "I've been thinking that since I was sixteen. I still haven't found him."

"Some of us have to wait a little longer. Your man will come. Now start thinking pretty for yourself. As a seamstress you should have the best wardrobe in town. Always wear your best dress. Make new ones that accent your best features. Pick out some man who might be a good husband and flirt with him. It can't hurt. Now I do have to go."

He lifted her face and softly kissed her lips. Her eyes widened and she reached for him, but he'd backed away and hurried out the door. A slow smile crept over her teary face and she began to nod.

Out on the street, Morgan continued up the boardwalk past Hannah's Place to the general store. Few ranchers would come into town and not have a list of supplies needed at the cook shack. Morgan had talked to the store owner before, but the man had said he'd been off the day that Roundtree had been killed and his helper had handled the store.

The clerk was there, a man named Hart, and he nodded when Howard introduced Morgan.

"Sure, I remember the day Mr. Roundtree died. Thought about it the next morning when they found him out there on the river trail. He'd been in the day before, which I guess is the day you're talking about. Had a few things the cook needed and then we discussed a new shotgun that we just got in stock. He was interested, but said he had three good scatterguns at home now he wasn't using. This new one is a great double-barrel model from Remington."

"What time was he here?"

"Not sure minute to minute. I'd come back from my afternoon coffee, so it had to be three o'clock or later. Say three-fifteen to maybe a quarter of four. He really liked that shotgun. I didn't know quite how to talk him into buying it."

"He say where he was going after he left you?"

"Not exactly. I remember him saying he had two hours to kill. He made a joke about that. Said his old pa always used to tell him that the best way to kill time was to work it to death. We both laughed about that."

"You saw him leave the store?"

"Sure. He helped me load some sacks of flour

and a box of other things in his wagon. I noticed a whole passel of new horseshoes in back. Never figured a big ranch would use that many hard shoes, but I guess they do."

"You see him drive away?"

"Nope. We got busy then and I went back inside." He frowned, then snapped his fingers. "Yeah, I was on my way home after I closed up about eight, and I saw his wagon sitting out in front at a saloon up there across from the courthouse on Fourth. It's the Lone Rider Saloon."

Morgan thanked him and tried the saloon. The apron nodded. "Yep, knew Isaiah. We go way back. Used to ride for him years ago. He'd stop by from time to time and shoot the breeze about the old days. He was in that day he died. Late afternoon."

"What time did he leave?" Morgan asked.

"Leave. Damn we started getting busy. We get a wild crowd in here. Had a small fight about that time. I had to break it up with a pool cue on a guy's head. Must have been about five, maybe a little later when Isaiah left. He went to the door and waved and I never saw him alive again."

Morgan walked out the door and stared at the hitching rail in front of the saloon. Some places had them; some didn't. How had the rancher moved from a wagon into a black closed buggy?

"Oh, damn," Morgan said.

He turned east and walked fast. He should have

thought of it before. Roundtree was riding in a black buggy when he was killed. It could have been rented at the livery by the killer or maybe by the victim. Morgan hoped it was the killer.

Fifteen minutes later Morgan found the livery owner in back, cleaning out stalls. The man pitched manure into a wheelbarrow and looked up at Morgan. "You stop them, the rustlers?"

"A couple of times. Thanks for your help. You get your horses back?"

"All but one. Still looking for her. She was just a cheap dollar mount anyway. I'm still watching."

"The fiver is ready for the next time. I'm interested in something else now. You rent black buggies?"

"Got a couple. Good for funerals."

"Two or three days ago did you rent one to Isaiah Roundtree?"

"Sure as hell did. Blood all over that sucker. Had to wash the seat off three times."

"He rented it in the late afternoon?"

"Yep. Said he had a private meeting with somebody and this was the best way to keep it private."

"Met with his killer. Did he give you any idea who it might have been?"

"Not a word. Guess that's what he meant by keeping it private."

"True. I hoped that somebody else had rented the rig and picked him up, and you might have a name for me. No such luck. Murder is never easy." Morgan handed the man a folded five dollar bill. "You keep on the watch for any more young cowboys who need a horse for a short job. Let me know the same as before."

"Yes, indeed. I can do that." The livery owner pitched some more manure and hay into the wheelbarrow. "You doing any good finding out who's behind the rustling?"

"Not much. You'll know when I figure it out. Making progress is about all I can say."

Morgan walked back to the hotel, then went over two blocks to B Street in the residential section of town, where he watched Josh's house again. No smoke, not much happening. Morgan settled down in a little clump of brush on a vacant lot down half a block from the house. A half hour later he started getting hungry. He couldn't remember if he'd had any lunch or not. When he checked his watch it showed 4:30. He'd give it another half hour. Josh might come home or go out; either way it would be some action.

Ten minutes later, the screen door on the front entrance squeaked and then banged as someone came out. The person turned and headed his way. Morgan dropped lower in the weeds. A woman. As she passed, he saw the painted face and low-cut dress. Maybe one of Matilda Jones's fancy girls. He could follow her but that wouldn't help much.

Morgan stuck by his post and at 5:15 Josh came

out wearing a shirt and tie, dark trousers and a dark jacket. Looked as if he was going to a funeral or a wedding. He went west to Fourth Street, turned toward town and then back east on Main.

Josh Eagleston tried three different saloons before he found the man he wanted. They sat at a back table and talked for two hours before Josh got up and left. Morgan had been working on a pair of beers and sat in for a time at a dime-limit poker game. When Josh left, Morgan eased up beside the man Josh had been talking to and pushed his six-gun into the man's side.

"Friend, I suggest that we head out the back door like we need to take a piss something bad. Then we can talk and nobody gets hurt. You stand up, go out and don't say a word to anybody. I'll be behind you. Understand?"

"Oh, yeah, I hear you," the man said.

Morgan eased away and put the Colt back in leather. He had been turned so no one in the place could see him draw and use the weapon. With the man almost to the rear door, Morgan followed. Outside the man waited. It was dark out, but there was no place in the alley to hide.

Morgan had a better look at the man in the faint moonlight. He looked about 30, clean shaven. He wore range clothes that were neat and clean. He didn't look like a saddle bum.

"Okay, now is the time to talk to me. What

were you and Josh in such a long conference about?" Morgan said.

"I don't know any Josh—"

That was as far as he got it out before Morgan drew and pushed the muzzle of the Colt under the man's jaw. The man stood as tall as he could but still the weapon pressed upward.

"Now I suggest you stop lying before you start and tell me exactly what Josh and you talked about, or I'll blow your fucking head off. You understand me?"

The man reacted with shock and wide eyes. "Okay. I didn't know how serious you were. You could get in big trouble causing Josh any pain or problems."

"Let me worry about that. Who are you and what did you and Josh talk about?"

"I'm a railroad detective. I work for the Northern Pacific. I'm out here from St. Louis, trying to get a line on what the ranchers call large-scale rustling. We figure that, if they can't ship the cattle, they won't steal them."

"Who do you work for in St. Louis?"

"Alonzo Stutz. He wants the problem cleaned up quickly."

Morgan kept the six-gun pushing upward on the man's chin. He cocked the weapon and the man's eyes went wide.

"Hey, I'm telling you the truth."

"Not a bit of the truth. The Northern Pacific doesn't go to St. Louis. The home base is Chicago.

You have ten seconds to tell me who you are before I blow you straight into hell."

"All right. Just take that iron out of my face."

"When you talk straight."

The man sighed. "Okay. I'm a cowhand down on my luck a bit. I heard Josh needed a recruiter to gather up temporary batches of cowboys for a week's work and then get shipped out. I'm here to find him cowboys."

Morgan lowered the six-gun and pushed it into the man's belly. "Now what's your name and where are you from?"

"I'm Dobbs Gilroy from Wyoming. Any law in Montana against that?"

"Just punishment for being a smart mouth. Tell you what you're going to do. There's a train through here in an hour or so. You're going to be on it. When were you supposed to deliver the next batch of riders for Josh?"

"God, he'd kill me."

"He won't have a chance. You'll be in Wyoming or Idaho or Washington or maybe even Minnesota before he knows you're gone."

Dobbs hesitated and Morgan jammed the Colt's muzzle harder into his belly. "All right. It was for three days from now. He says he has the cattle cars spotted and all he needs is the beef. I was to get twenty bucks for every cowboy I hired up to six."

"Good pay," Morgan said. "You get any advance?"

Shotgun!

"Yeah, twenty dollars."

"We'll see how far that will take you on the train. Let's take a walk."

At the station they found Kay Butterfield. The westbound hadn't come in yet. When Morgan explained the small problem, she grinned and went to the ticket window. She showed the man some credentials and he gave her a ticket. She came back laughing.

"You can keep that twenty dollars of dirty money you have, Mr. Gilroy. I have here a ticket for you all the way to Seattle. I also have a pair of handcuffs. You'll be handcuffed to the seat back and each conductor from here to Seattle will have the key. Oh, the conductors will take good care of you. I'll write a note to go along with the key. You'll have a great train ride free from the road."

Gilroy shrugged. "Hey, I've always wanted to see Seattle. Is it true that's on the Pacific Ocean?"

"Close enough you can smell it, Gilroy," Morgan said.

A half hour later, the train came puffing in and spewed out a great cloud of steam as it came to a stop. Forty angry passengers stepped down, unhappy to be four hours late.

The train had to wait half an hour to clear another train on the tracks. By then, Kay and Morgan had Dobbs Gilroy safely handcuffed to a seat in the passenger car and the key in custody of the conductor. The conductor had stared at

233

Kit Dalton

Kay's credentials for two minutes before he at last nodded and looked down at her.

"Never seen a female railroad detective before," he said at last. Then he grinned. "Good. You're prettier than any of them guys."

Kay and Morgan stood on the station and watched the train slide out of the station heading for Seattle. Their guest was still on board.

Kay turned to Morgan as they walked away from the station. "I'm starved. Have you had supper yet? If you haven't, I'm buying. Come on. I hate to eat alone."

234

Chapter Sixteen

Kay and Morgan had dinner in the dining room at the Cattleman's Hotel and tarried over coffee as she told him a brief story of her life. She finished her coffee and folded the napkin on the table.

"All right, enough of this. You're bored with the dull story of my life and I'm making like I'm on a first date with you and trying to impress you, which I'm not. We're working together. That's all."

Morgan nodded. "Agreed. We're working together. What's on your docket for tomorrow?"

"I'll take the first train out east or west and go to either Custer to the west or Glendive to the east and check out every siding that I see. I'll have a name, location and number of miles from Miles City for each one of them. Then I'll ride back and see if I have time enough to go the other direction. It will depend on what kind of connections I can make."

"Good. I still have to watch that damn Josh. He's up to something again, like he has the cattle cars all ready and is just waiting for some steers."

"Fine. It's been a long day for me and I'm about ready to go to sleep in my saucer here despite all the coffee I drank."

Morgan picked up the check and started for the cashier when Kay caught him. "I said I was buying dinner. I'm on an expense account."

"My expense account is better than yours. You trying to embarrass me here?"

"Yes," she said and grinned impishly. She pulled the check from his hand and paid the cashier, who looked at her and smiled, then frowned at Morgan.

On the way to the stairs, he groused at Kay. "I'll never get elected mayor in this town if you do that once more."

She laughed. "It's good for you. One day, maybe a hundred years from now, women are going to be doctors and lawyers and judges and senators and maybe even president. You best get used to the idea that women are real honest-to-goodness people just like men."

Morgan chuckled. "In a hundred years, I'll call your bet. I just hope that women don't become exactly like men."

Kay snorted and they walked up to the second floor. Morgan saw her to her door. When she had it unlocked and stepped inside, he said good night and retreated to his own room three doors down.

Morgan lit the lamp this time, pulled the shade and peeled out of his clothes. He had a quick sponge bath in the big washbowl and dried off. Then he slid on top of the sheets in his short underwear. It was going to be a warm night for so early in the spring.

He blew out the lamp and dozed. Sometime later he came alert and sat up. His right hand grabbed the Colt from beside his pillow. That was when he remembered that he hadn't even locked the door. He saw the door edging inward; then it came open all at once. Morgan rolled to the floor, the Colt up and ready to fire.

Slowly a figure came around the door holding a candle. It was Kay in a long white nightgown. The light from the candle showed Morgan crouched on the floor, his gun ready.

"Oh, dear, I didn't mean to startle you. It's Kay. Remember me?"

Morgan put down the Colt and stood. Kay looked at him a minute, then reached back and closed the door. "You forgot to lock your door."

"I was distracted."

She smiled in the candlelight. "I couldn't sleep. Could we talk for a few minutes?"

"Sure. You want me to light the lamp?"

"No, this is fine." She looked for a place to sit

and chose the bed. "I really do need to talk. You see, when I start a new assignment this way, I get all defensive and sharp and curt and try to show everyone that I'm just as tough and sure of myself and competent as the rest of you are." She patted the bed beside her. "Sit here so I don't have to shout."

He hesitated, then sat beside her. The nightgown covered her from neck to toes. The drape down her chest didn't even reveal any breasts.

"So you're not as tough as you seem?"

Kay sighed. "If you only knew. Half the time I'm scared right out of my chemise. I mean, I'm usually not a forward person, but in this business I have to take charge and order people around and do things that I ordinarily wouldn't even consider doing."

"Maybe that's why you enjoy it."

"Like coming in here to your hotel room. Not a chance in hell I'd do that back in Chicago with one of my fellow workers. But I used to do this all the time at home when I was growing up. I had a big sister and she helped me a lot. We'd sit with a candle between us on her bed and talk into the night. I learned a lot about life and about boys from her."

"But maybe not enough."

She ignored what he said and looked up. "My sister always held me. Would you hold me, just for a minute?"

He put his arm around her and she snuggled

Shotgun!

against him. She sighed. "Oh, yes, now that feels ever so much better." She clung to him a minute and sighed again; then she eased away a bit and looked up at him. "Morgan, you're not getting any ideas, are you?"

"What kind of ideas."

"You know."

"Just because a sexy lady comes into my bedroom in the middle of the night wearing next to nothing and asks me to put my arms around her and hold her, you think I'd get that kind of an idea?"

"Yes." Her voice was soft and small and far away and she leaned against him again. She had turned so he felt her breasts pushing against his bare chest. Her face came up toward his and then she kissed him lightly on the lips.

"Mmm, not bad. Needs more research." She kissed him again. This time her mouth edged open and her tongue darted out and licked his lips. Then his mouth opened too and her arms went around him. The kiss was burning hot in an instant.

Morgan could feel the heat radiating from her breasts. Kay moaned softly, put her arms around his neck and held the kiss as she fell with him backward on the bed.

Morgan lay half on top of her, crushing one breast. Kay eased her lips from him. Her voice was strong again.

"Look. I figured why put the burden on you.

We're working together and the sexual tension was getting to me, and so I figured we'd make love once tonight and have it over with. Then we can work side by side knowing it had been good, not wondering what it might be like and when and why. Do you agree?"

Morgan kissed her again. His right hand found one of her breasts and he stroked and fondled it gently.

"Yes, you're right, and you're an extremely pretty woman. I'd be wondering what you looked like with your blouse off. Your breasts are fine, so fine."

"Good. Let me sit up and we can light a lamp, I want to see all of you right now."

He slid out of his short underwear bottoms and she pulled the white nightgown off over her head. They sat on the bed, staring at each other.

"Magnificent," he said.

"Marvelous. What a fine body," she whispered.

He kissed her again, then worked kisses down her neck to her chest and breasts. She began to breathe faster as he licked her breasts, then nibbled at her nipples. They had doubled in size since he'd first seen them, and they pulsated with hot, boiling blood.

Her hands traced down his sides to his crotch and caught his erection, holding it gently, exploring his pulled-up balls and scrotum, then going back to his erection, gently pumping it back and forth twice.

Shotgun!

She pushed him down on his back and dropped one breast into his mouth. He chewed on one breast and fondled the other one and one hand flowed down to her crotch into her soft blonde muff. She made mewling noises as he worked through the jungle growth and came to her tiny node. He twanged it once and she yelped in delight.

He explored deeper and found her heartland and thrust into her deeply with a finger. She gasped, then purred and her hips did a small dance.

She came away from him, pulling her breast free of his mouth. She kissed down his chest to his belly, then kissed the tip of his penis and watched it jerk.

"Oh, yes, he likes me." She kissed it again, then sucked it in and pumped half-a-dozen times with her head taking in most of him and then coming away and lying beside him.

He rolled over on top of her, crushing her into the firm mattress.

"Dear sweet Morgan. I'm ready."

He shook his head. "Not nearly ready. You have to want it so bad you could scream." He kissed her eyes, then her nose. He licked at the inside of her ears until she pulled away, then nibbled on her neck where the fine hairs lay. His hands explored down her inner thighs, coming up slowly, massaging, petting, caressing her tender white thighs until she moaned.

"Now, darling, now," she said.

He continued his fingers working up both her satin flanks until they met, jumping over her moist slot to the node and twanging on it a dozen times. She gasped and shuddered, but didn't quite slam into a climax.

Then Morgan sat up beside her, spread her legs and lifted her knees. He went between them, bent low and kissed her mouth. Then he gently eased forward with his erection aiming at the glory hole.

She gasped as he entered her. Then in one quick thrust he drove into her so deeply that their pelvic bones grated together and she felt a tinge of pain. It vanished in a moment as he relaxed and lay there waiting for her to make some move. She writhed her hips against him. Then she tightened her inner muscles making him give a quick gasp.

He withdrew slowly, then thrust in all the way before he reversed directions and came almost out of her. He set up that pattern and a dozen strokes later her hips bounced upward to meet him and her whole body shivered, shook and rattled as if a string of empty boxcars clattered over an uneven track.

Kay gasped and moaned and keened a high note. Then she spasmed a dozen times until she nearly came undone. She moaned, writhed and yelped. Suddenly she finished. No tapering off, just nothing left.

Shotgun!

Morgan let her pant there for a minute. Then again drove into her and her inner muscles caught him on every thrust. Her climax had hastened his own and a few moments later he blasted her with his payload, driving deeper than before and bringing a wail of surprise from her.

He shivered and gasped, and then it was done and he fell on top of her.

They lay there for five minutes before either one moved. He rose then and she pushed to the side and they lay side by side.

Kay reached over and kissed his lips lightly. "Darling Morgan, nothing has ever been so wonderful, so good, so ecstatic for me before. Truly marvelous."

He smiled and kissed the nape of her neck. "You were fantastic. So responsive, so giving. But now can we still work together?"

She pushed away so she could focus on his face and nodded. "Can a duck fly? Is the Pope Catholic? Does water run downhill? Now I'll bust my ass for you. I'll do such a fine job that you'll get your due and I'll get a commendation by the road and all will be well on the Northern Pacific."

"What about with the Stockgrowers Association?"

"Yes, all's well with everyone except the rustlers." She snuggled against him. "May I stay the rest of the night? No more making love, just holding and comforting and being close. I really want that."

"I think I can blunt my basic instincts enough to hold you and not make love to you again tonight."

"Good."

They lay that way for ten minutes. Then she reached down and pulled the sheet up over them. He blew out the lamp and they lay in the darkness.

"What are you thinking right now?" she asked.

"I'm thinking you're a beautiful, sexy lady. I'm thinking that you're going to be a good help on the case. I'm thinking that we both have a lot of work to do tomorrow and maybe we better get to sleep." He chuckled. "I'm also thinking that I'd really like to make love to this wonderful lady again, but if she said once, then once it will be— tonight. But I'm putting in my reservation for other nights."

Kay nodded and kissed his cheek. "Yes, many other nights. Now I'm half asleep already."

A moment later she slept. Morgan listened to her even breathing. He could imagine the rise and fall of her marvelous breasts. Then he shut that out of his mind. For a moment he concentrated on waking up the next morning at six-thirty and went to sleep.

He was up and dressed the next morning before Kay awoke. He shaved in the cold water with his straight-edge razor and she sat up, letting the sheet fall delightfully from her shoulders and reveal her naked upper body.

Shotgun!

"Beautiful," Morgan said. "I don't know why we let our women wear clothes. You're so much more amazingly beautiful naked."

"Men are, too. But you're dressed."

"Convention, I guess. You want breakfast?"

"Yes, but all my clothes are all down in my room."

"I could go get them."

"No, just check the hall. Maybe no one is out there."

He unlocked the door and looked out. Two older women walked down to the stairs. He motioned her to come to the door. She had slipped the white nightgown on and stood beside him. He closed the door gently.

"Two men coming by," he said. He reached one hand over and cupped one of her breasts and she smiled. He kissed her lips and came away reluctantly.

This time when he looked through an inch crack in the door the hall showed empty. "All clear."

Kay darted past him and down the hall. She pushed in her unlocked door and hurried inside without as much as a wave. He finished shaving. Then he put on his hat and vest. After he closed and locked his door, he knocked on hers.

"Who is it?"

"Santa Clause. I'm early this year."

Kay opened the door, smiling. Morgan slipped in and saw that she wore only her chemise. She posed prettily for him, then slipped on bloomers

245

and a skirt and a blue blouse to match the skirt. She tied a dark blue scarf around her neck and put on her white cowboy hat.

Kay pointed to the hat. "New. I figured I'd fit in better with a hat like this."

"Looks good on you. Ready for breakfast?"

She nodded. "I'll take a notebook, two pencils, my reticule with my .32 six-shooter and some other necessities. Ready."

For breakfast they went to Violet's Fine Foods, the restaurant and bakery where the food had been so good. They both had pancakes, bacon and eggs and coffee. It was better than last time.

They walked to the train station, trying hard not to touch, and there she found that the next train was westbound and would be along in a half hour. Morgan told her to watch herself. She picked up two envelopes from the division point addressed to her.

"The crews and their schedules—I'll look them over." She watched him. When he looked up she grinned. "Oh, damn, this isn't supposed to happen. Don't get involved with the people you work with. I know that. You be careful today. I don't want to lose you now that I'm just getting to know you."

Morgan touched her hand and said he'd be careful. He walked away quickly. She was right. He made it a rule never to get involved with the people he worked with.

Morgan had given up learning anything more

about the movements or the contacts that Isaiah Roundtree had made that last day of his life. Any more work on that wouldn't be productive. He knew most of his movements, but none of them had offered any clues to the killer.

Josh was his next best target. He guessed that Josh would not be an early riser. Just as Morgan settled in the empty lot he had used before, he saw the first trails of smoke coming from Josh's house. Good, the bastard was at home.

Josh stayed home most of the morning. Once he went into the backyard and split some wood. It wasn't until 11:30 that he left the house and headed down Main Street.

Morgan tailed him, staying well back, keeping out of sight. Josh looked behind twice but Morgan turned and stepped out of sight just in time.

The cattle buyer evidently didn't cook much. His first stop was a cafe. Morgan had a cup of coffee in another eatery across the street so he could watch the cafe entrance.

A half hour later Josh left the cafe and worked his way down Main. He went into Hannah's Place. That was a stopper. Morgan couldn't go in without attracting Hannah, who would ask where he'd been, and there would be no way not to be spotted by Josh.

Morgan settled down in a chair across from her place. He remembered the body of Mike Corrigan, who had leaned back in one of these chairs. Morgan didn't lean back, just let his hat come down a little over his eyes to cloud his identity.

Josh left Hannah's Place after ten minutes, about time to drink a beer, look over the drinkers and gamblers and try to pick out a man for rustler duty. Maybe. Did he know that the Dobbs guy who had been hiring cowboys for him was on the train heading for Seattle?

Josh hit two more bars, then settled into a poker game at Lord Willy's Saloon across from the general store. It looked as if he would be there for a while.

Morgan went back to the saloons Josh had been in. He asked the barkeeps if anyone had been looking for cowboys or riders for a short job. Two said that a guy had been in that morning early and picked up a couple of riders. Two saloons later another the barkeep said he'd heard somebody was hiring for a short job. The last barkeep took the dollar bill Morgan offered and agreed.

"Yeah, we had a guy in this morning hiring. Strange-looking duck. Never seen him before. Told everyone his name was Willy. He and three cowboys rode out of town about eight o'clock. Didn't see what direction they took."

Morgan headed for the livery. Something was afoot. He rented a horse, saddle and Spencer rifle and rode out for the four largest ranches. They needed to be warned to get out range guards. He could get to the four largest ranches before sundown. That would be a help, and it just might prevent the loss of another batch of steers.

Chapter Seventeen

Morgan rode the first six miles to the Dempsy ranch and told the owner what he suspected. Dempsy thanked him and said he'd put out range guards. Morgan ate there, then hurried across the river four miles to the Bar B Ranch.

The foreman, a man named Phil Verde, had taken over the cattle operation for Mrs. Roundtree until she decided what she wanted to do with the ranch. Verde was a short, tough little man, no more than five five, and he looked as if he ate barbed wire for breakfast.

"Yeah, I'll put out range guards. I know where the bastards ran off the other stock. If they come we'll be ready for them with six rifles." Verde scowled. "Any idea who's behind all this rustling?"

"Not yet, but I'm getting closer. I'm sorry about your boss. He was a good man."

Verde nodded. "A damn good man. Now I better hustle up some hands here to do the guarding.

Shotgun!

You going to Corrigan's place?"

"Yes, if my map is right." Morgan showed the map to the foreman, who frowned a minute and then nodded.

"Pretty close. Corrigan is on the other side of the river about eight miles down. From there on it's small outfits both sides. Not sure how much they can help. If you want, I can send two men out to hit the other river places. Triple your efforts that way. I'll have them ride to hell and gone down there to alert some of them folks."

"Be damn glad for the help, Verde. Thanks." Morgan reached out his hand and shook the firm grip. "We're gonna beat the sons of bitches yet. I better ride."

Morgan found Mrs. Corrigan in charge at her ranch. She was a plump woman of 40. She had long hair tied in a bun at the back of her neck, a no-nonsense apron over her pale gray dress and a stern expression. She had a crooked nose, deep set eyes and a chin that could be used as an icebreaker. When she smiled it lit up her face. She said she'd put out three men with rifles and keep the rest of her men in their clothes most of the night.

"I'm sorry about your husband, ma'am. Real sorry," Morgan said.

She nodded, not letting her emotions show, and he rode for the next ranch, a small outfit across the Yellowstone. He found a place he could ford and rode through, then caught the outfit just as the lamps had been lit in the ranch house.

The owner squinted at Morgan and told him to come in the ranch house kitchen.

"Yep, know about it and we got two men out. Half my work force. Gimpy Zilk came riding by a half hour ago. He figured your horse was getting worn out by now so he's telling everyone on this side of the river and another man is doing the other side. You best sit a spell and have some supper."

Morgan ate. He found out the man's name was Floyd Lang. The rancher was about 50. He made a living ranching, but wasn't getting rich.

"Then owlhoots hit me again and I could go damn near broke," Lang said. "Hope they pick on somebody else if we can't catch them."

"We're going to try. The rails are on this side of the river, so chances are they'll hit this side tonight. Is there a siding anywhere near here where they could load the cattle?"

"Not for maybe ten miles west. Then there's a little stop called Riverrun with room for maybe six cars. At fifty head to a car, that would hold three hundred head."

"Can't get fifty head in a car no more, maybe forty," Morgan said. "However many, I'll ride out and watch that siding. Any you know about farther on?"

Lang shook his head. "Don't get down that way, but there's bound to be more sidings. Remember seeing them when I went in to Billings on the train once."

Shotgun!

"So I'll watch." Morgan finished the roast and potatoes and gravy, and he had another cup of coffee. "I better ride. About ten miles you say. I'll stick close to the tracks and shouldn't be able to miss it. Any night trains come through here?"

"Yep, both ways, used to bother me, but I sleep right through them now. The wife fixed up something for you to take along in case you get hungry. Watch out for the fruit jar of coffee. It's hot, but she wrapped it in a towel so you can carry it. She says that'll keep it hot for three or four hours. You'll see."

Morgan thanked the rancher and his wife for the kindness. Then he took the cloth sack with the food and the coffee.

He followed the river and rode for the siding. It was slightly after eight o'clock when he left the place. By the time he found the siding, the moon was full and his railroad watch showed him that it was almost ten o'clock. There was nothing at the siding except the six cattle cars and a small sign that said it was Riverrun. Morgan tied his mount to the first car and climbed to the roof and looked out over the prairie. He couldn't see far in the darkness, but he could hear sounds from a great distance away.

The wind whispered gently, then stopped. Morgan could hear no cattle lowing, no pounding of hooves on the sod. A night bird of some kind called to his right. From far down the river he heard a hawk of some sort screech and then the

Kit Dalton

sound of an owl. He could even make out crickets pleading for love, but nothing else.

Morgan sat down on the top of the car and stared into the darkness. He tried to remember the map of the ranches. There were more than a dozen down this way, many of them stacked outward from the Yellowstone and getting their water from a tributary to the larger stream.

The rustlers could be hitting these smaller ranches 10 to 15 miles outward from the Yellowstone, then driving the cattle farther west to another siding. This one seemed to be too close to the ranches to be practical for the smugglers.

For half an hour Morgan considered the situation. Then he climbed down from the cattle car and took out the sack of food. The coffee was still warm inside the towel.

Morgan ate three of the sandwiches, which were made of fried chicken stripped off the bones. Then he ate an apple. He repacked the food that was left, sealed up the coffee and stepped into his saddle. Down the line somewhere, he might want to reheat the coffee.

Morgan thought about the rustlers again. It seemed certain that if they hit tonight it would be on some of the smaller ranches that couldn't put out an army of range guards. They'd hit the smaller outfits—maybe three or four of them—drive the cattle farther west and stop at another siding.

Morgan thought as he rode due south from the

Shotgun!

siding. On the realistic side, the smugglers could count on pushing a herd of cattle no more than 12 miles a day or night. They couldn't make good time at night. So they might have had to drive them 12 miles to get to this point.

Then they might have to hold the cattle a day to let them rest, then drive them again at night. Or would they have some safe haven, some blind canyon in which to hold the cattle and move them later? There weren't any blind canyons in this flat country. The best the rustlers could hope for would be a small valley with herd riders.

Morgan rode out two miles, stopped and listened. The breeze had picked up a little and he tuned his ear to anything unnatural. He heard the birds and crickets, a tree frog and an owl.

Was there something else? He strained to hear. If it was something it came from upwind. He turned and rode into the breeze.

After half a mile he stopped and listened again. This time he grinned. He caught the unmistakable sound of a bleating steer unhappy about having to walk when he wanted to be sleeping. Then as Morgan concentrated, he could hear the marching hooves on the dry Montana sod. The cattle were coming.

He put his ear to the ground and listened. It was a steady plodding, not the drumming roll of a stampede. How far away? Which way were they coming from? Going to the nearby siding or to another one?

Morgan rode slowly toward the east, figuring the rustlers had made a hit somewhere out there and would move the animals to the west to get to a siding. Somehow he didn't think they were going to the close siding, not much over 18 miles from Miles City. Doing so would have been too risky.

He stopped the mare and listened again. Now he could hear the beat of the hooves and an occasional high-pitched bawling of a steer.

Morgan stared ahead, but could see nothing. He rode forward again, working up a small rolling rise. At the top he looked down and saw a long line of brown stretched out in the moonlight. The lead animals were less than 100 yards away.

He had decided how to handle this herd if he found it. He wouldn't stampede them. The animals were too far from their home ranges. Instead he rode sharply to the side to be out of the path of the animals, concentrating on finding the riders who pushed them forward.

Quickly Morgan spotted a point man on his side. There should have been a trail boss out in front, but evidently in this country there was no need for that. He let the animals plod past him about 50 yards away and watched for a swing or flank rider alongside the line of steer. They moved along four or five wide and stretched out farther than he had guessed. A good-size herd.

Soon he spotted a man riding alongside the

Shotgun!

animals. As he watched, a cowboy rode up from the rear, talked to the hand on swing and then moved ahead. Morgan figured this must be the boss, and he spurred his mount, riding hard up to the cowboy, who heard him coming and turned.

Morgan's Colt .45 was aimed dead center on the other man's chest, and the rider slacked off and lifted his hands.

"Who the hell are you?" the man asked.

"I've got the gun. I ask the questions. Give me that iron at your hip and be careful." The cowboy handed over his six-gun. Morgan pushed it in his belt and motioned. "Now ride out to the side away from the cattle. Ride now or I'll shoot you out of your saddle."

The man appeared to be no more than 30 or 35. He gritted his teeth, looked at the unwavering black hole of the gun and rode. Morgan took him 300 yards to the side, then told him to get off his horse. Morgan slid off as well.

"Now who the hell are you? You have a name?" Morgan asked.

"Josie Smith," the man said.

Morgan didn't believe him but it didn't matter. "Where you taking this herd?"

"To Billings. Cheaper to drive them to the stockyard there than to take them on the train."

"Not in the long run. You'll shrink a hundred pounds off every animal. What outfit you with?"

"The Double D."

"That isn't the brand on those cattle. I've spotted four different brands so far."

Morgan gave Smith a chance to go for a hideout if he had one. He let the muzzle of the Colt drop and looked away at the herd. The cowboy bent and drew a hideout from a holster fastened inside his boot.

Morgan saw the cowboy move and kicked sharply, his boot toe smashing into the man's wrist, dumping the derringer into the dust.

"Dumb move, rustler. You know you're going to hang, don't you? So you tried a stupid draw. Get back on your mount and we'll go to the point men and have them circle the herd to bed them down. No questions. And tell them that I'm from the siding. You're too early. The train cars aren't there yet, you understand? I'm taking over this herd, and anybody who doesn't like it gets shot. No sheriff in Montana would lift an eyebrow if I shot down all five or six of you right now."

They rode forward to the point men, and with Morgan at his side, the trail boss ordered the point men to start the steer in a circle so they could be bedded down.

When the men came by, they asked what was up, and the trail boss told them all that they were early, so they could take off the rest of the night. The men welcomed the news.

A half hour later, when the herd had been coiled into a compact group, Morgan told the boss to put one man on riding herd and bring the rest of them together. They picketed their horses and came up in ones and twos.

Shotgun!

"Thought you said we had twenty-five miles to go down the line," one cowpoke said when he came up. "Why we stopping here?"

"Orders," the man who called himself Smith said. "Orders that we follow with no more questions."

Morgan told the men to sit down in the grass and stood in front of them. He stared at them a minute in the moonlight, then took it to them hard.

"How many of you men know this is a rustling operation?"

"Hell, no," one man said.

"What? No such. I was told four days work on a drive."

Two more men voiced similar ideas. Two men toward the back edged away. Morgan drew his Colt and put a round between them.

"Steady, you two. You men who didn't know you were rustling, go over on that side. The other three stay put. So you'll know, the rustling operation is over. In the morning we drive this herd right back where it came from.

"Anybody who doesn't want to do that is a candidate for hanging as a rustler. Any of you three want to volunteer to be the first one to stretch a rope? I've got authorization to hemp stretch any neck I find with the wrong brands inside his rope."

Morgan watched the three men who knew they were rustling. One man boiled with rage. His right hand trembled over his six gun.

"Go ahead and draw it, cowboy. Nobody is faster with a holstered gun than a man with a Colt in hand. Want to try it?"

The cowboy stood slowly. "Not a chance. But you put that iron in leather and I'll take a shot at it."

"You ready to die?" Morgan asked.

"Here or on the end of a rope don't make me no never mind."

"After we get these animals driven back to their home range, the seven of you will be free to go. I won't have any evidence against you. Don't you understand that?"

"Oh, yeah, that's what you say now. Never heard of a lawman who kept his word."

Morgan watched all three rustlers. "Any time you're ready, deadman."

Morgan let the other man start his move first. Then his hand ripped upward, drew, cocked and fired. The rustler's weapon had barely cleared leather and his finger hadn't yet found the trigger.

The rustler took the bullet in the chest. It plowed through his vest and shirt, and the lead slammed into his heart, killing him before he could drop the weapon. He jolted backward into the grass, his open eyes staring upward at the stars without seeing a single one.

"My God, he's dead," one of the other cowboys said.

The shot boomed into the night and the herding

cowboy galloped up and skidded to a stop. His eyes were alert, and his weapon was out.

"Put it away, Larry," the trail boss said. "This was a personal thing here between these two men. Get back to the herd. Make sure they don't get nervous."

"You sure, boss? Looks like Barney there is down."

"He is, Larry. Now get back to the herd or just keep riding."

Larry frowned in the moonlight, then turned and rode back to the cattle.

"You other two rustlers—you want a try at your luck?" Morgan asked in the same icy voice he had used before.

"God, no," one said. The other shook his head.

"Anyone object to driving these animals back to their rightful ranges come morning?" Morgan looked from one shadowy face to the next. No one said a word. "Then I suggest that you get some sleep so you won't fall out of the saddle tomorrow. How far did you drive these animals?

"About twelve miles," the trail boss said. "We pushed them along faster than usual with no water stops."

"With daylight we'll be moving back the same way. You get the beef all from one or two ranches?"

"Three small ones. They join each other."

Morgan nodded. "We'll leave them near where the ranches join and let the ranchers do the sorting at roundup time."

Morgan motioned the boss to the side; then they walked out of six-gun range. "Now, one more chance. What's your name?"

"Josie Klemens."

"Where you from?"

"Wyoming. Times are hard down there now."

"You done any rustling before?"

"No, sir."

"Why now?"

"Man offered me three hundred dollars a herd at the cattle pens down the road a ways."

"Exactly where were you to deliver the stock?"

"Place called Deadwood Gulch. Nothing but a siding. Supposed to be twelve cattle cars there waiting for us."

"How far from here?"

"Another ten miles. Supposed to be there tomorrow afternoon at three."

"You could have walked half these steers to death. Who were you to meet at Deadwood Gulch?"

"Nobody said. I was just supposed to show up with the stock and somebody would give me three hundred dollars. The men were to get paid twenty dollars a day for three days work."

"I need to ride down to Deadwood Gulch," Morgan said. "Can I trust you to deliver these animals back where you found them or damn close?"

"Why?"

"Because I'll pay you to take them back where

you found them. I'll pay you fifty dollars cash money to return the cattle. Tell the men they'll get five dollars a day, not twenty, to deliver the cattle back where they belong. If they'll do it, you all are to meet me at Hannah's Place at noon the day after tomorrow. Can you remember that?"

"I can remember."

"Will you do it?"

"You pay us not to rustle the cattle and take them back where they belong?"

"Right."

"Sounds crazy to me, but it's better than getting hanged."

"Believe me, Josie, anything is better than being hanged. Remember, if you don't get the cattle back, and don't see me in the saloon, I'll put out a bounty on you and the others and you'll be wanted men for the rest of your lives. If they catch you, you'll hang."

Klemens held up both hands. "Don't worry. I came out here to make some money. I'll still make a little by unrustling these cattle. I'm not about to welsh on a deal like that."

"Good. Now how far is that siding with loading chutes and who do I meet there?"

"About ten more miles west. Three o'clock tomorrow. The cattle buyer will be there to help get the critters loaded on the cars. Then the train comes by."

"A cattle buyer is coming way out here? He must have dropped off a westbound and will wait for the eastbound. Sounds like a cattle buyer. I better get moving."

Morgan mounted up and saw Klemens talking with the men. Some of them seemed to be complaining but they soon quieted down. The threat of being hanged could change a man's mind about a lot of things in a rush.

Morgan rode for two hours, took a break walking the horse for half an hour, then rode her again. They had put a lot of miles in today. He angled back to the tracks and worked along just off the right of way. He figured it was after two a.m. when he spotted the cattle cars on a siding ahead. He moved in silently, leaving the horse a quarter of a mile back tied to some brush.

There were no lights, no buildings—nothing but the empty cars on the rail siding. The wind blew through the slatted sides making a strange whistling noise. When he was certain no one hid in any of the good places, he retreated 100 yards up a small creek in some brush and settled down for the rest of the night. He slept like a newborn colt after its first day of finding that its legs really did work.

Morgan was up with the sun. His railroad watch told him it was just after 6:30. A train had gone by during the night but it didn't even slow down for Deadwood Gulch. He had no idea when the cattle buyer would show up and get started loading the cattle. It would take three or four hours even if the men were used to the procedures. He checked the cars and the small pens built behind them. Each pen had a ramp that led upward to the cattle car. That would make loading go faster.

He ate the rest of the sandwiches and tried the cold coffee, but hated it, and he didn't want to risk a fire to heat up the coffee in the glass jar. He'd seen it done before. The heat transferred to the coffee and left the jar unaffected. Or did the jar break and put out the fire? He couldn't remember.

Morgan didn't want to venture out of the nest of brush and trees in case someone came up unexpectedly. He had a nap and a big drink of water for his lunch. Then about three o'clock that afternoon, he noticed something coming across the plains from the west.

Twenty minutes later Morgan made out a horse and a rider moving at a leisurely pace. The rider came straight to the cattle cars, dismounted, tied up his horse, and headed for Morgan's creek, evidently for a drink. Morgan let him go down in the grass to drink. Then he moved up behind the man soundlessly and pressed the muzzle of his six-gun into his neck.

"Well, well, well. Fancy meeting you here. I'd say you came all the way out here to load some rustled cattle on some rail cars. Isn't that true, Josh?"

Chapter Eighteen

Josh Eagleston looked up from where he'd been drinking at the creek and swore. "How in hell did you find me here?"

"Skill, talent, informants and a lot of luck," Morgan said. "Ease back from there and let me relieve you of any dangerous weapons."

"I'm not carrying. I'm afraid of guns."

"You best be, also you should be afraid of a rope with a large knot with thirteen loops around it."

Morgan patted Josh down, but found nothing but a small folding pen knife. He let Josh sit up on the grass.

"How much is the association paying you for this job?" Josh asked.

"A lot."

"I'll give you fifteen thousand cash just to forget about all this, catch the train and head west today. No questions asked, no reports given."

Shotgun!

"Why should I take a pay cut, Josh?"

The cattle buyer looked up sharply.

"Just joking, Josh. You can't buy me off. Not a chance. I'd be through in this business overnight if I did that. Word gets around fast. Tell me how you work it with the railroad. You know some of the trainmen?"

"Not a chance. Word would get around."

"It won't matter with you dropping through the trap on the wrong end of a rope. Don't worry. It isn't a long fall, usually about six feet."

"You can't prove a thing."

"I can prove plenty. I have three witnesses in jail right now. I have the sworn testimony of Josie Klemens, whom you hired to rustle five hundred head of cattle off three of the smaller ranches. You were due to meet him and the cattle here this afternoon. Here you are.

"I'll talk to the engineer when the train stops here to pick up the cattle, probably along about eight o'clock tonight. He'll implicate you to save his skin. You're going down fast, Josh. I can almost see that trapdoor being sprung right now."

Morgan watched the cattle buyer. The words hit Josh like bullets and he winced. When he looked up it was with a touch of concern.

"I didn't actually rustle any cattle, so—"

"Any person who participates in the planning, execution or sale of animals with knowledge that they have been rustled shall be charged with rustling the same as those who actually drove the cattle off the ranch property."

"Hey, that's not fair."

"Fair? Nobody said it was supposed to be fair, Josh, but that's the law. You're looking at a noose, sure as hell."

Morgan waited as the silence stretched out. "Josh, you don't look like a stupid person. There could be a way that you could live."

"How in hell is that?"

"Give me the names of the men behind this rustling scheme. Then I won't have you charged with rustling, only with receiving stolen goods, which is five years in prison at the most."

Josh looked up, a trace of hope around his eyes. "You could do that?"

"Probably. I'd have to talk with the judge and the district attorney, but there's a good chance if you give up the names we need."

"Oh, damn! This didn't start out so complicated."

"Who talked to you first?"

"I can't tell you." Josh looked around and grinned. "You really think I'd come out here alone, with nobody backing my play?"

"Absolutely. You had no idea this would not go as smoothly as all your other shipments."

The two stared at each other for a full minute. It seemed like an hour to Morgan. At last the cattle buyer sighed and looked away.

"Yeah, I'm alone. I'll talk if and when you get

Shotgun!

me back to Miles City and put me in jail."

"Might not be good enough, but it's a start. Now get comfortable. I'm going to tie you up."

"Why? I can't get away. Besides, the train won't stop unless I put out a green flag down the track a quarter of a mile and then stand beside the first car on the siding. It's arranged."

"Makes sense. You have to promise to stop the train. If you don't, you could have an unfortunate accident and cheat the hangman. You understand what I'm saying?"

"You'll murder me?"

"One way to look at it. You'll stop the train?"

"Yes."

"When is it due through here?"

"The cattle were supposed to be here by three. We'd load them in the cars and be done by seven. The eastbound should roll in here by eight."

"So we have a wait. How is the engineer going to see a green flag at night?"

"I'll put it in the middle of the rails. His engine light will pick it up and he'll slow down and watch for me."

"So we have some time to waste. You getting half of the money on the critters?"

"Half?"

Morgan grinned. "Figured out how I'd do it if I was in your shoes. I'd say I would pay only twenty dollars a head, then sell them at the usual rate by weight or forty dollars per animal. Pocket the twenty and split the other twenty between the rancher involved, the trainmen and myself."

Josh squirmed where he sat on the grass. He stared at Morgan a long time, then nodded. "Something like that. How did you know there was a rancher involved?"

"Just about had to be—one of the big three. Two of them are dead, so that leaves the guilty party, Lorne Dempsy. He's getting greedy."

"I didn't say it was him."

"You didn't have to. Let's go take a look at your mount. I'd say you must have a good bit of cash in your saddlebags."

Josh's eyes flared in anger; then he recovered. "Why would I bring cash out here?"

"To pay off the trainmen, the riders and your recruiter. Say the trainmen get five dollars a head. You have three hundred head. That's fifteen hundred dollars. Say there are seven men working the train and the engineer takes two shares. That's still over two hundred dollars a man. More money than a trainman makes for half the year. Enough for them to risk getting fired if they're caught."

"You're guessing, pure and simple guessing."

"Not since I talked to the railroad. This little caper of yours is about ready to be squashed."

"You talked to the railroad?"

"The division point manager in Minneapolis."

Morgan tied Josh's hands and feet, then went to the saddlebags and brought them back to the brush. He opened them and took out stacks of cash.

"How much is here, Josh?"

"Two thousand dollars. Enough to cover four hundred head if they got that many."

"Not a bad haul. You sell the three hundred head for twelve thousand to the stockyards. You keep six thousand for yourself and split the other six thousand giving fifteen hundred to the trainmen. Then you keep fifteen hundred for yourself and the rancher pockets three thousand. Great little scheme for as long as it worked. You should have taken your money and ran."

"Probably. I think I better tell you everything I know about this setup so I can save my neck. I will as soon as we get back to Miles City. That way I won't have an accident."

Morgan put the money into his own saddle-bags. He was amazed at how small a package it was: two inch-high stacks of bills.

Morgan came back, checked the tracks, then settled down in the cover of the stream's brush near the cattle buyer.

"I'm going to have a nap, Josh. Don't try anything stupid. I wouldn't mind blowing you straight into hell if you give me a chance."

Josh scowled at him. "Won't give you the chance. You can count on that."

By 7:30 that night darkness had slithered in around the prairie. Morgan untied the cattle buyer and found the green flag on his saddle.

They walked down the quarter mile and Morgan pounded the stake into the ground in the middle of the tracks. Then they walked back to the edge of the first cattle car.

"At least it's dark, so the engineer can't see that the cars aren't loaded," Morgan said. "This engineer pretty smart? Or is he as dumb as most trainmen?"

"The engineer on a train is the top paid man there and the smartest. We only work with one man. He picks his crew so there's no problems that way. That much I can tell you."

"Will he stop the train and give up when I confront him?" Morgan asked.

"Not a chance. He'll make a run for it. He'll know at once that you don't have any proof against him if he doesn't stop."

"Figured that. A bullet through his shoulder will help persuade him. I don't aim to lose him when he's so close to the trap."

Ten minutes later they heard the train coming far down the tracks. Morgan put his hand on the rail and he could feel the vibration. He caught sight of the train's light far off. It came closer and came to the green flag. It seemed to be going too fast. Then the train slowed and Morgan figured the engineer had seen the green flag. A few moments later it came grinding up to them still going 15 miles an hour.

It could have been some sort of visual signal. Morgan never did know. Josh stood eight or ten

Shotgun!

feet from the rails. The light from the headlamp of the train washed over him and almost at once the engineer threw the throttle forward, and the train wheels skidded with the added power as the train lurched forward.

Morgan drew and fired at the window, where the engineer had been a moment before, but now was out of sight. Morgan put four slugs through the window, but the train kept on grinding and rolling forward.

The train crew or the cattle buyer? The decision came in a flash of instant thought. Morgan could run, grab the side of a boxcar, jump on board and leave Josh free and clear. Or he could keep Josh and let the train men go.

Morgan tensed, ready to run, then shook his head. He chose to keep Josh, since he was more important in the scheme than the train men.

When the train rattled past and silence settled over the scene, Morgan growled at Josh. "You warned him, didn't you? I'm not sure what you did. The way that you stood, I would guess. Arms crossed in front of you maybe. Do you have any idea how many times and in how many places I can shoot you and not come close to killing you?"

Josh shivered in the fading moonlight. "No."

"I should give you a demonstration. I would, but I hate to tie up bloody shoulders and thighs. You think about what a big hole a round makes going through your leg. Ponder on it a bit."

Morgan retied the man's hands and pushed him back to the trees, where the horses stood.

"Nothing to do now but ride into the next little town and catch the next eastbound train to Miles City. Then we'll see how you like life in a jail cell. Come on. Get moving."

Josh told Morgan it was about eight miles to the next settlement, a stop called Yellow Creek. As they rode, the cattle buyer grew more talkative.

"You treat me right and I can tell you names in the railroad that might surprise you. The trainmen have to split their earnings with two other men."

Morgan nodded. "I could use the names. You tell me those and the rancher and any of his helpers, and I'll talk to the district attorney about your charges."

"No, not just talk to him. I want a bargain struck beforehand. I tell you the names and you give me a lighter type of charge—receiving stolen goods like you said before and no more than a four-year sentence."

"You've got it," Morgan said. "I think I can convince the district attorney. Now who are they?"

"When we get back to Miles City and after you've convinced the D.A. Then I'll tell you. I need some guarantees here. Out here anything could happen. I want to be sure."

Morgan hated bargaining with outlaws, but in this case he figured it might pay off. Without Josh's tip, they probably never would get the higher ups in the railroad. Morgan set his jaw, but knew he had to do it.

"You've got a deal. I'll be careful not to let anything happen to you until we get back to Miles City. Then I'll talk to the D.A. and the judge if I can. I can get the rancher. I have him now for all practical purposes. The railroad men I want."

The town of Yellow Creek was closed up and sleeping when they got in. One two-story building near the tracks was the only hotel. They had to wake up the night clerk. The man growled, but gave them one room with a big bed. It was all he had he said.

"When does the first eastbound train come through?" Morgan asked.

"Seven-thirty in the morning usually. Been late last three days. Some trouble with a washout over the way. Have to go slow across it."

"We'll be waiting."

Morgan took the bed. He tied Josh's hands and feet, then gave him one blanket, a pillow and all the floor he could use. Morgan checked his watch just before he blew out the lamp. It was almost midnight.

The next morning, they caught the train with two minutes to spare. It cost five dollars extra to put Morgan's rented horse on board. The ride to Miles City took under two hours, and Morgan managed to get the horse unloaded without losing Josh. He left the nag tied at the station

Kit Dalton

and hustled Josh up to the county courthouse and the jail on Fourth Street.

The sheriff looked surprised. "Who in hell is this?"

"Josh Eagleston, well-known cattle buyer and rustler. He's going to be staying with you for a few days. But I don't want anyone to know he's here. We still have a few more pieces in the puzzle to drop into place."

"Rustling? Josh was in on it? Damn, who are you going to trust these days? Will you file a complaint so I can justify keeping him here?"

Morgan did. Then he went upstairs and talked to the district attorney. His name was Ritter Udall. He wore a double-breasted black suit with a vest and a tie with a small knot in it. He stood a little over average at five-ten.

"You say Josh Eagleston had something to do with all this rustling?"

"Had mostly to do with it." Morgan sat across the desk from the top legal man in the county and spelled out the routine as far as he knew it.

"Josh can give us the rancher and two management railroad men in on the scheme. I already know who the rancher is, but any more proof and evidence and witnesses would be helpful to your case. For the railroad men, we need him. Here's the kind of a bargain I want to make with you in order to get everyone wrapped up."

The lawyer leaned forward. "You want me to bargain with a rustler?"

Shotgun!

"Yes, Mr. Udall. By doing that, we save the county money, we get a clean case of conviction, and we still put Josh away for five years."

"That is intriguing, isn't it? I hear they do this back east all the time—trade information for a lighter sentence. Not much of that happens out here. I don't see why not. Nothing wrong with it. I won't go to the judge and ask for a lighter sentence though. He burned me up one side and down the other the last time I tried that. Frankly, I'm terrified of our circuit judge."

Morgan grinned. "I would be as well. But if we nail Josh on receiving stolen goods, the top sentence would be what?"

The D.A. knew without looking. "Four to six years and usually it's five. Judge Dimmit almost always goes with a balance between the short and long range.

"Let's try it. You go talk to Josh this afternoon. I have some other tasks to get done. Then I'll have a talk with him after you give him your assurances. That's all he's waiting for."

The D.A. frowned. "The rancher involved. Who is it?"

"Lorne Dempsy of the Double D ranch, which explains how that good witness I had boxed in got himself shot to death at Dempsy's with all hands watching."

"When will you bring him in?"

"I need to fill up some holes first. A few things I'm not sure of, I want to get tied down. Then the sheriff and I will go pay a call on Dempsy and notify him of the charges. I doubt if he'll come in peacefully."

"Do the best you can. I'll see Josh in his cell sometime this morning."

Morgan left the courthouse feeling better than he had in two days. Things were shaping up. There was a chance he could see the end of this job down the line somewhere. He was half a block from the courthouse when a familiar voice called from behind him.

He turned and saw Kay Butterfield rushing along the boardwalk toward him. She grabbed his arm and pulled it in against her breast and grinned up at him. "I've got a great surprise for you. Can you guess what it is?"

Chapter Nineteen

Morgan had to look downward only slightly at the lady. He smiled at her windblown blonde hair. "A surprise? I've never liked surprises. I like things planned out thoughtfully and with care beforehand."

Kay laughed. "Oh, yeah? Like the other night in your hotel room?"

"Yes, I had that planned, too. It would work only if you thought it was your idea."

"Liar," she said. "That was about as unplanned as anything ever gets. I loved it. But this is a surprise that you're going to like."

"I hope so. What is it?"

"First I've got the name of the crew that has brought back every shipment of beef from the Miles City area. It's the same crew every time. The engineer on that steamer is something of a maverick, but he keeps his job because he's so good at it."

"He drives engine 427?"

Kay looked up, an expression of awed surprise on her face. "How could you know that? You must be able to read minds. I better be careful what I'm thinking."

"You're safe. I took four shots at the man in the cab of engine 427 last night, but I probably missed." Morgan told her briefly about what had happened since last he'd seen her.

"So you almost had them," Kay said.

"Yep, but I didn't have any evidence. I hope you didn't spook them with all the questions back at the division point?"

"Not a chance. I talked with my boss, who can get information with almost no one knowing about it."

"Good. He'll be of some help later. There are two men at Northern Pacific who are involved in the marketing of the rustled cattle. I should get their names tomorrow when Josh spills out everything he knows about the rustling."

"So Dempsy, the only big rancher left of the three, is involved," Kay said. "I guess rich is never rich enough."

"He won't get much richer, I can guarantee that. He'll hang for murder of that cowboy or for rustling. Doesn't matter much either way."

"Is Dempsy wise to your knowing about his part?"

"Probably not, but he knows I'm sniffing around. If you were in on this swindle and you knew it was getting risky, what would you do?"

"Quit and move to Mexico or New York?"

"You might, but I'd bet that Dempsy will be sure enough of himself to try to make one last big score. He'll try to sell four or five thousand head of rustled cattle."

Morgan thought a moment and nodded. "Yeah, that's the way he'd think. He's outrageous enough to think he could get away with it one more time. Only now Josh isn't there. He's been missing for a couple of days. Maybe Dempsy will go it alone. Send a message to the stockyards telling them that Josh is hurt or sick and he wants to deal direct and he has about three thousand head. Would the railroad send the cars?"

Kay nodded. "Oh, sure. An order like that would bring a line of cars a mile long."

"So Dempsy would have to arrange to get recruits for his rustling crew, or maybe use some of his own hands, rustle a big bag and move the cattle out to one or two sidings. Any big ones down west?"

"A couple. Good-size one at Yellow Creek and the one you saw at Deadwood Gulch. He could use both of them since they're just eight miles apart."

"Yes, so we keep an eye on the saloons. Rather, I do. You contact the division point and see when 427 and her crew goes out again. What's the engineer's name?"

"Elton Ferrand. The crew calls him Highball

for the way he drives that engine."

"Hope we get to meet Ferrand. You check when he runs again. I've got some saloons to work."

Kay squeezed his arm. "When are we"—she stopped and he looked down at her—"you know, again."

"Soon, real soon." Morgan squeezed her arm and stepped away and she turned and went toward the depot.

Morgan ate a quick lunch, then started talking to the barkeeps and spreading money around. None of the barkeeps had heard about anyone looking to hire cowboys. They said they'd send a note to his hotel box if they heard of any.

The last saloon Morgan went to was Hannah's Place. Hannah was there. She grabbed Morgan and they sat at her back table.

"Haven't seen you for a couple of days," she said. Her voice said one thing, but her eyes seemed to hold a question that she didn't ask.

"Been busy. Looks like your business is a little slow this afternoon."

"Yeah, gets that way sometimes." She wore a cream-colored blouse that stretched tight over her breasts. It had two buttons open on top.

"Like your blouse," Morgan said. "Almost as if you're advertising."

"I hoped you'd come in and I could get you working up a hard on right here in the saloon."

"I am."

"You real busy right now? Or could you spend

some time and have a little nap upstairs?"

"A nap sounds great. Let me get a couple of cold beers."

As they went up the back stairs, Hannah reached over and rubbed his crotch. "It's been too long, lover. Have you been fucking some bitch here in town?"

"Why would I do that when you're the best there is? Just relax a minute so I don't drop these bottles of beer."

In her bedroom the beer went on the dresser, leaving two wet circles on the varnish. Then they tore each other's clothes off, popping some buttons and throwing the garments around the room. Soon they dropped naked on the bed. When Hannah nodded, Morgan slid between her thighs and stroked into her in one swift move that brought a long wail from her. Then it was a race as they pumped and pounded at each other until they both exploded in climaxes at the same time, wailing, grunting and moaning until the spasms passed. They lay pinned together, panting and gulping in fresh air as they slowly recovered.

Hannah flipped her long red hair out of her eyes and off her breasts. "I keep telling myself that sex with you can't possibly be as good as the last time, but it always is. How can you do it? You get me so red-hot that I can't stand it."

Morgan lifted away a little and looked at her. "I can do it only because you've got the best fucking body I've ever seen. It's perfect. It's a love

283

machine that never stops."

"You say the most wonderful things. I think I'll buy you and keep you as a slave in my bedroom. I'll fuck you three times a day until I wear your pecker down to a little bitty nub."

They both laughed and came apart. Morgan got the beers and opened them. They drank, wiped their mouths, kissed and then drank again.

"Now this is what making love should be all about," Morgan said after he had finished the last of the beer. "A great woman, a fast furious fuck, then a cold beer. How can life get any sweeter than this?"

Hannah nestled against him, one hand playing with his limp penis. "If it's so good here, why don't you stay?"

"Can't."

"I know. You're not buying land like you told me. You're looking for rustlers, right?"

"Yeah. I didn't figure you needed to know all the dirty details."

"How is the job coming along? You know who the bad guys are yet?"

"Some of them. I just got back from following some rustlers to the west."

"Why did you lie to me about what you do?"

"Didn't want you to know. Then maybe I could catch the ones doing the dirty work without getting my head blown off. Somebody tried once already—or was it twice?"

"You could have trusted me."

Shotgun!

"I didn't know you then. Hardly know you now. How's your pa?"

"About the same. I know he can't ever get any better. Just a matter of waiting for him to die."

"Sorry."

"It's not your fault."

Hannah's left hand curled off the side of the bed and pulled a long thin knife out from between the mattress and the quilts. She held it low where Morgan couldn't see it. Then slowly she pushed the knife back in place and out of sight.

She rubbed his chest and played with his nipples. "How long can you stay?"

"How long do you want me to stay?"

"All day and all night and then all day tomorrow."

Morgan chuckled and caressed her breasts. "Not quite that long. I've still got some business to attend to. That's why the ranchers hired me."

"Been any shooting so far?"

"Some."

"You be careful. I don't want to see you stretched out in a pine box."

"I'd rather that you didn't see me that way, too."

Hannah rolled over on top of him. "Why don't you just let it be and quit the job? Then nobody would try to shoot you."

Her right hand fell off the side of the bed and she gripped the handle of the Chicago ice pick.

"I don't quit a job that's half done. I like to see it through to the end."

She pushed the knife back in place in the mattress and nodded. "Your real name is Lee Morgan, I've heard. You're right, Morgan. It's right to finish a job once it's started. I've got me one started and I'm damn well going to finish it. One way or another it's gonna get done—and soon."

Morgan pushed her back so he could focus on her face. "That sounds serious. Just what are you talking about?"

"Never you mind. Women's work. Nothing for you to even think about." Hannah moved so her breasts were over his face. "You want to have a little chaw of white tobacco there, partner? I've got strawberry on the left and vanilla cream on the right."

Morgan sampled each one.

"Now no more thought about work and jobs done or undone. Let's just concentrate on seeing how good we can do number two here and now."

They did, then drifted off to sleep. The striking clock on the dresser announced four o'clock before Morgan eased out of the bed and pulled on his clothes. Hannah slept on her back, her breasts uncovered and one arm thrown over her head. Her other hand covered her crotch. Morgan made as little noise as possible but she roused.

"Sneaking out on me?" Hannah said.

"Yep. Work to do, people to see."

"Rustlers to catch."

Shotgun!

"Not a word from you to anyone, you hear? That's what could get me shot quicker than anything. You promised."

"When?"

"Right now." Morgan dropped on the bed, one knee on each side of her stomach. He bent and kissed her hard on the mouth, then came away from her.

"Yeah, I promise," Hannah said.

Morgan lifted away from her and eased on his dark brown cowboy hat. "Now, woman, I'm off to do man's work. You stay here and be good or I might have to spank you."

"Oh, good. We haven't tried that yet. That really gets my motor running like a steam engine."

"Hold that thought." He went to the door, turned and waved, then continued down the steps and out the alley door.

He wasn't sure where to go next. He'd covered the saloons where the cowboys usually congregated. One was for train workers, and another one hardly had any business at all.

He angled up the street and too late saw that he was in front of Teressa's dressmaking shop. She hurried out to catch his arm. He couldn't very well walk away from her.

"Good, I found you. Mother's inside and she wants to talk to you. I think that she wants to invite you to dinner. I told her you might not want to come. You better talk to her yourself." She took his arm and he followed so she didn't have to pull him across the boardwalk.

Inside her shop, Teressa snapped the night lock on the door and pulled down the closed sign.

"Teressa, we talked this out the other day."

"I know and you were right. I shouldn't have presumed that you would marry me just because you kissed me. You know I'm not terribly experienced in this sort of thing. That's why I figured it was about time."

She had been fiddling with the back of her dress, a light blue shirt waist that came from her neck to the floor. She caught the neck in front and pulled and it came down. Her arms slid out of the sleeves and the dress hung around her waist, leaving her naked on top.

Her breasts didn't jiggle from the movement. They were no larger than lots of men's breasts Morgan had seen. They were half a handful, with small areolas and tiny pink nipples.

"So, Lee Morgan, I decided that we would make love, right here on the floor if you want to or in back in my bed. Which do you prefer?"

Teressa walked toward him quickly, catching him, pushing her breasts against him.

"Teressa, not me. You really don't want to do this. Sex between two people has to be more than an animal act. There has to be respect and tenderness and love and caring. Otherwise it's just a meaningless bodily function, like going to the bathroom."

"But I do care for you. I'd die for you. I've been

Shotgun!

totally in love with you since the first time I saw you in school back in Boise. Don't you remember those Valentines I sent you?"

"You lied to get me inside here."

"Yes. Anything is fair in love."

Her hand slipped between their bodies and she began rubbing his crotch, searching for a hardness. He was as soft as an old angle worm.

"That won't help, Teressa. I'm not going to have sex with you. You're not ready. I'm bigger and stronger than you are, and I just won't let it happen."

Teressa stepped back from him and pushed at the dress. It fell to the floor, leaving her naked. A muff of black hair protected her crotch. She spread her legs and caught his hand but he resisted her moving it down.

"Teressa, I'd suggest you get some clothes on. I'm going to lift the blind, and anyone coming up to the door will see you. Do you want that?"

Morgan turned and lifted the blind. Two women started in from the boardwalk. Teressa grabbed her dress and darted behind a display of bolts of cloth.

Morgan unlocked the door. "Teressa, I'll see you again but nothing is ever going to happen between us."

He opened the door, stepped back and let the two matrons walk in. Then he went outside. Just before he closed the door he heard Teressa greeting the two women like old friends.

Morgan worked the saloons again, including the ones that he hadn't been to before. Nobody had heard of any work. Tomorrow he'd come back in his range clothes. He'd figured that Dempsy would get into motion before now.

He whiled away another hour. Then he went to the hotel to meet Kay, as they had arranged.

She was radiant, and he thought of her as a quiet kind of beauty who was also terrific in bed. She couldn't wait to tell him her news.

"I got a wire back from division this afternoon. They say Ferrand will be going out again tomorrow to Billings. He'll lay over a day and then come back from Billings to Minneapolis the next day."

"Which means Dempsy has three days to get a herd of cattle to the sidings he has chosen. I'd bet a bundle he has it all laid out and in motion right now. He's going to try for one last big score before he hides somewhere."

"We'll be there to nab him," Kay said. "I'm riding with you."

Morgan shook his head. "Not a chance. I'll be going as a working cowboy. Can you do that? No way. You keep the railroad people informed of what's going on—that'll be your end of it. I'm the one in the field."

Morgan ordered and ate but he didn't remember what it was. His mind was on the next day. Somehow he had to get in the crew that was going to do the rustling and see how it all played

290

out. At the right time, he would stampede the cattle and thwart the sale of the cattle. As soon as the meal finished, Kay stood. Morgan rose automatically.

"This has been the worst meal of my life. You've been a thousand miles away. You haven't heard a word I've said. You were thinking, planning something, and it didn't include me. I might as well be a chair or a table. I hate you."

Kay stomped away and Morgan settled back at the table. Yes, he had to get on the rustling crew in some way. He'd work the saloons tomorrow and ask again. They would need to get out by tomorrow noon if they were going to meet the train on schedule.

He pulled back and thought about it. Was he pushing too hard? Was he making too many assumptions? Maybe Dempsy had no plans to make a final big haul. Maybe—but Morgan just had a hunch that Dempsy would. He'd seen the man twice before, and neither time had left him with a different impression.

Morgan decided on a good night's sleep. He would need it. He hadn't had much sleep the past two nights. Upstairs he opened his door carefully and looked in. In the dim light he could see little. He went in, closed the door, struck a match and lit the lamp that set on the dresser.

When he turned around, he jumped. Teressa sat on his bed as naked as she'd been that afternoon.

Kit Dalton

"This time, Lee Morgan, I'm not leaving until you make love to me. If you don't, I'll go back to my shop, take a candle and break my maidenhead. Then the doctor will have to believe that you seduced me, and so will father and mother. We'll have you up for a shotgun wedding before you get your trousers back on. I want you to understand me, Morgan. I'm through being an old maid. I want to get fucked right now, and I won't take no for an answer. Do you understand what I'm talking about?"

Teressa lifted up on her knees. Her legs were spread and Morgan could see the pinkness of her nether lips waiting for him.

Chapter Twenty

Morgan took in the scene with a wry grin. He expected Teressa to launch into a long plea, but instead she simply held out her arms. She didn't say a word. None were needed.

Morgan unbuckled his gunbelt, hung it on the bedpost, went to the bed and sat down next to her. She reached over and unbuttoned his vest and shirt. Then she massaged his chest.

"Oh, Teressa, you do wear a man down. I guess that, since you've gone to all this trouble, it might be the right time to give you your sexual education."

She finished unbuttoning his shirt and worked at his belt until she got it open. He said nothing more until she tugged off his cowboy boots, pulled down his pants and short underwear and gazed in amazement at his erection.

Morgan caught her shoulders and looked at her. Slowly her gaze came up from his crotch.

The blush that bloomed in her neck had spread up her cheeks and tinged her whole face. "Oh, my, it's so huge."

"Teressa, your first time should be slow and gentle, not like this. You must have dreamed about your first time at making love. What did you imagine?"

She smiled and nodded. The blush receded. "Yes. Oh, yes, I've dreamed about it so often. It would be soft and gentle, on a big bed in a grand house, and the man would be my new husband. We'd be in a bedroom overlooking San Francisco Bay or maybe the Pacific Ocean. I'd be wearing a fancy silk nightgown all frilly and full of lace and roses. First he'd kiss me gently, then sit beside me and tell me exactly what he was going to do. He would be slow and gentle and make me feel like a queen. He'd make me excited and anxious."

Morgan kissed her lips. He held the kiss a minute, then came away and let her respond. She kissed him back. All the time her big blue eyes were wide open, and she breathed in short gasps through her nose.

When his lips came away she nodded. "Yes, like that."

She leaned backward on the bed and patted the spot beside her. Morgan stretched out near her healthy young body and then gently kissed her again. As he kissed her, his hand touched one breast, and when she didn't move away, he let his fingers caress it. Then he fondled the nipple. To his surprise it stood taller and filled with blood. His lips came away from hers and she let out a long held breath.

"Oh, yes, that does feel good. It's supposed to, isn't it?"

"Yes, it should feel good. Your breathing will speed up and get deeper, and hot blood will be rushing through your body. Your breast should grow warm and give you a contented, glowing, happy feeling."

She nodded, her face serious as if it were a lesson she must learn. He massaged her other breast and felt it respond. Then he took her hand and put it on his erection.

She whimpered when she touched him. Then she looked quickly at him to see if it was all right. He nodded, then lifted her to a sitting position and sat beside her.

"Go ahead, touch him, stroke him back and forth."

She played with him, gently moving his balls, and she looked up to see if she was hurting him. As she satisfied her years and years of curiosity, he caressed her body, working on her breasts again. His hand slipped down the outside of her leg and she looked at him sharply.

"Oh, yes, I forgot. This is all right. Once I had to slap a boy who put his hand on my leg. But now it's fine."

Morgan bent and kissed her lips again and her hand came away from his crotch. When the kiss ended, she looked at his bare chest.

His hand came up the inside of her leg to her knee, then she clamped her legs closed. He bent and kissed her lips again and this time washed her lips with his tongue. She moved back suddenly.

"You licked me."

"Yes, it's all right. It doesn't hurt. Try it." He kissed her again and her lips opened. He let her lick his lips. Then he opened his mouth and let his tongue dart inside her mouth and she moaned for just a moment and eased away from him.

"That's all right, too? I mean people do that?" she asked.

"Yes. Sometimes it's a kind of signal that the woman is saying that she wants the man inside her."

Teressa bent to him and kissed him, her mouth open this time, and she let him explore her mouth with his tongue.

When she pushed away she grinned. "Like that?"

Morgan nodded. His hand still lay trapped between the inside of her knees. He took her hand and showed her where his hand was.

"I promise not to go too fast. This is the time you should relax a little. Remember, you wanted this. So relax and let your legs move apart."

"But—" She sighed. "Years of training. Sorry."

She eased her knees apart and he kissed her again and his hand slid up her leg. Teressa trembled. His hand slowed and massaged the soft whiteness of her inner thigh. She reached and caught hold of his erection and she tried to smile. He moved his hand and eased her shoulders back on the bed. He kissed her lightly and his hand went back to her inner thigh.

"Just hold me a minute," she said, her voice shaky.

He lay down beside her, pulled her on top of his naked body and put his arms around her. "Better?"

She nodded. Twice more she shivered and he could feel her whole body tremble. "Will it hurt?"

"Maybe a little, but no more than pricking your finger with a pin."

"Good." She rolled off him, caught his hand and put it back on her inner thigh. "Please."

Slowly he massaged the tender flesh, moving higher and higher until he felt the dark muff of hair.

He stopped his hand and kissed her long and deep, and he heard her breath catch. Then her hips began to rotate slowly, gently.

When his lips came away from her, he watched her eyes. "You still want to?"

"Oh, yes. Don't stop now, I'd die."

His hand brushed the furry crotch and her hips pushed forward. He stroked quickly across her nether lips and she gasped. Her eyes went wide, then she smiled.

"Oh, yes, do that again."

He stroked past them, then returned and petted her moist center, and she gasped and moaned in delight. His finger moved higher and found her hard node and he rubbed it back and forth twice.

"What in the world?" she asked.

"You've never touched it before?"

"I don't know what you mean."

"The other girls never told you about this little hard spot?"

"No. I never talked about things like that."

He settled in, kissed her and twanged her clit twice. He could feel her passion building. He touched it six more times. Then she wailed and her whole body spasmed in one huge climax. She shivered and the spasms came again and again, rattling through her like an empty train on an uneven track.

Her hips humped forward again and again. She cried out twice more and her whole body trembled as the spasms fired through her again and again.

When it stopped, she let out a long sigh, threw her arms around him and pulled him on top of her. She held him without moving for three or four minutes.

Then he kissed her cheek and whispered in her ear. "I guess you liked that."

"Oh, yes!"

Suddenly a frown clouded her face. "You

weren't inside me, were you? I didn't feel anything there. How could that happen without your big thing inside me?"

"It's just a sensitive spot on women. Did you like how it felt?"

"Oh, yes! I've never been so thrilled, so overjoyed in my life. I could have gone on doing that for a year."

He chuckled. "You'd probably get hungry."

She laughed and kissed him, then frowned. "But there's more. You haven't been inside me yet."

"No, and you should get much the same sensation inside as well. Some women do; some don't. Just depends on a lot of things."

His hand went down again and he stroked her love lips, then parted them and pushed one finger far up inside her.

Teressa gasped. "Well, now. That is something." She nodded. "That's just your finger. I still don't see how—"

"Your juices will help lubricate you."

Morgan kissed her and worked his finger around and around, spreading her juices on the exterior of her labia. Then he moved, spread her legs and knelt between them.

He looked at her and kissed her gently. "Are you ready?"

Teressa took a deep breath, shivered a little and nodded. "Yes, ready and wanting you."

He felt her hips moving under him. He bent and

moved forward, adjusted himself, then lathered the head in her juices and eased into her slot.

"Oh, my!" she said as he edged forward. "Oh, my God!"

Then he thrust forward an inch and she smiled. "I'm not too small. I'm going to do it!"

He pushed again, came out a ways, then stroked in a little at a time until he was fully inserted. He rested there and looked at her.

The smile on her face was wonderful. Her blue eyes radiated joy and awe. Her lips parted and she nodded.

"Oh, yes, yes, yes. I love it. I feel so marvelous. Why didn't somebody tell me about this years ago."

Her hips moved against him and he stroked gently, then harder, and as she relaxed and the pressure eased, he came almost all the way out and rammed back in and she squealed. Then he settled down to slow stroking, and she met each thrust with a forward motion with her hips and it excited him.

Before he came close she squealed again and climaxed once more, moaning and wailing as she pumped hard at him and her body vibrated in a wild series of spasms that left her panting. He held back until she was done. He saw the sweat bead her forehead and her eyes drifted open and she sighed.

"Heaven. I'm in heaven. I'm sure I am." She closed her eyes and then they popped open. "Hey,

don't you get a turn? Where's all this rooting and
grunting and panting I hear about?

"Coming," he said and stroked into her again,
harder now, riding high, speeding up until she
had trouble keeping up with him. In two minutes
flat he exploded in her, unable to keep it any
longer. More pounding strokes emptied him and
he tapered off, then eased down and lay full
length on top of her.

Teressa wrapped her arms around his back and
held him so he couldn't get away. He lay there,
pushing her into the mattress, flattening her even
more, and they both let their breathing return to
normal.

She opened her eyes and tried to focus on him
but it didn't quite work. "Oh, my," she said.
"Oh, my!"

"Yes, I agree." He started to move but she
held him.

"Stay this way longer. I love it here. Also this
is the last time I'm probably going to be able to
hold you this way—all naked and marvelous and
beautiful."

Five minutes later he moved slightly and
she unclasped her hands and let him
get up. He sat on the bed beside her
and she luxuriated on the covers, watching him.

"Oh, my. That was so wonderful. Am I properly
initiated?"

"Yes, I would say so. The basic course. You'll

think of alternatives and refinements later on—
after you're married."

"Now that is a great idea. Who in town would
be right for me? I've never really thought about
it before. I can pick out the right man, let him
know I'm interested and set about getting him to
propose."

"But no bedding him before the wedding. Men
can be slippery about that. Why marry a girl if
you can get her into your bed any time you
want to?"

She lay there frowning. "Yes, yes, I see. I
understand. But I can kiss him and let him fool
around a little bit, but not go all the way."

"It's been known to happen in the best of
families."

He lifted her up to sit beside him. "I was
supposed to have a good night's sleep. Could I
talk you into getting dressed?"

"If you'll watch me."

"I'll watch. A woman dressing is a little like a
ballet dancer dancing. Ever seen a ballet dancer?"

"No."

"They're so graceful, so natural, but it's such
hard work. They're really athletic. I've seen some
practices. The dancers work out hard. They do
exercises and stretching and everything."

She dressed slowly and he watched her. She
had folded her clothes and placed them neatly
on the chair. She slipped into them and stood in
front of Morgan for inspection.

Shotgun!

"You look good enough for polite society," he said. "Now go and pick out your husband and then tease him into asking to come courting."

Teressa kissed him gently on his lips. No other part of their bodies touched but Morgan felt a stirring. The kiss was gentle and chaste, yet at the same time one of the sexiest he could remember. She smiled, went to the door and peeked out.

"All clear," she said and slipped out the door.

Morgan picked up his clothes from where she had thrown them, stacked them on the chair and went over his plan for the next day.

The rustling crew. There had to be an emergency crew formed up or maybe two of them. They couldn't be cute and go up the tracks this time. They would form one from town, maybe another from Dempsy's own hands. Yes, he'd get some sleep and be at the cowboy gathering places first thing tomorrow.

It was early for him, but he slid into bed, closed his eyes, rolled over into his sleep position and promptly went to sleep.

Morning started at 6:30 when Morgan's mental alarm clock roused him. He shifted his bare feet to the floor, washed out his mouth with some water from the pitcher, then dressed. He didn't shave. He wore his dirty pair of jeans, a ragged blue shirt and an old brown leather vest. He discarded his good hat and put on a sweat-stained black hat. Morgan made sure his gunbelt was cinched up tightly. Then he tied down the bottom of his holster and went for breakfast.

By eight that morning, he wandered from saloon to saloon. Most of them were closed. He found two cowboys on the same trip he was. He asked them if they had heard of any work. Both said no, but there was some talk that somebody might be hiring this morning.

Satisfied, Morgan exchanged first names with them and they made a trio, working the saloons. One opened about nine, but there were only two old-timers in there nursing beers and playing poker with matches for counters.

Hannah's Place usually didn't open until 11, so they bypassed it. It was after ten that morning when they came into the Lord Willy's Saloon across from the general store. A dusty cowboy in a battered black hat stood at the bar finishing a cold beer. He watched them come in and look around.

The cowboy went to them. He looked about 30, Morgan figured. Dust on his shirt showed he had had an early morning ride.

"You men looking for some riding work?"

"Could be," the older one of the trio said. "You hiring for a roundup and the rest of the summer?"

"Nope. Filled up on regular riders. We need five or six for a special cattle drive we got going. Pay three dollars a day. Four, maybe five days, depends."

"Any regular work around?"

Shotgun!

"Not yet. Won't be roundup time on most spreads for another month. Might be some work then at most of the ranches. Any of you want to hire on for five days at three bucks a day?"

Morgan held up his hand. "Yeah, I'll take it. Better than nothing."

The other two cowboys nodded. The cowboy in the black hat grinned. He wrote down their first names on a sheet of paper he took from his shirt pocket. Morgan told him his name was Buck. The other two were Ned and Quint.

"I need three more men. Meet me out at Fifth and Main at one o'clock. You furnish your own horse and saddle. If you don't own a horse, rent one at the livery. Get some dinner first. Won't be no chow until near seven tonight. See you boys there."

"We get an advance to rent a horse with?" Ned asked. The cowboy who didn't give them a name scowled. "Wasn't supposed to, but reckon we can afford a fiver for each of you. It comes out of your pay."

The three of them had steak dinners at an eatery nearby and ate until they couldn't face another forkful.

"I need to rent a horse," Morgan said.

One of the other men did, too. They walked down to the livery. Morgan rented the same mare he'd ridden before, and he pretended he didn't know the livery man.

Morgan and the other riders were ready and

waiting at the corner of Main and Fifth by 12:30. It was a block past the county courthouse. With a full day's growth of beard and his hat pulled down, Morgan figured no one at the sheriff's office would recognize him even if they came close by.

Three more riders came, then the ramrod who had hired them.

"Everybody had a good meal?" the boss asked. They all nodded. "All right, let's ride. We'll be heading west after we ride south about three miles. One rancher up ahead is a hard head and we don't want to get in any trouble about crossing his land."

Nobody objected. They settled into a fast walk that would eat up five miles in an hour. Morgan wondered about the remark about the ranch owner. The first place they would hit out of town this side of the river had to be the Dempsy spread. Maybe the ramrod would never let these men know they were rustling cattle. It had happened at least once that way before.

They rode for two hours, maybe ten miles from town, well into the Dempsy range. They saw pockets of cattle here and there, but no other riders and no ranch buildings.

A mile farther on, they saw some horsemen ahead and the ramrod headed straight for them. As they came closer, Morgan saw there were six riders. One of them left the others and rode out to meet them.

Shotgun!

Morgan recognized the man at once. He didn't know the other man's name but he was one of the lead riders for Dempsy. Morgan ducked his head and stayed at the back of his group. He didn't need to be identified and shot.

Chapter Twenty-one

The two riders at the front of the group talked a minute. Then the man whom Morgan recognized as being a lead rider for the Dempsy ranch turned and rode back to the other bunch of cowboys. Morgan's ramrod waved at his men and they struck out more to the south and then due west.

So there were two rustling crews out. Morgan had been right. Dempsy was going to try for a big score. What Morgan hoped was that the rancher had no idea that Morgan considered him a prime suspect in the leadership of the rustling.

The six-man crew settled down to ride and Morgan tried to evaluate the men in his group. The two he signed on with were innocents; he'd bet a month's pay on it. They were simply cowboys looking for work. They had no idea they were being dragged into a criminal scheme they could get hung for.

Shotgun!

The other three were harder to figure. One of the riders was over 30. He had a Texas drawl and Morgan figured him to be wise enough in the cattle wars to know what he had signed on for. His name was Tex, as far as Morgan knew.

Another of the men in the group was a little heavy to be a cowboy. But he had the suntanned face of an outdoorsman and he rode with a style and flourish that spoke of many years in the saddle. Morgan figured he was maybe 28. He had a baby face and somehow Morgan couldn't fathom him not knowing about the rustling purpose of the drive.

The last man in his section was over 40. He had a three-day growth of beard and rode with supreme confidence, but sometimes looked as if he'd been away from the trade for a few years. He smoked constantly, lighting one store-made cigarette from the last one. The others called him Pete and Morgan knew that he'd been over the mountain more than once.

The route continued over the rolling high prairie to the west. The riders saw more scatterings of animals, a range mixture of cows and calves, two- and three-year-old steer and an occasional range bull.

By the time they had ridden for three hours, Morgan figured they were 14 to 15 miles from town. That would put them well beyond the Dempsy spread and into the Corrigan outfit. With Corrigan dead and his ranch in disarray, it would be the ideal time to make a big haul of stolen beef. They rode another half hour and began to see more and more cattle. The ramrod called a halt and motioned them around him.

"This is where we start. Work in pairs. Move out and bring back to this point all the three-year-old steer you can find. We've got four hours to dark, so let's make good use of the time. First team back will stay here and ride herd on the steer, keeping them in this place. When we get this quarter mile worked, we'll drive the catch forward and work another section. Now let's get moving. Don't go chasing off after a steer. Get the easy ones and we'll move ahead. Let's go."

They fanned out. Morgan worked with Ned and they brought in six steer, went back out and came in with three more. Then they moved ahead a quarter mile. The little herd they had cut out stood at 18.

They worked the next chunk of range and then another one and another. Morgan's mare was not a cutting horse but she seemed to enjoy working the steer. By the time they moved the sixth time they had over 100 head of steer. That was 4,000 dollars worth of beefsteak on the hoof. They moved again and then twice more, each time rounding up more steer and driving them forward, always working to the west. The steer held the brand for Corrigan's ranch.

Dusk made it harder to find the steer and cut them out from a group of cattle. The animals

Shotgun!

seemed to gather together when it grew dark.

Two hours later the ramrod yelled at the riders, and when they brought in the last steer, he said that was all they would take that night. Each time they had moved the cattle, they had formed into a line five or six wide. The length of the line of cattle stretched well back into the darkness. Morgan figured that they had well over 200 animals.

"We'll keep them moving due west for four hours," the ramrod told each of the teams of men. "Spread out at point. Flank and drag and keep them moving. Most cattle want to lie down at night but we need to move this bunch a good ten miles before we let them rest.

"At two miles an hour?" somebody asked.

"If we're lucky. Now let's keep them moving."

Mile after mile they drove the sleepy cattle. Morgan couldn't remember when he'd worked so hard. All the time he was trying to figure his next move. He could stampede the herd anytime, but that wouldn't get him to the next step. Were the riders simply to drive this herd to the train? Or was there some stop along the way? That was what he wanted to find out. A 200-head herd did not make a big score—not even if the other crew brought in another 250 head the next day.

So what next? Watch and wait. That was all Morgan could do. They had the rest of tonight, tomorrow and the next day before the train with the right crew would be heading eastbound out of Billings. Watch and wait.

About midnight they had the cattle moving well after a slow down crossing a small stream. Every steer in the herd had wanted to take a drink and almost all of them had. That cost at least a half hour. When they had them back on track, Morgan noticed that they had slanted more to the south again.

He had no way of telling. But from the various southern angles they had taken since their first due south trek, he figured that they must be at least ten miles from the railroad tracks. What were they doing this far away from their eventual destination?

They had been rotating around the herd every hour, moving one stop. Each man got his share of the dust at the back end of the line as he hoorayed, tugged and prodded stragglers back into the march.

Now Morgan had the right-hand point at the head of the line. The ramrod came back from where he had been riding ahead of the animals. He pounded his black hat against his knee, freeing it of some of the dust. Then he eased it back in place. He rode up knee to knee with Morgan.

"You've done a trail drive or two, I'd say," the ramrod said.

"One or two."

"Won't be long now. I figure we have a little over a mile to go. We'll swing sharply to the south at the next creek. It's about ten feet wide along here."

Shotgun!

They were silent a moment and Morgan heard somebody yell and hoot as if trying to stop a running steer or get one started to move.

"That's the other crew bringing in the sheaves," the ramrod said. "We both should hit the creek about the same time."

It took them a half hour to get to the creek, and they saw the tail end of another line of steers moving upstream on the waterway to the south.

"Damn, he beat us here," the ramrod said. "I owe him a buck."

They swung the animals upstream, following the others, and herded them along for a half hour. Morgan heard a guitar playing somewhere ahead. He listened, but couldn't make out the song. Music meant a crew was fed and at ease, probably getting ready for sleep.

They kept the animals moving and then in the gloom ahead of them they saw a small valley between two low hills. Even in the dim light, Morgan could see a lot of brown backs. They were using this small valley as a holding area. It would take several men riding herd to hold the animals here, but it was better than the open range. Morgan had no idea how many head were in the herd, but there were a lot.

The riders pushed their animals into the herd ahead and some ran forward to find the water they smelled. Others merged with the stock there and soon their trail drive was over.

Morgan was aware of men talking in the darkness. He had no idea how many cowboys were in the area—10, maybe 15. He watched, but couldn't make out any in the darkness.

The ramrod talked to each man as he came up with the herd. "This is a way point for us. We stay here tonight and most of tomorrow. So find a soft spot of grass and get some sleep. If anybody is hungry, the cook will have chow for you in ten minutes. Put your horses in the rope corral over on the right. Unsaddle them and keep your saddle with you."

The men put their mounts in the corral and carried their saddles off a ways and dropped them. Morgan found Ned, who had some questions. "Why the hell we stopping here? I thought this was a straight drive through to the train."

"Most probably the train isn't there yet," Morgan said. "They keep the cattle here and trail them down to the siding to load them. This ain't Dodge City, where they used to have cattle pens along the railroad to hold five thousand head waiting to be loaded on cattle cars."

A poor excuse for a chuck wagon had been set up near the stream by some willows. The cook had steaks that had to weigh a pound and a half, boiled potatoes, slabs of fresh bread and enough carrots to choke an elephant. Gallons of coffee completed the meal.

Morgan ate his steak, cleaning off the tin plate. He had a third cup of coffee, then settled down with his saddle for a pillow near where Ned had dropped after the midnight meal.

Ned lifted up on one elbow. "Somehow this don't seem like a regular drive. I mean, I ain't been at this work more'n three years, but I never seen nothing like this. Why the night driving?"

Morgan wanted to tell the man about the rustling, but he decided to wait. If the cowboys got caught and accused of rustling, Morgan would get Ned and Quint off free and clear. If he told Ned now, he figured the rangehand would cut and run as fast as he could.

"Night driving isn't all that unusual," Morgan said. "I can't figure this out all the way either. Evidently that rancher needed a herd here and brought it in a little at a time. No law against that. Hell, I always figure if I don't understand something I can only get in big trouble asking a batch of questions. Let's just get some sleep and see what happens tomorrow."

"Yeah, I guess. Still seems odd. Aw, hell, I'm too damn tired to fight it."

They both went to sleep quickly. They'd been in the saddle for almost 12 hours.

The next morning, Morgan came awake at 6:30 as usual and groaned when he sat up. He hadn't slept on the ground with his boots on for a few months. This was a job for some 20-year-old kid. He looked around. From the little slope, he could see the valley angling off to the south. At first glance he figured maybe 1,500 head in the herd, most of them still lying down.

Men seemed to be spread out everywhere. He
lost count after getting to 22. Why so many men?

He smelled breakfast and kicked Ned out of
his slumber. They went over to the cook wagon.
At least they were eating well. Ham and eggs,
country-fried potatoes, bread and jam and lots
of coffee. Morgan went back for seconds and the
cook grinned. He was fat and sweating; his hairy
chest bulged under a dirty undershirt. His dark
hair straggled out from a wide-brimmed Stetson.

"Dig in. I figure half them hombres won't wake
up for breakfast anyway."

Nobody seemed to be in any hurry. Four men
were assigned to go out and ride herd around the
animals. The men on duty came in for breakfast. Morgan and Ned found Quint. They checked
their horses, took them to water and brought
them back to the rope corral and left them.

About ten o'clock some of the men lined up
and were paid off. They saddled their horses and
rode off to the north. Morgan counted ten, who
evidently were cut lose. He hoped to see their
ramrod but he didn't show up.

Shortly before noon, the black-hatted man
found them. "You three and my other three
and the rest of this crew will move out
right after chow. Eat up. We got to push
that herd eight miles and do it before dark.
Change in plans. The chuck wagon is about
ready."

Shotgun!

They ate again—another steak, scalloped potatoes with cheese and peas and slabs of bread and jam and coffee. Morgan went back for a second steak again.

"I cotton to a man who likes my eats," the cook said and guffawed.

Ned looked at Morgan as they saddled up. "Eight miles. That means we're eight miles to the railroad?"

"Be my guess. If that's where we're headed. What else do you do with market-ready steers?"

They double-checked their saddling work, then mounted. Morgan and Ned rode out to look at the cattle. They were still bunched, but some were moving around hunting graze. There were five men holding them in position. Morgan rode up close to them and sat watching the steers.

Without trying he saw three different brands in the mix of cattle. The Box C from Corrigan, the Bar B from the Roundtree spread and a Slant S. There could be three or four more brands in the mix.

Promptly at 12:30, the ramrod came out and started the cattle down the trail. It took some urging. They were still tired from their all night walk. Ropes were used to whack the reluctant cattle on the backs to urge them to stand and get moving.

They strung out six wide and more than half a mile long as the cowboys pushed them forward. Morgan counted 12 riders working the herd. More than enough, but soon he discovered that three or four of the riders didn't know what they were supposed to do. The ramrod galloped up to two of them and screamed at them, telling them exactly what to do. Then he rode on.

The riders drove the long line due north, then slanted slightly to the west and kept the animals moving along at a steady pace.

Morgan knew from experience that there was no way to hurry a batch of cattle in a trail drive. He amended that. There was one way but it was spelled stampede and almost nobody used that method.

He figured the first hour on the drive they covered a little over a mile. At that rate, they would never find the railroad before dark. The second hour went better. The cattle were more used to the pace. The drovers worked them better and soon they had established an even two-mile-an-hour pace.

The prairie was easy—no sudden canyons or ravines or big rivers to worry about. The tracks were on this side of the Yellowstone River, so there was no worry about a ford. The drive moved along well.

As Morgan rode on one side, he figured what 1,500 head of prime steers were worth. Even at 40 dollars a head, that would be 60,000 dollars—more money than the average trainman would make in a lifetime.

So what did Morgan do when the herd hit the

Shotgun!

cattle pens? He didn't have the slightest idea.

An hour later the riders gave the cattle a break, letting them stand in place instead of the usual noontime rest. Morgan drifted back and talked with Ned. He told him from the top what this rustling scheme was all about and that he might need some help when they got to the pens.

"Christ, they got twelve other guys here. Might be more at the loading pens. What the hell could two of us do against all those?"

"That's what I'm trying to figure out, Ned. Can you use that six-gun on your hip."

"Tolerably."

"Good. When we hit the siding, you and I are going to get away from the cattle and do something. I don't have the slightest idea yet, but I will."

"What about Quint?"

"If you can find him, get him on our side. Don't tell him the whole thing. Just that we need him and we'll keep him from getting hung for being a rustler."

They moved the cattle again. Two hours later they spotted the siding. It wasn't the one that Morgan had been to before. Twenty cattle cars had been dropped off next to some makeshift loading pens. It would take forever to load that many cars, even with experienced cowhands.

Quint had moved up on the same side of the herd as Ned and Morgan, and they signaled each other. When they were half a mile away from the pens, Morgan caught the attention of the other two and motioned to the side. The three of them turned and rode away from the line of cattle, heading in a long arc toward the rails.

They heard some pistol shots behind them. But Morgan hadn't seen a rifle on the trip in any of the saddles, so he felt fairly safe. They got away cleanly, crossed the tracks and headed back toward the siding. They could see the cattle cars, but no horses or other men seemed to be around.

"What now?" Ned asked.

Morgan pointed to a stream that ran into the Yellowstone 200 yards from the siding. "We get into the brush down there on that stream. They won't be able to see us and we'll be close enough to do something if and when a train stops for those loaded cars."

"I used to work for the railroad back home in Ohio," Quint said. "If it ain't locked, I could throw a switch and put that engine right up there into that siding before the engineer realized it and cause all sorts of a mess."

Morgan shook his head. "Might kill too many cattle. Somehow we've got to get them back to their rightful owners. Good idea, but let's keep thinking."

They watched from the brush as the line of cattle neared the pens. Morgan knew that the rustlers couldn't jam all those 1,500 steer into 20 cattle cars. Even 30 steer to a car would move only 600 head.

Shotgun!

As the cattle arrived, they were angled into the chutes and into the cattle cars. A ramp at each car let the animals walk up and into the cars. The engineer had positioned the cars exactly right for the loading.

"Loading doesn't matter," Morgan said. "The train is what we need to worry about. We have to stop it, disable it or capture it."

"We can capture the engineer," Quint said. "Usually he's the only one on the train who can run the engine. Sometimes the fireman knows something about driving the train. We take both of them, and the train will sit there a long time."

"Good," Morgan said. "As soon as the train pulls in, and even before he starts switching cars, we grab the fireman and the engineer at gunpoint and bring them down here in the brush. We do that from this side so the rustlers won't even know about it."

"Will the trainmen have guns?" Ned asked.

Quint shook his head. "On most lines they won't let the trainmen carry even a pistol. There's probably a rifle locked up on board somewhere. The conductor might be able to get it. By then it would be too late."

Morgan grinned. "I think we have a good team here. As soon as engine 427 drives into this flag stop, we'll have a big surprise for the engineer."

Quint looked up. "You said you're working for the cattlemen. Is there a way that you can keep us from getting hanged for rustling cattle?"

"You're with me. I brought you along to help me capture the train. Who can say any different? Not a chance in hell that either of you can be charged with rustling."

Down the tracks Morgan heard a train whistle. It was far too early for the train to be coming. What was this all about?

Chapter Twenty-two

The three cowboys looked to the west, then to the east. The train whistled again, and this time they could tell it came from the east. It wasn't the train they were waiting for. They watched as it appeared far off, then came closer and at last roared past without so much as a wave from the engineer.

"Those things still amaze me," Ned said. "Never saw a train where I came from. One of these days I might even ride on one."

The three cowboys watched the progress of loading the steer into the cattle cars on the siding. It didn't go well and now and then they could hear somebody swearing a bloody streak. The rustlers had bunched the cattle well behind the siding, and from time to time a batch were driven forward to be loaded.

"Since we don't know when the train is due, we better make our plans," Morgan told the other two. "How long do the engineer and fireman stay in the engine after it stops?"

Quint scratched his cheek. "Usually the two of them stay there all the time. If other folks want anything they have to go to the engineer. He's sort of the captain of the ship."

"So we can wait until the train stops, then walk up to the cars and work up to the engine and jump on board and surprise them," Ned said.

"Should work." Quint frowned. "I ain't never shot at anybody before. Think there could be any gunplay?"

Morgan shook his head. "Wouldn't imagine so. The trainmen don't carry weapons, you said. So if we do it fast and get them out this side of the train, the rustlers at the loading chutes won't even know what happened."

"Good. I don't aim to get myself killed," Quint said.

They waited. Ned had a nap. Quint sat up, edgy from this sudden turn of events. Morgan leaned against a tree and watched the loading operation through the screening leaves. He could see out but no one could see him.

The shank of the afternoon drifted past and Morgan saw that the rustlers had all of the cattle cars filled. More than half of the steer still chewed their cud on the slopes above the train tracks.

Morgan consulted his railroad watch—ten minutes before seven. This far north there could be another two hours of daylight. He had no idea when the train was scheduled to arrive. They could switch the cars at any time, day or night. He settled down to wait. The big steak dinner had served him well. He hadn't even thought of food until now. He bent and had a drink from a spring that flowed in from the side of the stream. That would have to do him for some time to come.

A half hour later, the three cowboys heard another train whistle. This one came from the west and soon a train pulled into view. It had two passenger cars up front and behind it came a string of 20 or 30 cars. These flatland trains could have a long line of cars pulled by one big engine. The train slowed down a quarter of a mile out and then ground to a stop, with the engine close to the head of the loading chutes.

The three men had worked up the creek under cover of the brush when they saw the train coming. As soon as it stopped, they broke from the brush near the train cars and ran forward. All were on the near side of the tracks, away from the siding and the cattle cars.

Quint went up first, bouncing between the coal car and the engine and holding his six-gun on the engineer. Morgan went right behind him. The engineer turned with surprise, then anger.

"Hold it," Morgan barked. "We're taking over this train. Just do as you're told and you won't get shot. Otherwise you'll be buzzard breakfast. Now keep the brakes on and get down out of there. We're going for a walk. You, too, fireman."

"You can't do this to Northern Pacific property," the engineer said, but Morgan's six-gun rammed into his belly and stopped him.

The two trainmen left the cab and dropped to the ground where the rustlers couldn't see them. Morgan and Ned prodded the two men toward the brush. Then they ran through the stream to the other side for more concealment and hustled the train men 200 yards down the creek. There they tied the trainmen hand and foot. Ned agreed to stay as guard.

Morgan ran back to the train and tried to figure out what to do next. He heard a shot and rushed forward, stepping up to the coal-car connector and looking out at the siding with its loaded cattle cars.

A man in a suit and white shirt ran from the passenger car and fired a shot in the air. "Hold it right where you are, you men with the cattle. The next cowboy who moves gets shot. Everyone understand?"

As he spoke, six more men left the passenger car and fanned out. Each of the other men carried a rifle aimed at the rustlers.

A cowboy who had just delivered more cattle to the pens spurred his horse and angled away from the men. Two rifles cracked and the rider slumped in his saddle as the horse went down belly shot.

Two of the suited men ran down the line of cattle cars and pushed six men who had been loading the last car back toward the near end of the siding. Other railroad men had brought in two riders and had them leave their horses.

Morgan looked at the last man in the line of gunmen. He looked smaller than the rest. Then the person turned and Morgan grinned. He jumped down from the train and two of the riflemen turned toward him.

"Kay Butterfield. Am I ever glad to see you," Morgan called.

She turned to the other railroad detectives. "It's all right. This is the man I told you about."

Morgan hurried up to her and Quint came along behind him. Kay gave him a big hug and then they detached themselves.

"About time you got here. We had three men against about fifteen."

She looked at the cab. "But you captured the engineer before our man could get to him. I'd say we worked this out pretty well."

"How come you're on board?" Morgan asked.

"Some luck and some good planning. I wired the office about the probable last-ditch try by the rustlers. We knew it would be on engine 427's run. They cut the day's layover in Billings and had the 427 come back a day early. We figured this might upset the rustler's plans. Then I took the train to Billings and caught the 427 when it left this morning. Billings supplied us with four detectives, and we picked up six more along the way."

In front of them the rustlers had been relieved

of their weapons and their wrists were in shackles. The rustlers were marched to the train and put in the end of the second passenger car, which had been brought empty for that purpose.

"What about the cattle?" Morgan asked.

Kay shook her head. "I don't do cattle, just rustlers and crooked trainmen. We have the whole crew of this train tied up in the second passenger car. Now if we could add the engineer and firemen, we'll have our work done.

Morgan walked with Kay to the woods, where he held the two trainmen. Morgan told Ned to take the two prisoners back to the passenger car and to turn them over to the railroad detectives.

Kay lingered in the woods when Ned left with the engineer and fireman. "Glad you were here. It helped."

"At first I didn't recognize you in your suit."

"I'm still the same. See for yourself." Kay stepped up to him and kissed him, pushing her breasts hard against him.

When the kiss ended he grinned. Morgan kissed her again and caressed one breast through her white shirt. "You seem to be all there."

"Wish we had time right here," she said. "I love to make love out in the woods like this."

Morgan grinned and caught her hand. "I'm going to remember that. Right after we get the rest of this rustling problem cleared up, we're going to experiment and see how excited you can get with your bare little bottom in the soft grass under the trees somewhere."

Shotgun!

"It's a date. Now what are you going to do with all of these cattle?"

"Drive them back to where they belong. Trouble is it's going to take more than the three of us."

Kay grinned. "I figured that. Check the first passenger car. You'll find some help."

He frowned. At the first passenger car he stepped inside and found a dozen cowboy hats with riders under them.

"You men looking for work driving some livestock?" Morgan asked.

"Yep, we been awaiting for you," one of the men said. The ten cowboys got up and filed off the train. They picked out horses from those left by the rustlers and then concentrated on unloading the cattle cars.

Kay had even thought to bring along a fireman and an engineer to take the train on into Miles City.

"See you in town in two or three days," Kay said. She stepped on board the passenger car as the train got up steam and moved along the tracks.

Morgan turned to the new riders and Ned and Quint. "Looks like we've got some work to do. Let's get these cattle unloaded and let them rest until about noon tomorrow."

"What about chow?" one of the new riders asked.

Morgan looked at the chuck wagon, which had

come up almost to the tracks. "We'll soon find out."

They walked over to the chuck wagon, where the hairy cook in the white hat, dirty underwear shirt and clean hands looked up in surprise.

"Looks like I'm working for a new boss. They said you, big eater." He motioned to Morgan. "Some guys in suits brought out six burlap bags filled with all kinds of food. Looks like I'm expected to feed you guys for three more days. What the hell is going on here?"

Morgan told him the situation. "We're damn lucky you didn't get hauled into town for rustling."

"Hell, all I do is cook. Don't do nothing else. Nobody can prove I did. Hell, I cook good." He pulled out a big pocket watch and checked the time. "Looks like nobody ate anything since noon. If you gents want to come back in an hour, I'll have a late supper for you."

Morgan nodded and hurried down to the chutes, where the men continued to unload the livestock that had been put on only hours before. Most of the animals bawled and headed for the creek and a long drink. The men had the cattle all out of the cars and back in the herd by the time the cook rang the big triangle hanging from the chuck wagon.

Morgan got in line for his tin plate. When he came up to the serving table, he told the cook some bad news.

Shotgun!

"One of the steer broke a leg getting unloaded," Morgan said. "We had to shoot it. Couple of the men hung the carcass and bled it out. You might want to go down and see if you can carve out a steak or two."

The cook nodded. "Sure as hell I can do that. We'll have beef for breakfast, dinner and supper tomorrow. After that I wouldn't feed it to my dogs."

Morgan took over the job of trail boss. He talked to all of the cowboys and asked them what arrangements had been made. One man said they'd been promised three dollars a day for a five-day drive.

Morgan told them it would be more like a three-day drive, but that each one would get 15 dollars for the job. That made them pleased. He assigned three men to riding herd and set up two more shifts of four hours each.

Just before dark he rode into the herd and checked the brands. He found brands from five different outfits. He wasn't even sure where some of them were. He decided that he'd take the cattle to the Corrigan ranch, leave them there and notify the different ranchers to send a crew over to reclaim their cattle. It would take a small roundup and then a sorting out of the brands.

In a day or two the cattle couldn't travel far. Then Morgan remembered the map he'd made of the different outfits. He pulled it out and checked it. He knew where the Roundtree and Corrigan places were and found that the others were close by.

He changed plans. They would drive the herd up to the boundaries of the first outfit that had been stolen from, then rest the cattle. He'd ride in and tell the owner about the theft and recovery and have him send out a crew to cut out his cattle.

Then they would drive what was left to the next closest ranch and work it that way. By the time they finished at Corrigan's the rest would be driven across the river into the Roundtree spread and they'd be done. It might take five days at that. If they ran low on food they could slaughter another beef. The owners wouldn't mind losing a couple of steer to gain back nearly all that they had lost.

The next day they let the cattle rest until noon, then started them out on the drive. The men knew their jobs and all went smoothly. They only made six miles before it grew dark. Since there was no big rush, they bedded the cattle down and ate steak again and went to sleep early.

The next morning they were up in the dark and had the cattle moving shortly after daybreak. They made nearly ten miles that day and were coming close to the first downstream ranch. It was the Slash S brand. Morgan rode in early the next morning and met Shackleford, the owner.

"You got some of my steer? Figured I'd lost some but I didn't know where."

Shotgun!

They rode out with six hands and worked through the herd. All of the hands helped and in two hours they had cut out 150 head. Shackleford sat his horse dumbfounded.

"I'll be damned. I knew I had lost some animals, but not this many. That'll make the difference between me going broke and staying in business another year. A hundred and fifty head is worth over six thousand dollars. Been a time since I've had a pay day like that. Tell the association that you're worth whatever they paid you."

Shackleford gave a yell and spurred out to catch up with his herd.

The next ranch was even smaller than the Slant S. It was the Circle B, run by Charlie Barnard. He and his men helped cut out his distinctive brand, and when the total ran over 200, he shook his head in wonder. When the last count came, the Circle B total showed 285 head.

"Just goes to show you that most ranchers out here don't have one goddamned idea how many steer they have until roundup time. These damn rustlers knew what they were doing. I'd have missed maybe half of what they took. Course, I can't be certain they didn't get some more off me before."

The third small rancher had only 50 head that they found in the mix. The herd had been whittled down a little, and when they cut out the Lazy L cattle, they also divided the two brands left, the Corrigan ranch and the Bar B. They would drive them in separate groups the last few miles to the respective ranches.

The ramrod of the Corrigan ranch saw them coming. He'd been on some range work, and when he rode over and saw the 500 head of steers with his ranch's brand on them, he shook his head in wonder.

"Mr. Corrigan figured the rustlers had tapped us some, but he had no idea how many. We can probably double that number for what's been stolen from us here. Any way we can get back at the rustlers? If they did get away with five hundred before this, that's twenty thousand dollars somebody owes the Corrigan ranch. Somebody should pay."

"We'll be working on that. There's a good chance that most of the losses can be made up from the man behind this whole scheme, just as soon as we get it all tied up neatly. Figure out how many animals you lost and their projected worth and be ready for us."

At the Bar B ranch, the foreman came out to meet them. They left the herd well inside the DD range. It was another 500 animals and the foreman and Mrs. Roundtree both thanked the men.

From there they hit the trail the seven miles into town. Morgan had promised the men pay and he didn't have that much cash. He found Kay Butterfield waiting for him at the livery barn.

"Figured you'd take care of your animal first," Kay said.

Shotgun!

She reached in her reticule and brought out a stack of five-dollar bills and waved them at the cowboys. "Pay day just as soon as you get your horses turned in. We're not even sure who owns some of these mounts, but the livery man can straighten that out. Some have DD brands, others no brands. When you get your animals tended to, see me over here and be ready to sign your name or make your mark."

Morgan leaned against the barn door and smiled. Kay wore a Western-cut shirt tucked neatly into a pair of jeans, which had been tailor made to fit her sleek curves. On her head sat a Stetson without a chin strap and her .32 had been housed in a new gun belt that let the iron hang on her right hip.

"Lady, did you think of everything?"

"Not quite. We've still got to corral the head man on this scheme. You said it has to be Lorne Dempsy. I'd guess there were no stolen DD brand steer in the herd you sorted out."

"Not a single one. He's our man, but how do we prove it?"

She frowned. The men came up then, signed for their 15 dollars and hurried for the saloons, cafes and bawdy houses.

When the last man left, Kay thanked the livery man and she and Morgan wandered up the street. It was a little after three in the afternoon, but Morgan was hungry. He steered Kay to Violet's Cafe and he ate half a fried chicken and all the dinner trimmings, including a mound of mashed potatoes and chicken gravy. He settled back.

"Tomorrow will be early enough to go get Dempsy. He's not going to run anywhere. How did they take care of all those prisoners you brought back over at the jail?"

"It is a bit crowded, but they managed. The district attorney said he's questioning each man. Two of them had no idea that they were in a rustling operation. One of them was a kid of no more than sixteen. The district attorney put him on the train for his home in Illinois. The other one will be charged with a lesser offense, but should get some prison time. We could have eight men eligible to hang one of these days."

"Where are all of your little railroad-detective helpers?"

"They went back to their regular posts. This was what we call an emergency call so we can mass our forces."

"Whatever it was, it worked. I was out there riding blind. I knew I had to do something, but wasn't exactly sure how it would turn out. When it ended with you and ten railroad detectives, I felt a lot better."

"You look so tired you could go to sleep on a red-hot stove," she said.

"Bet I could. A soft bed would be heaven right about now."

Kay watched him, a slow smile breaking

around her mouth and touching her big blue eyes.

"I'm not going to make any offers because I want you fresh and strong and vigorous when I get you alone out in the woods."

Morgan caught his head as it dropped forward. Then blinked. "Too damn early to be getting sleepy," he said.

Kay grabbed the bill for their dinner and hurried to the cashier, where she paid the tab. Morgan was fighting to stay awake and barely winning.

Kay walked him back to the hotel, unlocked room 212 for him and guided him to his bed. He fell forward on his stomach, and the second his head hit the pillow, he slept.

Kay chuckled, pulled off his boots, then rolled him over. She got his gun belt off and loosened his pants belt. Then she slipped out of the room.

She had a thousand pages of reports to complete. Her boss wouldn't be happy with the 150-dollar bill for paying those cowboys, but he would make it back later when the ranches shipped their steer east.

She wondered if she should have curled up beside Morgan and woken him up after a few hours. She shook her head and went into room 218. It had been a full day. Tomorrow morning they would go call on Lorne Dempsy and see what he had to say about the charge that he headed the rustling operation.

Chapter Twenty-three

Early the next morning, Hannah Johnson sent her barkeep to the livery to bring back a carriage. She wore a black dress with a black hat and veil. She stepped into the buggy in the alley in back of her saloon and told the barman to forget he'd even seen her that morning.

Hannah's grim expression mirrored her thoughts. She would do what had to be done, no matter what the cost. She had to follow through and complete the task she had set for herself five years earlier. It had to be today. Everything had come crashing down around her. It had to be today.

She touched the new revolver in her reticule. It was loaded with six rounds. There would be no chance for a mistake. It had to be today.

She drove carefully, letting the gray mare trot for half a mile. Then she held the mare down to a

Shotgun!

walk. She was good with horses because she had been raised with them.

Her grim expression turned angry as she thought of all she and her family had been through. It would be over soon.

Hannah would not dwell on unhappy thoughts. This should be a time for rejoicing. Her mission and whole purpose in life was about to be fulfilled.

It took Hannah nearly two hours to drive to the Dempsy ranch. When she arrived, it was just after 8:30. The hands had been fed and all were on the range, getting ready for the roundup, which would come soon. She drove up to the ranch house without seeing anyone and tied the mare to the short hitching rail there. Then she went to the kitchen door. Hannah walked in without knocking and found Lorne Dempsy seated in a chair next to the kitchen table.

"You stupid asshole!" Hannah shouted the moment she saw him. "You've ruined everything. Why did you try for one more big score? I told you that it was finished, that they were too close to us. You went right ahead and did what you wanted to do. Ten of your men are in jail. The train crew has been arrested. And the fifteen hundred steer you tried to ship on a six hundred steer train have all been driven back and distributed to their home ranges. It's all over. We're finished. Now all we have to do is wait for the sheriff to arrive and arrest you and half your men for rustling.

"You fucking, limp-prick bastard. Why didn't you at least include a couple of hundred of your own brand steer in that last herd you tried to sell? You're an idiot. The trouble is, you're my idiot. I picked you out from the other ranchers as the most dishonest and corrupt of all of them. I didn't know you were shit-assed stupid as well."

Through the angry words, Lorne Dempsy shifted his bulk in the chair once. Then he had a sip of his coffee. Hannah saw a whiskey bottle nearby and knew the coffee had been liberally spiked. Lorne had developed a drinking problem several years earlier.

Dempsy looked up at her. "First, I don't take talk like that from no fancy-pants woman."

"You don't? So what are you gonna do about it?"

"I am going to shoot your tits off and see how you like that." He fumbled for his six-gun and drew the weapon, but the table and the big chair got in his way. Before he could lift the gun to aim, Hannah had pulled the revolver from her reticule and fired. She had aimed at his chest, but her sudden trigger pull jerked the muzzle to the right and the bullet slammed into his right shoulder, bringing a shrieking wail of pain and spilling the weapon from his hand.

"That's just starters, you stupid rustler. You still don't know who I am, do you? That was another reason I picked you to handle the field-work in this rustling scheme. You were so dumb you didn't even wonder who I was or try to find out.

"You should know before I kill you. My last name is Johnson. Does that mean anything to you? Johnson, as in Ralph Johnson, the JC brand. The cattle spread that used to be between you and the Bar B range. Remember that?"

"Quit yakking and stop my bleeding. Damn, woman, you just shot me. I'm bleeding to death. Get some cloth and tie up my shoulder."

"No. Concentrate on what I'm saying. Do you remember the Johnson ranch?" Hannah saw movement out of the corner of her eye and turned just as the cook edged into the room, a rifle in his hands.

"Kill her!" Dempsy thundered.

The cook lifted the weapon. Hannah turned and fired. Long hours firing a handgun with her father at their ranch paid off. She remembered to squeeze the trigger gently. She fired three times and the cook fell dead in the doorway.

She turned the weapon back on Dempsy. "I asked you a question, Dempsy. Do you remember the Johnson ranch and the JC brand."

"Yes, yes, I remember. Little spread but he controlled a mile of water along the Yellowstone and I needed the land."

"So you stole his calves and some of his cows. You eliminated any chance for natural growth and you rustled his calves as soon as they could graze and live on their own. Then at roundup time you branded them and put another nail in the JC brand's chances for survival."

"So? Ranching is a tough business. Your old man was never cut out to be a rancher. Not mean enough. Not ready to take any advantage you can get over the next guy."

"Like you?"

"Damn right like me."

Hannah aimed carefully and shot Dempsy in his left shoulder. The bullet knocked him halfway out of his chair. His scream came from deep within his soul—the kind of tortured, agonized voice that showed that he knew he would never survive the rest of this day. Tears streamed down his cheeks. He blubbered, he screamed, he swore at her.

Hannah sat down with her back to the kitchen wall and watched the man suffer. A slow smile crept over her features.

"I hope to hell you enjoy pain, Dempsy. You're going to get more than your share in the next few hours. I figure I can shoot you at least ten or twelve times before I miss and hit something vital and kill you. It'll be our little game."

He quieted down and reason returned to his eyes as he watched her. "This was all your idea. You told me it was a way that both of us could get rich with no risk. No risk, you said. You planned how to do the rustling with crews and then ship them down the railroad and out of the state so there would be no witnesses to testify against us.

Shotgun!

"You seduced Josh and then blackmailed him into helping us so we could sell the cattle. You said Josh got half, but I know you kept most of his money and half of mine. You bitch!"

"You cleared over forty thousand dollars in the deal, Dempsy. You're not going to be able to enjoy spending the money."

"You said we had to give a quarter of the money to the railroad men, but I know for a fact you kept most of that," Dempsy wailed. "They got a hundred a trip, not the eight or nine hundred they should have. What are you going to do with all your money, bitch?"

"I'll find a way to use it. I thought you had a family? Where are they?"

"My wife and daughter went to Billings for a month. I knew there was trouble coming. Your father—wasn't he sick, lost his mind?"

Hannah shot Dempsy again, this time in one of his massive legs. The round jolted into flesh and hit bone, but never came out the back.

"My father was a saint. You're a devil. Don't you ever talk about him again or I'll kill you right away." Her brow sparkled with beads of sweat. Her eyes flared and her nostrils twitched as she sucked in breath enough to fuel her hatred.

She watched him a minute, then opened the cylinder on her revolver and replaced the spent cartridges with new ones. Then she closed the weapon and spun the cylinder.

"Now, old man, where do you keep your cash.

343

This will look like a robbery."

"I don't keep cash here, just in the bank in Billings."

Hannah lifted the weapon and fired. The round slammed so close to Dempsy's head that it missed his ear by an inch.

"Oh, God!" He trembled so badly that he couldn't hold his hands still. "All right, in the den, the desk drawer far in back. In an envelope. Hundreds. My reserve fund."

Hannah moved then, picked up Dempsy's fallen six-gun and put it in her reticule. The barrel stuck out the top. She watched him a minute. He couldn't move if he wanted to.

"Don't go anywhere. I'll be right back." Hannah left the room, then found the den and the desk. In the back of the wide top drawer she found a white envelope with more than a handful of hundreds in it.

She put the bills in her reticule and went back to the kitchen. Dempsy had pushed his chair toward the cupboards and had a door open, but he hadn't reached the shotgun yet. She came in time to grab it before he did. She broke it open and found two unused shells in the double barrels.

"Still playing games with me, Dempsy? Should I use the shotgun and blow your face apart? Yes, I would like that. But we're not ready to end the game yet.

"You mentioned my father losing his mind. He did when he realized he'd been cheated and forced to lose his ranch because his neighbors were thieves, robbers and bastards. The men he had thought were his friends turned out to be the very ones to kill his mind, bankrupt his ranch and send him on a five-year trail of torture.

"I'd like to send you down that same trail, but I can't. I can only let you see a few hours of what it's like. I've been taking care of my father these past five years. He doesn't know who I am. He can't speak at all. He looks out the window and shits in his pants. That's the reality of what you've done to my father and me."

Hannah moved for a better angle and shot the big man in his other leg. By that time Dempsy was beyond pain. He screeched in surprise, then looked at Hannah with eyes that were not rational. His head bobbed in a way she had seen her father do early on in his sickness.

"Dempsy, can you hear me?"

He didn't reply. She checked to be sure he was still alive. His breathing came steadily but a little ragged. Blood still dripped from his shoulder. A dead man wouldn't bleed. He was still alive.

Hannah heard something outside and ran to the kitchen window to look. Six men and a woman rode into the ranchyard. They looked around, saw her buggy at the hitching rack and headed that way.

"Hello, the house," someone called. "This is Sheriff Attucks. I'm here with a warrant for the arrest of Lorne Dempsy. Just come out with your hands up and we won't have any problems."

Hannah took the shotgun, poked it out a partly open door and fired one round over their heads. The seven people dropped off their horses and used the animals as their protection.

The same voice came again. "We know you're in there, Dempsy. That buggy of yours is still in the shed. You might as well come out and save us all a lot of trouble. I've got deputies with me with rifles and we can shoot that place apart if you want us to."

To demonstrate, one of the deputies put a rifle slug through the top of the screen door. Hannah retreated to the kitchen window, where she could look out past the curtain without being seen.

Then the sheriff spoke again. "Come on, Dempsy. I don't want to have to shoot you. You can afford a good lawyer from Billings and he might get you off with five years. You'll still be a middle-aged man when you get out."

Hannah looked at Dempsy. He hadn't moved since she'd shot him in the leg the last time. She watched outside again. The deputies left their horses and sprinted to both sides. They would circle the house and come in the back door or maybe a window.

"Oh, damn," Hannah said. She'd planned on arriving early, settling with Dempsy and getting away before the hands came back or the sheriff arrived. She hadn't planned right.

What now? She could leave Dempsy in his

present state, hoping that he would be helpless the rest of a long life. She frowned, thinking of his wife and daughter. She couldn't put that kind of a burden on them. She didn't hate the women in his life, only Dempsy. She lifted her brows, took his big .45 out of her reticule and checked the loads. Then she turned the cylinder to a live round and held the heavy gun with both hands.

She shot Lorne Dempsy in the head from three feet away. She saw the bullet hit. Then she dropped the gun on his lap, turned and ran for the stairs to the second floor. She carried the shotgun with her.

From the third-floor window she watched the slow movement of the lawmen as they worked their way up to the building. She recognized the sheriff and one other man. She was not surprised to see that he was Lee Morgan. He worked up behind his horse, then sprinted the last eight feet to the kitchen wall.

She heard them come into the house. She cocked the shotgun and looked out the window. The grass had started growing. The prairie would be green all over soon. Soft white clouds shifted across the sky.

A moment later she heard someone on the stairs. She lowered the butt of the shotgun to the floor. The trigger was too far away. She knew what to do. She'd been raised with guns.

When she heard someone slipping up the stairs to the third floor, she looked down at the twin muzzles of the shotgun and lifted the butt three inches off the floor and let it fall.

Morgan heard the shotgun blast just as he topped the stairs. The shot had come from the left. He ran that way, dropped to his hands and knees and looked around the doorway from floor level. He saw the woman near the window. The smell of the shotgun blast remained thick in the room. The ceiling was peppered with buckshot holes, some of them showing red. He couldn't see the woman's head.

Morgan rose and hurried into the room, holstering his six-gun. He looked down in shock and horror. He recognized the long carrot-red hair flowing down her back. However, the sharp green eyes, the high cheekbones, the strong chin and full red lips of Hannah Johnson had all been blasted away, leaving only a bloody, pulpy mass of bone and lacerated flesh.

It took them a half hour to load the three bodies into a wagon and hitch up a team. The sheriff talked to the first cowboy who rode into the ranch yard. He couldn't believe it. He sat on his horse, tears dripping off his cheeks.

"Who done this? Who done this? Who done this?" He said it over and over.

Back in town, Morgan and Kay sat in the sheriff's office. They had just come from Hannah's Place and made the discovery in the upstairs bedroom. Ralph Johnson was dead. He had been shot early that morning with one round to the head. He had died instantly. In Hannah's bedroom they had found three of the Chicago icepick knives.

"She told me about her father one time," Morgan said. "How the other ranchers had squeezed him out by stealing his newborn calves when they were big enough to make it on their own. In three years he was broke and the bank took over the place.

"Ralph Johnson went insane over the loss, and Hannah had been taking care of him ever since. She evidently worked up the rustling plan to get revenge on the big ranchers who ruined her father."

Kay shuddered. "But how could anyone kill her own father?"

Morgan shook his head. "It's tragic and unthinkable for us, but she had watched her father slowly lose his mind, then lose control of his body. She had cared for him for years. Then she'd hired help to care for him. To her, he wasn't the father she remembered and loved. He was only a mass of skin and bones with no mind and no reason to live. She may have figured it was time to put him out of his misery and let him rest in peace."

"God, after five years, I don't see how anyone could blame her," the sheriff said.

"I just realized that she wore black today," Morgan said. "She was in mourning for her father, evidently determined to kill the last of the big ranchers who had driven her father mad."

"Then you think she killed Corrigan and Isaiah Roundtree?" Sheriff Attucks asked. "Sure like to clear them off my books."

"Oh, she killed Roundtree, for certain. The Chicago ice pick proves that. Corrigan shot himself, but she could have had a hand in that. With what we know about Hannah, she could have seduced him and somehow blackmailed him, maybe threatened to tell his wife."

"Maybe she even had somebody take a picture of them in bed," the sheriff said. He looked quickly at Kay.

"Sheriff, I'm a big girl, I've heard of this sort of thing happening before."

The sheriff nodded, relieved. "Wouldn't be hard to check. Only one photographer in town. I'll have a friendly talk with him. He couldn't be charged with anything."

"So what happens now?" Kay asked.

"We have some trials coming up. Eight or nine men in my jail. I forget how many. District attorney may reduce the charges on some from rustling to receiving stolen goods. Still we could have four or five hangings in a few weeks. Takes longer now to convict a cow thief than it used to."

"Now we have to figure out how to compensate those other ranchers who lost cattle to the rustlers," Morgan said. "We probably should talk to the district attorney about that."

Morgan and Kay stood and the sheriff came

up automatically. A few minutes later they were ushered into the office of top law enforcer in the county and his face was grim.

"I heard what happened out at the ranch and here in town. Hard to believe, but it happened. Nothing there for my office to do."

"We were wondering how the other ranchers can get some cash for those stolen cattle."

Morgan reached in his pocket and brought out the 2,000 dollars he had taken from Josh Eagleston at the rail head and 5,000 dollars of the cash he'd taken from Hannah's reticule before the sheriff had gone upstairs.

"Here's a start. Two thousand I took from Josh Eagleston before he could pay off the railroad men, and five thousand that Hannah had with her. I'd like a receipt for it please. Can we bring suit against the Dempsy ranch to compensate those ranchers for their losses? Some of the smaller ones could go broke if they don't get some cash money for their stolen cattle."

The district attorney stroked his chin and nodded. "I would think that would be proper. You'll have to get a town lawyer to draw up the law suits. I'd think if you can prove how many cattle were stolen and sold, then get each ranch to estimate how many cattle each outfit lost, most judges or juries would award damages in the asked-for amount."

"We know there were 2,486 cattle shipped from this area on our rail cars and sold at the St. Paul stockyards during this rustling," Kay said. "None have been shipped in the last two weeks since Morgan has been on the job."

"What sort of damages does that mean?" the district attorney asked.

"At forty dollars a head average, that's 99,440 dollars."

The district attorney nodded. "The Dempsy ranch and cattle should be worth more than that. You'd be looking to sue the Dempsy ranch?"

"Since he's the only one with assets, he would be the favored one," Morgan said. "Oh, Hannah's Place also could be attached. What's it worth—ten, maybe fifteen thousand? And Hannah may have a bank account somewhere."

"So set up your suits with those three elements to claim against."

Morgan nodded. "Now, is there a lawyer in town?"

"Adolph Ingles is your man. Down a block or so across from the depot. He has an office upstairs."

It took Buckskin and Kay an hour with the lawyer to spell out what they wanted to do. He grinned when he heard about the size of the claims.

"Yes, yes, we should be able to get a judgment on a case like this almost without any argument from anyone. Should be heard in front of a judge, I would think. What I need is the approximate number of cattle that each of the ranchers lost. Do you have that?"

Shotgun!

Morgan grinned. "Mr. Ingles, that's how you're going to earn your money. We'll give you the maximum number of cattle rustled, and you get the figures from the ranchers to total that. Corrigan and Roundtree will amount to probably two thirds of the total, but be sure none of the smaller ranchers get cheated in the process."

Ingles nodded. "Do my best. I better be getting a brief filed with the court, stating our intentions of suing, and then get on my horse and do some riding to the various ranches. How many do you think were involved?"

Morgan shrugged. "Hard to tell. Probably all ranches to the west of town, but you'll have to check on that. Six or eight ranchers, I'm sure."

Morgan and Kay stood. "So, Mr. Ingles, we'll leave it in your hands. Right now we need to go to the jail and talk to one of the rustlers. I wish you luck in your lawsuits."

Kay frowned as they headed down to the jail. "What do you mean we need to go to the jail?"

"Josh said there were two railroad-management people involved in the rustling operations. I figured you'd want to be there to see if you could identify the names."

"Two Northern Pacific management-level men?" Her pretty face took on a grim expression. "Come on. Let's find out who they are."

Chapter Twenty-four

In the jail, Josh Eagleston scowled at Morgan and Kay.

"You really busted this operation apart, didn't you? I heard about Dempsy. He was a fool to try for one more big roundup. I told him not to before that last run. Some people just never will take advice. Hannah was a surprise to me. I didn't know she was involved in any of it."

"So now you know," Morgan said. "The district attorney talked to you, I understand."

"Yeah." Josh almost smiled. "They separated us in here. I'm in this cell with two others who won't hang. The other guys got a bit rough one day when they found out some of us were getting off with a prison term."

"So you're signed and sealed and will testify against them and all that. That was my part of the bargain. Now who were the two trainmen involved on the management level?"

Josh looked at Kay. "Who's she?"

"Kay Butterfield is a Northern Pacific railroad detective. She's more interested in those names than either one of us. So who are they?"

"One man in the traffic-and-rates department who collected on every steer shipped. His name is Overland Wales."

Kay gasped, her eyes wide and slowly she nodded.

"The other one I've never met, but he works in the rates-and-charges department or something like that. Neither of them know the other is involved. That one's name is Yale Courtaine."

"Oh, my God," Kay whispered. She shook her head as if not believing Josh's words.

Morgan looked at Kay and she headed for the door out of the cell block.

"Okay, you paid off. Have fun in prison. It's a hell of a lot better than stretching a hemp rope. Oh, if you want to donate a few thousand of your ill-gotten gains to the court for distribution to the injured ranchers, the judge would be more lenient. Say twenty or thirty thousand would help."

Josh looked up without comment and Morgan couldn't read his expression. Outside, Morgan and Kay walked down the street, rivaling the speed of a land tortoise.

"Wales, I can believe. I've never liked him and he got his hands under my dress one day in his office. But Courtaine is a real surprise."

"Josh knows them both," Morgan said. "How

can we get some better evidence against them than the testimony of a liar, cheat and convicted rustler?"

Kay walked along thinking. "We need to get them here on some pretext, something to do with the loading and transportation. Wales would be the one who might do field trips and check on operations. Yes, he could have an excuse to come this direction."

Morgan worked his brow. "Maybe Josh could send him a wire saying there was some problem getting the right cattle cars here for the usual loading operations, and with the big season coming up, he would like a personal conference with Wales about the situation since some million and a half in shipments would be involved in the regular business this spring and summer."

Kay grinned. "That would get him moving. He'd know at once that Josh was having troubles with his rustled stock."

They both chuckled and increased their pace toward the depot. Kay put the wire together, and she said it should get Wales on the move that same day. "I set the meeting in a cafe on Main. It's kind of a hangout for some of the trainmen when they have a half-day layover."

"How long would it take Wales to get here if he rushes?"

Kay twisted her mouth up and frowned thinking about it. "Say he gets the wire in his office about two o'clock this afternoon. It's about 620

Shotgun!

miles or so from Minneapolis to Miles City.

"If he could average thirty-five miles an hour that would be about eighteen hours. But he won't be able to get here that fast. I'd say by getting on passenger only trains—we do have a few now—he could make it in about twenty-two hours or so—say about noon tomorrow."

Morgan smiled. "Good, we'll be waiting for him. Now, for all of your good work, I think it's time that I take you to lunch."

Kay looked up at him from blue eyes. Her short blonde hair danced around her head a moment. Thin frown lines creased her forehead.

"I wonder if you can afford it? I mean, I'm a big eater and how are you going to get your fee now that three of the five men you made the agreement with have died? Surely the two small ranchers can't come up with your fee in cash."

"I've already been paid," Morgan said. "Now don't worry your cute little self about it and let's eat. I'm starved."

Kay held his hand and stopped him on the boardwalk. "First, a promise. After we eat, can we see if we can find that sunshine spot near the river where we'd be all alone?"

Morgan turned to her and whispered, "Where we could get your bare little ass in the grass?"

"Oh, yes, that's the specific idea."

He looked away. "Kay, I don't know if I'm in the mood or not."

She poked him in the ribs and they both broke

357

up laughing. They found Violet's Cafe, ate with relish and came back outside in 20 minutes.

"We don't want to waste all this sunshine," Kay said. They picked up the horses they hadn't turned in yet and rode east along the river. They were out of town quickly and in a wilderness of brush and small trees along the sides of the Yellowstone.

They rode a mile upstream, then investigated the brushy shore again. Ten minutes later they found the perfect spot. They were a quarter mile from the railroad, on a bend in the river. The brush had grown on three sides of the patch of grass that had sprung up after a flooding of the river early in the spring.

"Perfect," Kay said. "No one within two miles of us, and even if a train goes by, they won't see us down here."

"Not even a saddle blanket?" Morgan asked as he stepped down from his saddle.

"Not even," she said. They ground tied their horses and walked down to the stream. Here the water was chattering as it dropped down a foot of riffles to a deeper pond beyond. Kay sank down in the lush green grass and reached for him.

"Oh, yes, this is the place." Her face had flushed and her eyes looked brighter than usual. She touched him and he felt the heat of her hand. Already her breath came quicker and she sat with her legs spread in the divided skirt. "Something about being in the woods and outdoors just makes me feel so wanting to make love. Does the outdoors affect you that way?"

"Only when I'm with a beautiful, sexy, marvelously built lady like you."

Morgan kissed her, and her arms moved around his back and wouldn't let go. She leaned backward in the grass and drew him down so he lay atop her. The kiss lasted and their tongues fought, and he could feel the heat of her body.

"Quick, darling. Quick, right now. Let me get this damned skirt off and then I want you with all your clothes on, fucking me fast and hard."

She pushed him away and sat up, and a moment later she pulled off the skirt and her pink bloomers. Then she wiggled her bare bottom in the grass.

"Oh, yes, my bare ass in the grass, just like you promised." Then she tore at his fly and opened the buttons. She looked up at him.

"Pull him out and let's fuck, right now, long and hard and fast!"

It was an invitation no man under 95 could ignore. He knelt between her firm white thighs and moved to her crotch. She held her outer lips apart for him and he drove in with one swift stroke.

"Oh, damn, but that is so fine. Again. Come out and slam into me that way again. I love it."

Morgan did it again and then twice more and then he felt Hannah begin to get close to a climax. He stayed in and stroked deep and hard, hitting her clit with each thundering stroke.

Kay gasped and shrieked and then the climax ruled her, shattering her with a series of tremblings that pushed her forward until she fell over the edge and her whole body tightened and then spasmed again and again and again. He stopped stroking and watched her.

Her face was twisted into a strange expression and she gasped air through her mouth and tried to scream at the same time. Gradually she tapered off and humped at him gently with her sleek white hips, but before he could begin again, her body spasmed once more in a series even stronger than the time before, leaving her slack and empty and exhausted.

"Oh, God, I'm dead. You killed me and threw me into a volcano and I'm burning into a cinder. Oh, God, but that was good."

Morgan lanced deeply into her and pulled almost out. Then he repeated the process and gradually shortened the strokes until she writhed under him and humped her hips at his and pounded up hard, then harder.

Morgan felt the tension grow. Every muscle in his body strained. He tightened his hips. He pounded again and again and then the world exploded and he drove into her until he had emptied the last of his load. He fell over the delighted woman, spent, drained and ready to sleep for days.

He awoke a few minutes later. A train whistle

Shotgun!

brought him up and to a sitting position. He stared at the train tracks, but Kay had been right. They were too far away and a fringe of light brush shielded them from any prying eyes.

Kay sat up, too, and watched the train speed past a quarter of a mile away.

"I feel terribly wicked," she said. "Making love out here in the woods and people over there who can't even see us."

Kay stripped off the rest of her clothes and Morgan patted her breasts. She pushed him aside and undressed him, then sat there staring at his body.

"So perfect, so marvelous, so male!"

He pulled her up from the grass and they waded into the cold water, splashing each other and screaming. Then they sloshed downstream to the deep pool and sank into the water for a moment. Afterward, they ran back to the sunny spot and lay in the grass to warm up.

Before they were dry they made love a second and third time before they dressed and rode back to town. They walked the town from end to end on each side of the street and Morgan bought Kay two silk scarfs.

"You shouldn't," she said, then tied one over her head and carried her cowboy hat. "I shouldn't take a gift from you, but I love it. She stopped him in the middle of the boardwalk and then backed him against the wall of the barbershop.

"Tell me, what magic did you use to get paid your big fee?"

"I had an advance on expense money," he said.

Kay frowned and shook her head. "That doesn't do it. What about your fee?"

"It's paid," he said, laughing. "So let's not worry about it. How about some ice cream at that little cafe up there that advertises it in the window?"

Kay gave up and they had strawberry ice cream with homemade chocolate cookies. They had an early supper and went back to his room. Kay frowned at him, fluffed her hair, then went up to him and put her arms around his neck and kissed him.

"Now that you're properly motivated, tell he how you got paid?"

"You don't give up, do you?" Morgan watched her a minute. "If you weren't so good at making love—"

She hit him in the shoulder. "Tell me."

"You remember that money I turned in to the district attorney?"

"Yes, two thousand from the cattle drive and five thousand you found in Hannah's purse."

"I'd been worried about the problem of getting paid. They could go back on their word with the three big ranchers dead. But when I examined Hannah's purse I found money in it. Not the five thousand I gave the sheriff, but ten thousand. I kept five thousand of what I figured was rustling money. They owed it to me. That was my fee. This way there would be no questions, no problems."

Kay raised her brows over pretty blue eyes, then slowly nodded. "Your fee was five thousand dollars agreed to by the Stockgrowers Association?"

"Exactly."

"So not exactly according to the letter of the law, but it doesn't look like you did anything wrong." Kay looked at him a minute, then charged him, flailing him with her fists in soft blows.

"You beast! You make five thousand dollars for two weeks' work! You know how long it will take me to make that much money on the railroad?"

"Eight years. Now settle down." He caught her hands and held them. "But you don't get shot at by an assassin or put your life on the line two or three times on every assignment. How many times have you been shot, stabbed, beaten up and knocked out? Some folks think I'm worth my fee."

Kay scowled for a minute, then shook her head and the scowl vanished. "Damn, five thousand dollars." She lifted her brows. "Yeah, I guess you're right. At least I don't get shot at and stabbed and beaten up."

She stayed in his bed that night. She snuggled close and they kissed good night, but didn't make love. It was a totally enjoyable and peaceful sleep for them both.

They met the train at noon and Kay stayed in the background as Morgan contacted Wales after she pointed him out.

"Mr. Wales," Morgan said. "Let me carry your bag. My name is Morgan and I'm a friend of Josh Eagleston. He's tied up right at the moment and asked me to bring you to a hotel room where you could talk. He has some major problems with the railroad cars. Two, maybe three weeks left before the roundups begin and Josh's season ends. He'd like to get it straightened out today."

"Hotel room? The wire said we'd meet in a cafe. We usually meet in a bar."

"Josh is trying to get a little more class here, I'd say, Mr. Wales. I just work for him though. I'm supposed to take you to the hotel room and wait for him. He'll be there just as soon as he can get away."

"Damned irregular. How has he got so damned independent? Give a man a break and let him make some money and he turns into a rich slob."

They didn't talk again until they got into Morgan's hotel room.

"I'll leave the door ajar an inch or so," Morgan said. "That way Josh will know we're here. It's a signal we use. Josh said he ran into some trouble on the last shipment, but he's got the supply problem of the cattle worked out."

Wales sat down in the straight chair. He had a small case, which he clutched securely. "He better have it worked out because, like you say, there aren't more than three weeks in which we can ship these cattle. I can get him all the stock cars he wants, but the sidings are the problem. Say he had a herd of a thousand and we have cars enough for three hundred—what does he do with them?"

"That's a real problem all right. He should be coming soon."

"Josh is a wonder though," Wales said. "How he got the idea to get the cattle this early and ship them is a masterpiece of work. The cattle rustling is the simple part. Getting the contact with the buyer, the railroad for the cars and then the train crew to do the pickup is all orchestrated so neatly."

"Josh didn't do it all. I bet you helped him, Mr. Wales."

"Well, I did what I could. Expedited the movement of cars, got our engineer and his crew scheduled for the right trains and did the communications. The telegraph is a wonderful invention."

"Never thought I'd get involved in rustling," Morgan said. "How did you get pulled in, Mr. Wales?"

"How? Strictly business at first. Josh ordered cattle cars from me for a buy and I figured he was two months early, so I came out and did some investigation. No rancher was ready to ship yet, so Josh had to be rustling. I confronted him and worked out a split on the profits."

The door opened and Sheriff Attucks walked in with his six-gun covering the railroad man. "Mr. Wales, I'm arresting you for rustling. I have two credible witnesses. Three if we count me and four if we count Kay Butterfield—one of your railroad folks. Come along now. I've got another noose that will fit your neck neatly."

Wales scowled and stormed around the room a moment. "Where's Josh Eagleston?"

"Josh is in jail. He might even be your cellmate," the sheriff said. "Get along now. I've got important work to do, getting eight trials ready." The sheriff marched Wales out of the room.

Kay rushed into the room and kissed Morgan. "Are you all right?"

"Fine. I got Wales to admit he was in on the rustling. It's all the rest of the evidence the sheriff needs. Did we have lunch yet?"

She shook her head and they headed down stairs and then along the street. A block down the way, someone came in front of them and stopped.

"I heard what you did. It was wonderful." It was Teressa Yardley looking pretty and pleased with herself.

Morgan made quick introductions. "Teressa and I went to school together back in Idaho a thousand years ago."

Teressa nodded. "I just wanted to tell you that I

have a gentleman caller, a real beau. I'm not sure but he certainly seems serious. He's a partner with Mr. Roto in the Roto Hardware. He's a year older than I am and he's never been married. We met at the church dinner the other night. I'm quite smitten with him."

"Well, congratulations, Teressa. I hope you'll be happy with this young man. Say hello to your parents for me."

They walked on past. When Kay looked up inquiringly, Morgan said, "She recognized me the first day I was here, so I bribed her with lunch one day so she wouldn't ruin my attempts not to use my real name. We're friends."

"Good. Oh, the district attorney saw me this morning and said both of us should stop by and give him depositions on any evidence we have in the rustling since we might not be here when the trials come."

"Any hurry?"

"He said today or tomorrow."

Morgan smiled. "Good. That will just about take care of the Montana rustler's scheme."

"Does that mean you'll be leaving town real soon?"

"Might, might not."

"I wired my office that I'll be here two more days, wrapping up the case. Oh, we decided that Yale Courtaine is one man in this scheme who will get away with it. We just don't have any evidence to charge him."

367

"We got most of them. I'll stay around a couple of days to be sure it all works out right."

"Good. Tonight we stay in my room."

Morgan nodded, caught her arm and steered her toward the cafe. He was starved—for food and for a whole day of hard loving.